Contemporary Iraqi Fiction

Middle East Literature in Translation

Michael Beard and Adnan Haydar, Series Editors

Selected titles from Middle East Literature in Translation

Contemporary
Iraqi Fiction

AN ANTHOLOGY

Edited and translated from the Arabic by

Shakir Mustafa

SYRACUSE UNIVERSITY PRESS

FICTION

English translations copyright © 2008 by Syracuse University Press
Syracuse, New York 13244-5160
All Rights Reserved

First Edition 2008
08 09 10 11 12 13   6 5 4 3 2 1

The paper used in this publication meets the minimum requirements of
American National Standard for Information Sciences—Permanence of
Paper for Printed Library Materials, ANSI Z39.48–1984.∞™

For a listing of books published and distributed by Syracuse University Press,
visit our Web site at SyracuseUniversityPress.syr.edu.

ISBN-13: 978-0-8156-0902-5
ISBN-10: 0-8156-0902-7

Library of Congress Cataloging-in-Publication Data
Contemporary Iraqi fiction : an anthology / edited and translated from
the Arabic by Shakir Mustafa.
    p. cm.—(Middle East literature in translation)
ISBN 978-0-8156-0902-5 (hardcover : alk. paper)   1. Arabic fiction—Iraq—Translations into
English.   I. Mustafa, Shakir (Shakir M.)
PJ8046.5. E5C66 2008
892.7370809567—dc22   9/08
2008005417

Manufactured in the United States of America

. . .

To Iraqi writers at home and abroad,

and to their new audience

Shakir Mustafa, assistant professor of Arabic in the Department of Modern Languages and Comparative Literature at Boston University, grew up in Iraq and taught at the universities of Mosul, Baghdad, and Indiana before attaining his current position. He has published books on Jewish American fiction, literary translation, and Irish drama.

Contents

Acknowledgments

This anthology testifies to a collective effort in a number of ways. I am grateful to the writers who were gracious in offering permission for translation and in providing texts, book reviews, and other helpful material. The encouragement of friends and family has been exceptional. I owe thanks to Margaret Obank and Samuel Shimon, editor and assistant editor of *Banipal*, the London-based journal of Arab literature, where several of the translations first appeared. Their enthusiasm for translating Arabic literature has been instrumental in the completion of this anthology. I am also grateful to my friends Herbert Mason and the late H. James Jensen, for reading and commenting on some of the translations, and to my wife, Nawal Nasrallah, who read and commented on all of them. Finally, I extend warm gratitude to Annie Barva for her careful and sensitive editing of the manuscript and to Dino Cavallari for the cover illustration, based on Mayselun Hadi's story "Her Realm of the Real."

Introduction

Iraqi Fiction Today

Iraqi fiction has been particularly well suited to keeping pace with troubling realities in Iraq. The past quarter of a century alone has seen a long
and brutal war with Iran from 1980 to 1988; the two Gulf wars of 1991 and
2003, a thirteen-year economic embargo that crippled the country's infra-
structures and the population's spirit, the decline of the country's middle
class, the demise of a cruel regime, and a current foreign occupation that
must remind many Iraqis of their country's vulnerability. It is only natural that recent Iraqi fiction has drawn heavily on such events and on the
sentiments they elicit. This is not to say that fiction writers have stayed
away from all other themes and concerns. Fiction as a dynamic force is
capable of imposing itself on the most engulfing of preoccupations to enable wider and perhaps more meaningful visions of reality. Iraqi writers
have continued to write about love and music and gardens and the spirit,
but one would have to wonder about the credibility of their writing if it
did not also reflect the weight of the dismal reality a step or two from the
writers' desks. Adverse circumstances have also narrowed the opportunities for publishing in Iraq, and many writers have had to publish their
books elsewhere. In the Arab world, the market for fiction is depressingly
small, and writers, including prominent ones, are lucky to sell a few thousand copies. Lack of publication opportunities in Iraq has opened up the
Arab market somehow, but it has robbed Iraqi writers of a good portion of
their usual readership.

Iraq's troubles, nevertheless, have energized its literary scene. Writing
under the kind of relentless surveillance the country has suffered since

the early 1970s gradually stagnates creativity, and it fell to events of historic proportions to help writing in Iraq escape the confines of mundane themes and treatments. National catastrophes are not necessarily beneficial to creative expression; indeed, they can be quite detrimental, but in Iraq they have opened up new terrains, and narrative writing has flourished. Fiction writers of the 1950s and 1960s dominated the field and somehow imposed their aesthetic, perhaps because their fiction was uncontroversial in terms of themes and mostly traditional in terms of style. Ali Jawad Al-Tahir, a scholar and critic, suggested in the mid-1960s that Iraqi writers needed to shake off the strictures of social realism to produce work with more universal appeal.[1] A number of writers managed to produce such new fiction, and the 1970s witnessed the emergence of several capable voices, including some represented in this anthology: Muhammad Khodayyir, Mahdi Isa al-Saqr, Abdul Rahman Majeed al-Rubaie, Samira Al-Mana, and Jalil al-Qaisi.

The new fiction is by no means less realistic than that of previous eras. Commenting on contemporary Iraqi writers, Ferial Ghazoul remarks that "[m]odern Iraqi fiction has thrived on realism, partly because its rise coincided with the prevalence of the realist trend, and partly because the real got lost in the dominant political and social discourse." Recent Iraqi fiction, she adds, "has veered towards the fantastic, the surrealist, the Kafkaesque, the labyrinthine, the uncanny, not out of renunciation of the real, but out of verisimilitude. Life in Iraq is depicted in juxtaposed scenes rather than plots. Continuity is privileged over causality . . . the confidence in a hopeful future has given way to a consciousness of the absurd and monstrous."[2] Khodayyir may exemplify this realism with particular poignancy in the vignettes of *Basrayatha*, his defamiliarized portrait of his home city, Basra, thinly disguised by the suffix -*yatha*.[3] Other examples include the visibility of magic realism in works such as Mayselun Hadi's

1. *Fi al-qasas al-iraqi al-mu'asir* (On Contemporary Iraqi Fiction) (Beirut: Al-maktabah al-asriyyah, 1967), 148–55.

2. *Banipal* 14 (summer 2002), 3–4.

3. *Basrayatha* (Baghdad: Manshurat al-Amad, 1993, 1996). In Syriac, the suffix -*tha* is the emphatic noun ending. Syriac is one of the languages that was spoken in pre-Islamic Iraq.

"Calendars" and Lutfiyya al-Dulaimi's "Shahrazad and Her Narrators." Al-Saqr also frequently redefines the real and the imagined, as in "Breaking Away" and "The Returnee."

A sense of the tragic and a sense of the absurd in the past two decades have apparently liberated Iraqi literature and art from traditional and predominantly social themes, as well as from an aesthetic tepid in its adherence to realism. Salih Altoma rightly claims that for much of the second half of the twentieth century, traditional themes and treatments actually narrowed the opportunities for wider circulation of Iraqi writers in other languages.[4] With the new wave of authors, reformist or didactic impulses gave way to more complex representations, and fiction writers grew bolder in approaching both private and public subjects. The fiction of the late 1960s and 1970s brought Iraqi writers to wider audiences in the Arab world and beyond. It is not surprising, then, that more Iraqi works were translated during this period and that Iraqi fiction started to reach other readerships.

Another development that has proved to have positive outcomes despite the hardships associated with it is migration. Wars and sanctions have forced many writers out of the country and brought them into more extensive contact with the cultural traditions of their host countries. Direct contact with Western cultures in the past two decades has revitalized Iraqi writing. Samuel Shimon's *An Iraqi in Paris,* Salima Salih's "Those Boys," and Al-Mana's "The Soul," for instance, deal with matters of identity, roots, and belonging that would have been unimaginable if these writers did not live and write in the West. About half of the writers translated here live and write outside Iraq, and many of them have become citizens of the countries where they live. Their fiction, however, draws on their multiple sources, and some of these sources of course relate to Iraq and the native tradition. The pieces selected for inclusion in this anthology show such relations, and much of their appeal lies in their portrayal of significant aspects of the Iraqi experience in exile.

If national disasters could not thwart Iraqi writers, then the stifling presence of censorship during Baathist rule could. Writing proved a chal-

---

4. "Iraq's Modern Arabic Literature in English Translation, 1950–2003," *Journal of Arabic Literature* 35, no. 1 (2004), 89.

lenge because the regime not only prohibited criticism of the state and its symbols, but ruthlessly punished those who fell short of compliance. Writers were among those who disappeared, were imprisoned, or, alternatively, were rewarded according to their positions toward the state. Abdul Sattar Nasir, for instance, suffered a year of solitary confinement in 1975 for publishing a short story built around a parable that denigrated the kind of absolute power embraced by the Saddam regime. International pressure on the Iraqi government finally secured Nasir's release. In this anthology, the shadow of the censor can be seen in some of the parables in which writers can be indirect and noncommittal. Parables that employ elements of fantasy and settings well removed from the country's contemporary times and places have enabled Iraqi writers to communicate subversive visions by manipulating the contradictions of Baathist rule that posed for years as progressive and that paid lip service to the necessity of criticism, self-criticism, and correction of policies. Hence, a story that depicts political oppression, such as al-Qaisi's "Zulaikha," can be read as depicting other regimes, pre-Baathist or foreign altogether.

The use of parables by Iraqi writers has sometimes encouraged ventures into tropes such as magic realism and fantasy, which blend various modes of representation. In Khodayyir's "Yusuf's Tales," for example, fantasy is pervasive but frequently anchored in the writer's own city, ruined by useless wars and deliberate neglect. Ghazoul uses the term *uncanny* to describe the coexistence in Iraqi fiction of opposed techniques and forces such as realism and fantasy; she further notes that their use is both "an aesthetic quest and a political camouflage."[5] The freedom that émigré writers have enjoyed in the past two decades, especially in the West, has made the quest more visible and the camouflage unnecessary. Al-Mana, Nasir, Mahmoud Saeed, and Ibrahim Ahmed, to mention a few represented in this anthology, needed no parables to voice their critiques once they were out of the regime's extensive reach.

The urge to tell stories, however, remains healthy enough to propel Iraqi writers past domestic troubles. Arabic traditions have been resource-

---

5. "Iraqi Short Fiction: The Uncanny at Home and Abroad," *Journal of Arabic Literature* 35, no. 1 (2004), 1–3.

ful in this respect, and some writers deliberately identify with them. The eternal narrator Shahrazad is there, and so are autobiographical narratives and the allusive parables of the medieval Arabo-Islamic traditions. Storytelling and indeed writing become issues in a number of the selected stories: al-Dulaimi's "Shahrazad and Her Narrators," Khodayyir's "Yusuf's Tales" and "The Turtle Grandmother," Hadi's "Her Realm of the Real," Al-Mana's "Sexual Complacency," and Nasrat Mardan's "Bar of Sweet Dreams." Attention to writing as a profession and a mission shows the writers' involvement in a virtual debate on energizing their techniques, even in specific details such as the choice of an ending.

Experimentation in fiction writing has been universally embraced in the Arab world, and it certainly indicates writers' awareness of world developments in their profession as well as their efforts to contribute to such developments. Khodayyir's novel *Basrayatha,* for example, has fictional pieces such as the character sketches in this anthology's selection, but other parts also draw heavily on historical material and use pictures of actual places in the manner of tourist guides. It is not the purpose of this anthology to demonstrate the extent of experimentation in fiction writing in Iraq, but the volume shows enough to give the reader an idea of how seriously Iraqi writers take their craft. Daring experimentation with form has not always been matched in matters of content, however. Especially in representing women, Iraqi fiction has generally reflected the conservative atmosphere that has dominated Iraqi society since the early 1980s.

Women writers are an exception here, though. The selections from al-Dulaimi, Hadi, Ibtisam Abdullah, and Al-Mana, for instance, show an array of female characters capable of asserting their own visions in a world governed by patriarchal values. A central preoccupation in the works of these writers is the rights of women to a life of productive energies that open up the possibilities for liberated feminine subjects. Their female characters make a point of taking on life on their own terms. They vary in their psychological makeup and in the forces that shape them, but they collectively reflect in Iraq and in exile a vision of life sensitive to the contours of women's complex condition. In Al-Mana's *Shufuni, shufuni* (Just Look at Me, Me—a Novel, 2001), Fatima lives in Britain and Spain because the possibility of living in Iraq has been curtailed by the cruelty of the ruling Baath regime and by the society it has nurtured. Her alternative life in London and Malaga is a painful substitute for a life in a homeland she longs for but cannot tolerate when she returns. Among al-Dulaimi's heroines, Hayaat pins her independence against the community's pressures on her to comply with social norms that suppress her and her daughter, and Shahrazad crosses worlds and centuries to preserve a feminine vision in the face of relentless attempts to domesticate it. One reason why writings by Iraqi women truly represent a rising trend in Arab intellectual discourse on the role of women is that they transcend the conventional calls for the liberation of women to make the case for their wider participation in shaping their societies.

In the works of male writers, women do occupy critical spaces, but their significance in some cases seems to hinge on relevance to men's perceptions. Saeed, al-Qaisi, and Mardan's female characters are nearly invisible, and it is the male partner who seems to endow their presence with meaning. Al-Saqr is certainly an exception because his female characters motivate the action and derive much of their energy from their own independent existence. In "A Dreamer in Dark Times" from the novel *The Witness and the Negro,* Najat assumes a central position because of her status as a witness, not as a victim. The American military authorities are more interested in locating the person who shot the MP than in the fact that Najat was raped. Over the course of the novel, she is forced to look at scores of African American soldiers and starts to shed her racist attitudes. She loses interest in locating her victimizer and begins to work on saving herself and her future.

Universal values and impulses in Iraqi fiction certainly augment the connections between Arab writers and the wider world community. English-reading audiences need a better knowledge of contemporary Iraqi fiction to see the pervasiveness of such universality in contemporary Arab writing. Translating these writers' stories prompted my feeling that the market sorely needs representative Iraqi works collected in one volume. Of the dozens of active Iraqi writers, only a few have been translated into foreign languages, even fewer into English, and almost all of them have been represented by single works in anthologies of Arabic literature or fiction. Iraq's writers deserve wider audiences. In a review of *Banipal,*

Robert Irwin says about one of the writers translated here, "Mohammad Khodayyir is a marvelous short-story writer, whose somewhat Borgesian fantasies about his native city, Basra, are well worth reading."[6] Other articles have also welcomed the effort to translate Arabic works into English in order to breach a deplorable cultural gap.[7]

The anthology includes representative writers from Iraq's diverse groups. Groupings in themselves are not important, and they are recognized in the anthology only when the fiction reflects particular religious or racial matters. Non-Arab writers, for instance, are called so when their work indicates relevance to their ethnic background. Turkmen, Christian, and Jewish writers are included in addition to Iraq's Arabo-Muslim writers. Jewish Iraqi writers would technically be considered citizens of another state, Israel, but the two writers translated here, Samir Naqqash and Shmuel Moreh, were born in Iraq and wrote in Arabic, and their stories represent significant aspects of Muslim-Jewish relations in Iraq. Two additional criteria have dictated selections for this volume: merit and appeal to English-speaking audiences interested in the literature and culture of this particular country and the region. A fair number of the country's major writers are included not only because they are better known, but also because readers will find their reputations well justified. However, the anthology also represents writers with no or few translated works. It includes a number of women and younger writers because they have been generally underrepresented in English translations.

Common Themes in the Anthology

The divisions named here should help readers, especially instructors, interested in treatments of specific themes. There is considerable overlap in

---

6. *The (London) Times Literary Supplement,* November 8, 2002.

7. See, for instance, Isabelle de Pommereau, "Arabic Literature Finds an Audience in Europe," *Christian Science Monitor,* December 29, 2004; Amal Amireh, "Problems and Prospects for Publishing in the West: Arab Women Writers Today," *Al-Jadid* 2, no. 10 (August 1996); *The Observer,* October 31, 2004; and *The (London) Times Literary Supplement,* October 29, 2004.

these themes, of course, but the divisions still identify central concerns in the fiction collected here.

Family: Women, Men, and Love

Representations of family life and of love relationships in many of the selections show the centrality of the theme in Iraqi life. A touching piece is al-Saqr's "The Returnee," in which a husband sees the presence of his departing wife in a stray cat. Another is Al-Mana's "Sexual Complacency," which portrays a woman's realization of intimacy apart from feminist and patriarchal assertions. Al-Qaisi's "Zulaikha" derives its title and much of its appeal from the protagonist's belief in the redeeming power of a woman's love. Intimate relationships, however, seem constrained because of war, as in Abdullah's "The Other in the Mirror"; poverty, as in al-Rubaie's "A Man and a Woman"; or exile, as in Al-Mana's "The Soul" and al-Saqr's "Breaking Away."

War and Its Aftermath

The presence of wars and other forms of conflict, such as the embargo against Iraq following the Gulf War of 1991, is visible enough but usually not dominant. The Iraq-Iran War forms part of the background for Abdullah's "The Other in the Mirror," Hadi's "Her Realm of the Real," and Khodayyir's stories. The first Gulf War appears prominently in al-Saqr's "Morning Exercises," and the second in al-Dulaimi's "Hayaat's Garden." More of a central experience in the selected pieces is the thirteen-year-long embargo. Its presence is felt in Hadi's "Outage," Abdullah's "The Nursery," al-Dulaimi's "Lighter Than Angels," and Saeed's "Bitter Morning."

Political Oppression

Coping with one of the worse dictatorships in the third world taught Iraqi writers how to portray political oppressiveness without risking harsh retribution. Hence, treatment of politics in the selected fiction is subdued and indirect. For instance, the carnage of the Iraq-Iran War glimmers in the background, but one does not get a sense of any specific critique of the Iraqi regime's role in causing much of it. All the stories that pose more direct critique of political oppressiveness have been published outside Iraq: Al-Mana's "A Dormant Alphabet," Nasir's "Good-bye, Hippopotamus," Ahmed's "The Arctic Refugee," Saeed's "A Figure in Repose," and Mardan's "Bar of Sweet Dreams."

Childhood

Children and childhood are key themes in several of the collection's stories: Abdullah's "The Nursery," al-Saqr's "Morning Exercises," Naqqash's "Tantal," Salih's "Those Boys," and Shimon's "The Street Vendor and the Movies." Memories of childhood are also prominent in Khoddayir's "Friday Bounties" and "The Turtle Grandmother," al-Saqr's "Breaking Away," and Moreh's "A Belly Dancer from Baghdad." In these stories, the child becomes the face of multifaceted realities where the past, present, and future converge. The teenager of "Those Boys," for instance, seems comfortable with an Iraqi-Arab past and a German present, and the children of "The Nursery" and "Morning Exercises" seem destined to a future as troubling as the present.

Interfaith Relations

Religious diversity in Iraq has facilitated representations of interfaith relations. Many of the selected stories hint at such diversity, and others make it a central issue. In "The Street Vendor and the Movies" and "Hayaat's Garden," Christian-Muslim connections seem adequately well established to contain differences and occasional friction. Similarly, "Tantal" and "A Belly Dancer from Baghdad" present Jewish-Muslim interactions that testify to centuries of coexistence.

Western Perspectives

The West as a theme appears natural enough even in the work of writers who continue to live and publish in Iraq. Al-Saqr's "Breaking Away" is a clear example. Western perspectives, however, receive more complex treatments in Al-Mana's four stories, Salih's "Those Boys," and Shimon's "The Street Vendor and the Movies." These stories depict life in the West as a formative force that affects characters and shapes action. Connections with the home culture are still visible, but Western values have left their indelible marks.

A Note on Language and Spelling

Only works written originally in Arabic have been translated here. This explains the absence of Kurdish works: those works on Kurdish themes and sentiments with which I am familiar were originally written in Kurdish. Kurdish, Turkmen, and Assyrian are languages spoken in Iraq and used in literary discourse. Works with relevance to the Turkmen and Assyrian ethnic groups translated here were originally written in Arabic.

I opted for the simplest of transliteration methods with few or no hyphens or diacritical marks. The purpose has been to represent names in Roman characters as close to the originals as possible. I generally acknowledged but did not foreground *al-* in the last names al-Dulaimi and al-Qaisi, and I have dropped the *al-* after the first reference in the introductory notes to these writers. For other writers whose surnames include *al-* as an initial element, I followed the spelling and capitalization preferences of the writers themselves or the common form used by the media, even when this causes some inconsistencies in my own presentation. I thus used "al-Saqr" because it is not a tribal name and "Al-Mana" and "Altoma" because that is how those authors themselves write their names.

Contemporary Iraqi Fiction

Muhammad Khodayyir

Muhammad Khodayyir's loyalty to his city of birth, Basra, is proverbial. He has stoically endured the harsh conditions Basra has suffered since the early 1980s and wrote a fine tribute to a city left in ruins after the 1991 Gulf War.

According to Khodayyir, a storyteller's aspiration is a humble one: to be a middle man. The storyteller's memory, he says, is a grocery store crowded with dusty cans, and his or her texts are not constructed or created, but exist in the world, packed with thoughts and images. The writer's mission lies in exorcising their potential narratives at the appropriate time and place (see Al-Hikayah al-jadidah *[The New Tale], 1995).*

Khodayyir's stories lend authority to his critical reflections. Their craft conjures up layers of voices, places, and eras that continuously stir what we know or remember. "Yusuf's Tales," for instance, is at once about the present and the past; the writer's city, Basra, and the ideal republic for writers and printers; living and writing; the carnage of war and the glittering marble of the mind's eye. Similarly, "The Turtle Grandmother" blurs the line between the narrator's tales and the grandmother's stories he recollects. In these fictional works, the real and the imagined are not strictly drawn territories, and dead poets join living storytellers in narrating.

Central to an understanding of Khodayyir's vision is the setting of much of his recent work. It is Basrayatha, a Basra of sorts, a city of the imagination with pristine stone edifices and marble towers, but also the one bombarded for years with artillery shells, missiles, and the rhetoric of divisive hatred. The legacies of the Iraq Iran War and the Gulf War are certainly driving forces behind the emergence of the imaginary city. The appeal of "Yusuf's Tales" is that it also circumvents the calamities of war by portraying a utopia based on the privilege of producing books. Interestingly, the principles on which Yusuf's postglobal publishing house is erected correspond to Khodayyir's theory on the origin of texts to which I referred earlier. The text simply exists in the world, and the writer merely facilitates its release. If Yusuf speaks for Khodayyir, then the publishing tower stands not only for a future fantasy, but also for the actual city in which war made intellectual activity a worthless surplus.

"Yusuf's Tales" and "The Turtle Grandmother" are translations of "Hikayaat Yusuf" and "Ru'ya kharif" from Ru'ya kharif *(Autumnal Visions; Amman, Jordan: Mu'assasat Abdul Hameed Showman, 1995). "Friday Bounties" consists of excerpts from Khodayyir's novel* Basrayatha: Surat madina *(Basrayatha: Portrait of a City; Baghdad: Manshurat al-Amad, 1993, 1996).*

Yusuf's Tales

When we reconstructed the city after the war, we set aside a plot of land one by two kilometers overlooking the river.* On that we built the printing house. We raised its twelve stone tiers so that visitors would see it polished and glittering in the sunlight next to the massive marble city towers. Work on building the house went on day and night for years, and now it pleases dozens of skilled workers to sit on the broad steps around the building to bask in the early-morning sun and reminisce about those joyful days. Laborers and craftsmen then disperse on the wide city boulevards leading to their workplaces as soon as the central city clock chimes fifty strikes.

Our city authorities have attracted from neighboring towns and cities scores of blacksmiths, founders, masons, carpenters, engineers, and bestowed on them enough honors to raise their status among the public. But printers, transcribers of manuscripts, and writers have received even greater honors. Theirs is the highest building in the city, and their chief is none other than the famed master we know as Yusuf the Printer.

On this sunny spring morning I walk briskly to the printing house, climbing up the many stone stairways and maneuvering my way through

* The writer dedicates the story to storyteller Yusuf Ya'qub Haddad.

those relaxing on the steps. One impulse has so possessed me that I am oblivious to several colleagues who are also heading for the southern gate. Yusuf the Printer has promised to share with me a secret he has kept locked away in one of the house's chambers.

My eyes hover over the impressive mural on the arch of the gate, colored in firm chalky strokes, to seek out one more time a tiny detail, an Arab transcriber bending over an open manuscript. At exactly this time of day when I report to work, I look up to see the ink in his inkwell sparkling in the sunlight. Other details of the mural conspire with sunlight at other moments all day long. The transcriber detail diminishes as I go through the reception and service offices, then into the overwhelming openness of the inner hall. The hall is a thousand square meters, pierced through the center by a massive elevator shaft whose metal pillars are visible behind thick glass panels. The printing presses occupy the entire lower floor.

I cross the hall to the lift, my rubber shoes gliding over its solid glass floor. The colored plastic chairs all over the hall are vacant at this time of day and look brilliant under lights coming from hidden spots in the ceiling. The printing machinery is visible through the glass floor, with forklift trucks and carts rolling through the aisles and separate areas for paper storage, binding, and the mechanical repair workshop. The printing presses and the heads of the workers are bathed in that murky basement light familiar in the press work area and that the eyes of our veteran printer have known since they first made contact with a printing machine. Below, massive wheels, oiled and gleaming, are spinning huge reels of papers and printing cylinders, and paper cutters are delivering to agile hands the first runs. Phosphoric lights from computer screens and monitors shower over faces, machines, and outstretched arms. From above, I can hear nothing—the glass ceiling rules out the clatter of wheels and the fluttering of paper, not to mention the sucking of inks and the dancing of characters and forms on screens and sheets of paper.

Four elevators run up and down inside the central shaft, but only one leads to the printing floor. The giant glass elevator ascends through the lower and middle tiers set aside for proofreaders, calligraphers, cover designers, illustrators, the photo lab, and the offices of the administrative staff, then through the eighth floor where the restaurant and clinic are. The elevator slows down as it reaches the top four tiers housing writers, transcribers, editors, translators, and manuscript readers. From the elevator you can see the occupants of these floors in their glass cubicles or in the corridors, and even have a glimpse of faces you might not have a chance to see elsewhere. The faces of the city's gifted few who willingly shun publicity: learned scholars M. J. Jalal and K. Khalifa; the storytellers K. M. Hasan and M. al-Saqr; the poets A. Hussein, M. al-Azraq, S. al-Akhder, and S. al-Chalabi; and elite journalists and publishers.

The occupants of these top tiers change, which explains why no visitor or worker has ever had a chance to see the city's intelligentsia all together at one given time. Their rank occasionally includes guests who collect manuscripts and rare books and who wander agog among the cubicles. But, as a rule, all writers, editors, and manuscript copiers from this city and neighboring cities can stay at the printing house only long enough to finish their work, but then leave so that others may take their places. Only Yusuf the Printer has been a fixture here, and he might be making the rounds right now on the printing floor or relishing seclusion in one of the cubicles.

I am a fellow at the printing house while I work on my novel *Khamarawayh's Last Portrait*, although I knew Yusuf before the war when he owned a small press in the city's old business district. Besides the local newspaper he edited, he used to print his own fiction and his friends' nonfiction there. When the city came under intense bombardment in the last year of the war, the press was closed even though it was producing Yusuf's autobiography at the time. Our meeting at the house after the war was brief and memorable. He looked old, a profusion of white hair hugging both sides of his red, slender neck. He supported himself on a smooth cane and had a flower in his jacket lapel. It was at that meeting that he promised to reveal to me the secret he had kept at the house.

I get off the elevator on the tenth tier where I work among the affiliated writers. In one cubicle I see Abdulwahab al-Khasibi proofreading his only collection of short stories, and from another I hear a diligent translator's renderings of Tagore's reflections. Then I walk past the cubicle occupied by Balqis, the young poet. She's barely fifteen years old, becalmed and not of this world, like a dreamy bird I once saw in a pomegranate tree. She surprises me when she looks up. All I can think of then is Tagore's line: "The bird wishes it were a cloud, and the clouds wish they were birds."

On the eleventh tier, the transcribers' floor, I see the tired face of an old friend, Ubaid al-Hamdani, and I wonder if he's copying the manuscript on medicinal herbs he found in a discarded box in a subterranean vault. Ubaid once told me about the Muslim medieval storyteller al-Hariri who penned seven hundred copies of his own Maqamat. On this tier of the house, only the aged silence rules the transcribers' cubicles, and the invisible creeping of mice hankering after volumes of ambergris paper.

I walk for hours looking for Yusuf the printer. As I reach the twelfth floor, I pass by the quarters of the writers who have acquired permanent status. They are the only exception in the house. And why is it that these permanent residents will not complete their work, even if the house were to become a *madrasa* of sorts or a workshop for writing or printing? I am considering a number of possible answers when I catch sight of the veteran printer. He is in the elevator ready to descend to the printing floor.

"I have been waiting here for you for hours," he says. "The first step dooms the ones that follow. As soon as you step into a corridor, you end up coming back to it, and when you move up to the next tier, you achieve no actual upward movement."

That is humor befitting an old man familiar with ascending and descending. His sparkling eyes make me think of a giant press where thousands of machines run day and night to put out a single book composed of endless volumes. I give Yusuf a wan smile. After all, it is he alone who knows the rules and secrets of the printing house.

Then he says: "I read your novel. I think you'll rewrite it. You had Khamarawayh commit suicide the moment he entered the chapter of the letter K instead of allowing him to materialize anew under a different name."

His words surprise me.

"When you're unaware of the value of letters," Yusuf adds, "you sever the chains of words beyond the repair that imagination or grammar can provide."

I reply: "I'll write the novel again. That will please me, of course, since it'll help me prolong my stay at the house for one more year. I'll also have more chances to get to know the recluses of the upper tiers."

"You'll stay," he says gleefully. "Your affiliation will be extended."

I have to ask him about the permanent writers of the twelfth tier.

"They're as permanent as ghosts, not individuals with names and accolades. Their works are part of this ever-reappearing ghostliness. As soon as they finish a page, a certain part of their existence vanishes. If they complete a book, they'll disappear entirely. But you see them every morning rewriting one page after another just to relish their presence at the house. What intoxicates them is the vineyard of inks, these ghosts of writers composing transparent pages. If you want, you can join them and never leave the house."

I am fumbling for an appropriate reply when he remarks: "We won't succeed in completing a book if we don't really defend our characters. The name 'Khamarawayh,' for instance, is hermeneutic since it reveals a part of the character's truth. A character could escape death by hiding his or her name behind that of another and not letting that name get swallowed up in the magician's melting pot. Her name alone betrays her transparent symbolism and the shackles from which she'll never be liberated. Give your character more than one name and more than one form, and your book will escape the rottenness of an ending. We fail because our books start to decay before they're finished. We impose on them our imperfection—we die and let the book die with us. What a dismal outcome for an honest and painful ordeal."

"Yes," I say, overwhelmed. "We let our characters live for us."

"When you approach the truth of genuine creation . . ."

I have the feeling that Yusuf suddenly stops talking, and then he presses a button on the elevator keypad. The elevator goes down through a series of tiers and stops at an unmarked one, the basement possibly or an entirely different floor. One thing I hear clearly is a suppressed roar. We leave the elevator and come to a suite with black walls. Yusuf takes out a small key and opens the door. When he turns the lights on, I find myself in front of a small printing press, old and manual, and cases of lead letters stacked all around it. The room is airtight, sound and light proof, and connected to a smaller side room with a table laden with zinc printing blocks.

"This is my secret, my friend," Yusuf says. "The treasure of the house." He is looking at me, searching for signs of wonder, joy, or interest, then he says: "Here I can work the way I like. I salvaged this machine from the devastation of war. It was in a room in my house. The one I trust most."

The silent machine generates an aroma of ink, acids, oils, rubber, leather, and paper—the remains of several printings of the rare books that this press put out. A structure crouching like a lubricated mythical animal. The mysterious energy the machine emits captivates my spirit, shakes my limbs, and sends my heart racing, as if I were feeling with the ends of my fingers the ancient leaves of a volume bound with deer hide. *Kalila wa Dimnah,* the *One Thousand and One Nights,* Ibn Sina's *Qanun.* Yusuf's voice comes to me again, "On this press the Ottomans printed the first issue of *Annafeer* newspaper, and the occupying British authorities used it to print out colonial communiqués. Perhaps it even fell into the Iraqi rebels' hands afterwards. When I bought it in 1940 from a merchant, some of its parts were missing or damaged. A blacksmith I knew made alternative parts, and a famed smelter cast new sets of characters. Today, it will print my tales."

He then pulls out of an open drawer a newly printed sheet and gently places it on the machine. I bring the page close to the bulb over the press. "If you want to print a genuinely great book," I hear Yusuf say, "one for yourself and for the ages, you have to set its characters with your own hands patiently, confidently. You will need only a few copies. Ten would immortalize you for ten centuries."

The page feels as if it were printed on a rough stone tablet. The nicely lined text is surrounded by wide blank margins stained with faint streaks and spots of ink and fingerprints. The page has a full tale printed on it and ends with a dark star rather than a period.

Yusuf is still flashing a euphoric smile. "One story fills out and never gets beyond a page," he says.

I think about what he has said and soon realize the discipline and skill involved in his work. You can read Yusuf's tales where you choose without ever having to turn the page. The title of the story I'm reading is "The Mirror of Turdin." Here's its plot: A giant mirror that the astronomer Sulayman al-Saymari made from a rare polished metal and placed on a green hill outside the city of Turdin was to reflect the three stages of the city. Its past image in the morning, its present one at midday, and at sunset the sun was to display changing reflections of the city's future. The city's old image gradually appears as the sun ascends, revealing first the Ziggurat, then the irrigation canals of the Hanging Gardens, the Procession field, and the Virgins' Altar. As soon as the details come into full view, the display starts slowly to vanish. At noon, the show lasts but a few minutes, long enough for the inhabitants to recognize the city where they currently live. But the display at sunset is rare and unpredictable. It came up twenty years ago for just seconds in front of a lucky shepherd and his flock. The future city flashed and dazzled the human and animal eyes in an instant that would remain folded in pastoral time. The description of this future place that the city dwellers wrested from the shepherd was more bewildering than the image's resistance to appear. He spoke of that city as a colossal and glittering golden hand lining houses in the shape of a cone. Then another golden hand, more brilliant and much faster than the first, would undo the work before the eye had had a chance to behold it. Since then, people go out to the fields surrounding the mirror hours before sunset and wait for the emergence of a city to come.

In the nights to follow, the patient printer will put on his overalls, smeared with patches of ink and oil, and select letters from the cases. He'll bend over the single-page forme to set the reversed characters of the tale with his blackened thumb, then align the rows within the wooden frame. And while we relish the leisure of our nights, he'll secure the type forme to the bed of the press, feed in the ink, and lay a blank sheet of paper. He'll turn the spiral handle gently down in the faint, saffron light of the bulb over the machine.

Years later my hands will hold one of the ten copies of the magnificent book of tales, illustrated with paintings etched by a house artist. I'll read it on the stone steps outside the building in the deliciously warm sun of the early morning.

The Turtle Grandmother

This autumn brings along a vision unlike those it brought in previous years. Those past visions belonged to the riverbank: the Severed Head, Functionless Clocks of the Public Squares, Isle of the Statues, the Hanged Flies. A series of apparitions saturated with morning dew, quivering like the heart of the big river.

All the faces but one in this autumn's vision are buried in fog and fear. The face flows clearly—maternal, tranquil, resigned. A crowd with light personal effects rushes from a bridge or a ferry and instantly disappears in all directions when it hits the coastal pavement. The crowd leaves behind an old woman plodding like a turtle.

The vision is invoked and examined again, as if in slow motion. Its components pass along with fresh details as the mind's eye lingers on a small segment, the kernel of the vision: the ancient face of an old woman. Framed in that recollection of the face are other particulars: the wavy surface of the river, the boats, giant wood poles of an old bridge, braided metal cables whose loose ends disappear in the water. Other indistinct details look like a squadron of planes or a cloud of fears. A few hours later the crowd rushes and disperses again with new details, and the same ancient face springs from nowhere and trudges like a freshwater turtle on the bridge leading to the ferry pier.

Before sunset, I went out to ponder the site of the new vision. Tranquility had pinned anchored ships to the surface of the turbid water. A breeze would occasionally rustle the wilting leaves. I arrived at the pier, the place that ceaselessly figures in all of this autumn's vision, with its familiar images: the wood poles, the braided cables, an old ship with rutted metal sides, and the quivering, tethered boats. And a bench right on the edge of the water.

I waited for a while, but nothing happened. No herald dazzled the eyes. The last ferry from the other bank docked and unloaded a few commuters. Darkness fell, clouding the big trees along the coast, and lights from the scattered ships became visible. The bridge leading to the ferries looked deserted, and the wings of a few birds combed the air above the river one last time. The repeated appearances of the vision sharpened the image of the old woman till it became identical with that of the archetypal grand-mother, the midwife of hundreds of newborns, the turtle grandmother with the laborious walk and the dark, green face. Forty years later it was the same face, without a single wrinkle added.

It was the spring of 1941, when British warships dropped off their Indian soldiers to seize al-Ashar. My family sent me away with the midwife to our relatives in Nahr al-Khoz, a village near Abu al-Khaseeb. The mid-wife brought me to a mud house in the middle of a palm tree orchard. We arrived at night, but in the morning I was surprised by how big the house was—five rooms with a long outside wall that separates the house from a nearby river. I also found out I was not alone there. In addition to the old couple who occupied one of the rooms, there were ten boys from the or-phanage evacuated by the city's committee for civil security. They were handed to the midwife when the public's resistance to the occupation forces intensified. The police force and civil servants had already aban-doned the city, and bandits were on the loose, looting public and private property. That morning, the midwife gave us our first breakfast. We sat on the ground around a long table about a foot high. It was a simple meal during which my eyes kept moving from the rim of my metal milk cup to the quiet faces. Swarthy, slim boys, the eldest barely ten.

After breakfast we left for the river. One of the house's three doors led to stone steps that went all the way to the river. It was not a big river, almost completely shadowed by the palm trees flanking it. The overwhelming lull of the palm tree orchard pressed on our bodies. In the evening we came back to the low table and followed with our eyes the midwife's heavy movements behind us as she dispensed bowls of hot soup and pieces of warm bread. We drank water from an earthenware pot and mugs. One of us said, "She's a turtle." In that secluded place the compari-son stuck to our minds like the fluid of the *bember* fruit, transparent and gluelike. When the old woman finally took her seat at the head of the table, the meager candlelight fell on her green face, revealing small scrutinizing eyes under scant eyebrows. But she looked like a sturdy tree whose turtlelike and peaceful visage were only meant to hide her real age and her trying chores between bellies and pudenda. She remained unchanged till the ferry delivered her to this autumn's vision.

I came back to my apartment later that evening and saw that none of my friends had arrived yet. I peeked out the window overlooking the bus station and followed the laconic energy of those returning or going home. Humans and buses looked almost unwilling to move, and their eventual departure made the vacant waiting sunshades appear even more desolate under that oppressive humidity and the wan lights of lampposts and hotel facades. From my elevated point of view I could see something falling ceaselessly. I couldn't pin it down, but it dimly fluttered so close to my eyes, it assaulted my ears with inaudible resounding, it brushed against my skin upwards and downwards. The room had virtually no furniture other than a long, low table. I sat on the ground at one end and started drawing the face of the turtle grandmother. I must have been sketching for a while before I heard my friends' feet approach the door. They were three of the company that had assembled every night. The sketches changed hands, and they asked if they knew her.

"One of you will eventually remember her," I said. "Many years ago we used to call her the turtle grandma."

Remembrance didn't seem to hit any of them. The rest of the group arrived, bringing more clamor and merriness. One of them asked on entering, "Tell me who said, 'A battle of your soul against the specter of fidelity, of mine against the specter of friendship'?"

"I don't know. Victor Hugo?"

"James Joyce."

The gang, the nightly gang, was complete now. All ten of them sat on the floor around the low table. From the next room I fetched their favorite wine, well chilled, and put the bottles on the table.

"Tonight, you'll drink in pottery mugs," I said and handed out brown ceramic cups. We raised our cups to a friend's toast, "To clay."

We filled our mugs again, and I raised mine, "Let's drink to the lost turtle." My eyes on the rim of the mug, I watched them take quick sips of wine. They come every night, sometimes bringing their own food and wine, then take off late at night in different directions, leaving me to my loneliness. I'm probably the only single person among them. They have homes to go to, wives and children I know nothing about. They don't talk about their families, and when they go, they leave behind no shadow or trace as if their presence were a chance meeting never to be repeated. Their names dare my memory, and I have no recollection of where they work or live. Before they came tonight, I was not sure they would come. Their uncertain gathering at the outset of the night concludes with their ghostlike dispersion at its end. They come from a very distant place.

I went back to the window and looked at the bus station. A small number of people sat under the sunshades or moved around them. The last bus was about to take off. That mysterious thing kept falling down. One of my friends was ending a speech I wasn't following, "Homelands are occasions for enduring friendships." They were getting drunk; the hands holding drinks and cigarettes became less steady. The leaning posture at the table, the closeness, and the overlapping of their shadows on the wall made them look like ghosts radiating with loyalty. An age-long and cherished closeness. The ceiling fan dissipated cigarette smoke and the wet drunken breaths, its squeaks blending with the low-pitched exchanges of final rough words.

They had grown old, and I noticed for the first time tonight premature crevices cutting through their faces whenever they changed their position at the table. The years' searing fingers had touched the faces and left permanent marks. Before tonight, they weren't aware of their past as it lingered in the shadows of alleys, palm trees, and dreams. Tonight, they took hold of the years and felt with their own fingers their long tracks on the smooth surface of the mugs' baked clay. Viewed from up here, they seemed to be looking down an abyss that glimmered under their hesitant stares. Even though I was less concerned with the passing of time, I was, like my friends, conscious of the years' slow flow as I contemplated the vision possessing me the past few days. Oh, I see that now—they're part of this vision—the tired friends, aging, docile drunkards, the intimate ten. Here, there, everywhere. Their voices and scattered words came from a very distant place.

Night was nearing its end. I must have fallen asleep because I noticed my companions were gone, their cups turned upside down next to the empty wine bottles. Still hovering over the table, smeared with a dry pink coating, was the face of the turtle grandmother.

I left the apartment at daybreak heading toward the ferry pier, taking in the river's cool breeze as I approached. There, in the same place, became visible a floating bridge on which a row of big military trucks crossed toward the eastern bank. A long caravan loaded with soldiers and military ware heavy enough to keep the parallel floats in continuous friction and squeaking. At the end of day I came back to the river. The bridge was still there, and the trucks were still crossing.

None of the companions showed up at my place that night. Or the night after.

Friday Bounties

The Night Supplicant

Friday, memory of a name, the name of memory, the repository of day's bounties and night's secrets. Friday, the day's answer to the night's query, uncircumscribed expansion and inevitable reunion. Creation, selection, recognition, ascendance, congregation, a path of righteousness. Of Friday I remember the walled roof of a house, a meal in the open, and a whole family having dinner on that roof under the sky's swings, with stardust descending like a forked tongue out of the caved mouth of Being. The child's flying bed bumps into trembling stars, fences, television antennas, water pots, doves' nests. The whispers of mosquito nets, the oozing of bodies, the surprises of the street below.

At the end of day, the night supplicant comes. A beggar collecting dinner leftovers, the surplus of households that close their doors after sunset.
More than the handfuls of rice and bread and fruit, Friday for the beggar is
light for the eyes and warmth for the feet. We feel his presence in the al-
leyway with the tapping of his cane and the resonance of his voice in front
of silent doors. We have never seen him. His voice alone conjures up a
blind form wading through the dark, Friday in Friday out. He is alone, but
he knows the doors and lingers in front of a few. His clandestine appearance fares well along our faltering imagining of him as a light being,
superhuman, carrying a sack loaded with unfathomable commodities.

His is the begging deposited by past nights outside our doors. If the
house rejects you, you become a beggar, a supplicant in the alley of mu-
nificent bounties.

I remember a beggar who came to our house—dark brown face, failing eyesight, a running nose, patched sandals, dusty headwear, a musty
coat. An ancient madman. He was the first visible beggar, one of our forgotten relatives, I was told. The first and last visible beggar I saw and
around whom my consciousness formed the notion that every family has
a mad relative or an absent beggar. For storytellers, all the relatives are
touched with madness or paupery, and all their days are Fridays. When
storytellers don't have relatives, they themselves become the beggars, and
their stories the bounties.

The Day Supplicant

As soon as the night's beggar disappears, the day's beggar takes over.
This beggar is not alone like his predecessor, but one in a group, and this
is one reason for the name. He'll be relaxing in a café, bathing in a public
bath, sitting in a barber's chair, slipping into the souk crowd, attending a
feast, visiting a movie theater, worshiping in a mosque. He'll have a name,
a description, an appearance, a number. The day's beggar won't lose the
amenities of the tribe. For outcasts perishing in their loneliness, Friday is
but a nameless day. They're exiles within their own walls, beyond the collective bounties of the holy name. When you fall outside the name, you're
ostracized, an outcast, like those confined to beds or behind bars.

Let's break the shells behind which habit hides to see how habit works. We'll watch how our hands extend to the *misbaha* to tell its beads, or to reach for the moustache, or to scratch, pull, or sneak into one thing or the other. We bend to tie a shoestring or count money in front of mirrors. From the day we saw the light, our bewilderment has grown at the machine that controls us, exposes us, and binds us to the screeching wheel. Break the chain, and you're on your own, a stranger to the faces in that common ball. Break the chain that separates you from the answer and alienates you from Friday's collective ritual, from the metamorphosing myth. But the question extends and reaches to the foot of the myth and beyond the city, to before the café, the public bath, the restaurant, the barbershop, the movie theater.

Heavy on our chests, our myths overwhelm lips worn out from narrating the tales of the marshes, the boats and fishing, the tilling and harvesting, and the pursuit and exile and murder. The most famous is the jolly myth of the long journey to the city, the wandering in its bazaars, entering a restaurant, praying in a mosque, and then the return to the village with fresh tales.

The myth begins with the farewell gathering Thursday night in the village guesthouse for the member of the tribe leaving for the city in the morning. The chosen one is the recipient of anxious looks, loaded with envy and expectations. The embers under bundles of cane in the hearth are fanned by the tribe's breaths and yawns and by the flickering of the lantern and the appearance of the knights of this collective spirit sporting their forked swords or long-barreled rifles. The jolly myth travels with mosquitoes and thick *egals*, colorful wool rugs and rolls of thin cigarettes, coffee pots and the brown faces shaped from the rivers' clay and the bowels of dead fathers. And the sperm that traverses the wombs of hard and fighting females, maternal and paternal grandmothers, mothers, green from tattooed dots and crosses, and happy girls taught at schools floating on isles of thatched canes. At the end of the night, the men, tired from coping with the urge to travel, leave the chosen man with the tribal totem that has crept out of the big coffeepot on the hearth. In the morning the two will take the roughest roads to the faraway city.

His back bent, the villager sits watching the waiter put dishes down on the table. The hardened fingers turn pieces of bread soaked in stew. The aroma of barbecued meat, pickles, and raw onions brings in the absent family to join the father in devouring the appetizing luncheon with one mouth. The table surface glistens with sunlight, and on it the father lines up the souls of his dogs and cats and hens, and the souls of his wife and children, next to the ghost of his hungry totem, so that they all will savor that leisurely meal. The restaurant is big enough to house all the feeding troughs of the village, and mirrors make it bigger and fuller with people. Food companions crowd the place, licking bones and fingers and lips. The villager belches, surveys the place and its mirrors, hanged pictures, and darting waiters, and tells himself, "I ate for all of you."

The literati and social reformers have forgotten the last villager lost in the crowds of Friday bazaars, and with the disappearance of the last character of a city villager in an Iraqi story, we lost the prototype of the first flea-market hawker, the porter, the *dellak* at the public bath, and the cotton carder. The early migrant villagers settled in the city, but their children inherited different occupations in the spice market and the copper market, and among moneychangers, carpenters, goldsmiths, and pottery makers. Above all, they laid their hands on the Indian secrets of mixing spices.

The Friday Market

A giant call wakes up the entire city, its source the massive common grounds vacated by all the weekday souks for the Friday market. It's the hub of all markets, but has no order, weights, measures, or pricing system. Secondhand items line up in a topsy-turvy land, a carnival of trivial finds. I go to the Friday market to ascertain the existence of a type I expect to see among the market loafers. I want to see him embodied, and I want to follow him at the end of the day to the little storehouse of trivia he has made out of his tours into the market. I know he exists. I can picture him amidst all these useless things. In that tiny museum you'll find a big bronze key whose teeth form some secret word that invokes the echo of a door slowly closing on the crushed bones of the past. And a mousetrap that keeps me remembering night after night an old story about a flute player whose tunes led a herd of mice to their demise in a river. A small stone grinder, a butcher's knife, scissors, an inkwell, a bookbinder's needle, a kohl container, pins, coins. Things dead and gone with no relevance to everyday life.

The trivia man lies in bed, his eyes fixed on a chandelier hanging from the ceiling, with dangling glass snakes whose heads have the bright stones of colorful, poisonous dreams. Like me, he dreams of a giant mousetrap that devours an army of mice all at once. A cage three-by-three meters, but only a half-meter high, with hidden retracting springs at one end connected to side levers that support the raised gate. A mere brush with one of the springs would cause the levers to snap and bring down in a flash the trapping gate. The mice will then become an easy prey to a crushing plate the size of the upper side of the cage. The plate is automatically released when the gate closes, its sharp spikes shredding the small, stunned bodies.

I read about such a machine in Edgar Allan Poe's "The Pit and the Pendulum" and Kafka's "In the Penal Colony." I have no idea what inspired Poe and Kafka with these terrifying notions, but I know that storytellers of great truths are familiar with the vicinity that houses depositories of worthless finds collected from the Friday market.

Al-Sa'ada Public Bath

To relinquish everything, to be liberated, the quiet settling, the total liquescence—states generated by the very act of stepping into a public bath. Along with clothes the bather discards in the changing vestibule all that has hung onto him, sheds the temporary and nominal, and melts in an indiscernible, steamy presence. The bath's parlors have been designed to duplicate the labyrinths of the quest for annihilation in the last white basin of anonymity, where the body, infinitely bare, looks like a sugar lump.

The bath I have in mind is in a roofed part of the souk. A low doorway obstructed with a curtain leads down to the warm changing parlor scented with oleander blossoms, cotton bolls, and cinnamon sticks and on to the heated stone benches covered with cedar and wet towels. When I step out of the parlor and into the sauna, I imagine myself among nude buddies, the children of the stone bridges, as we stand bewildered at our gathering and our identical nudity. Then the bathers would move into the parlor of dissipation and discontent, spread between the lumps of steam as the heat swells their sexual prizes. We would overflow then with complaints of illusory pains, decrepitude, exhaustion, servitude, and filth. A languid move of the hand would brush away dirt and hair like dead skin. In the mollification parlor we would regain our bodies—hairless and obese or marked by tattoos and scars. Bodies overflowing or happily settling within the human boundaries or consumed by their increasing thinness, waxlike and shadowless. Idols bent on their evaporating existence.

Then we would come into the middle hall beneath the bath's pentagon dome, light flooding its high windows. Steam would condense up there and fall on us in warm dribbles that induce semisenselessness. We would then disengage and become more prone to dreaminess. Then comes the ingenious parlor where I know the fabricating fellow. His lies would turn into a penis writhing on the bath tiles, bouncing from one water bowl to the next till it finally vanishes in the woods of steam and daylight feathers falling from the bath dome. Outside the public bath this man has no existence; neither does the laughing fellow, the crying fellow, or the cynical one. They are the mutant men of the bath, half human, half viper.

Then bodies become one nude form that slips into a big basin under a shower of waters hot enough to awaken in the veins the pleasures of breaking the fetters of the body. Desert drowsiness, cotton numbness, stationary and artificial trees, a fading sun, smooth marble floor. From a distance, a giant ball flickers like the egg of a mythic bird, emitting scented vapors. White doves alight on the rim of the basin, then transform into bathing maidens. The shapely bodies with little feet cast reflections on the marble of the pool, then transform again into birds that fly away. Behind the ball, the image of a white ship emerges gliding on the marble floor, and then it swallows the birds and disappears into the rising vapors. What remains visible then is whiteness alone. Drops of scented rains fall, and invisible anklets resonate, and out of the vapors red mouths take shape and caress the united bodies. For the bathers, a recurring dream comes back, and they remember the way back through the corridors and the basins and the benches and the drapes. A complete return eludes them, but they are finally delivered to the changing parlor, where they get back their clothes and go through the bath's curtain one more time.

The House of Names

The reader of electricity and water meters told me about a house in old Basra; it was behind the fish and vegetable market, close to a carriage stop where coachmen and appliance fixers would get together for rest. He would enter that house, its door open all day, to find to the right of the corridor a door on which the word *toilet* is written in chalk, and on the left another bearing the phrase *door to the staircase,* also written in chalk. The meter reader does not have to come all the way to the house yard, roofless and slab-stoned, since the water and electricity meters are under the staircase inside wooden boxes on which somebody wrote the words *Water Meter* and *Electricity Meter.* Flooding daylight exposes the writings on the other closed doors surrounding the yard: *Saintly Woman's Chamber, Bibi Karima's Chamber, Salih's Chamber, Marhoun's Chamber, The Bride's Chamber, Bathroom, Kitchen.* The oddest of these writings was on a door bearing the inscription *Chamber of the Lame.*

It was a child who went about practicing his writing by naming the house parts, especially its doors, with these chalky, fuzzy lines, exactly the way he labels parts of the landscape he draws in his school sketchbook: *fish, river, woman, car.* When he misspells names, images from his childish imagination creep into these chalky nominations. It's his way of driving away from his folks' house the silence, gloom, and emptiness once they are out. Although the meter reader has never seen a human being in the house, or an animal for that matter, no one with a hunched back coming out of the "Saintly Woman's Chamber," or a fiery figure darting out of "Marhoun's Chamber," he always felt the names signified the occupants' presence and the suppressed turmoil of life behind the doors of that ever-open house. Somehow like the bundles of leftovers dumped at night in the rusted garbage container at the door's entrance.

And as it happens in stories, one of the house's doors was left without a name to hint at what lay behind it. The chamber of warm secrets into which the child of the future has fallen, the one who wrote the names. Let's descend the steps into the room where a woman labors among three other women clustering around a stove. The patient women display their skill in supplication and small talk as the mother resists this collective invoking of the vocabularies of labor, relaxation, the promises of family life, and the pleasures of wet nursing. And resists the smells of medicines and the fumes of steam rising from the *tasht*, the talcum powder, the clean white sheets. The light falling from the room's single bulb flutters like a blade at the end of a thin line, never to fall. The mother's rhythmic breathing lifts her like white wings over the puddle of plasma and sterilizers and pincers and scissors. A sharp cry and the alighting of the fresh live lump end the feast.

The Friday child is born. Years later the boy will scribble on the unnamed room where he was born the name that has originated in his navel. For some reason he'll call it the "Honey Chamber," a vision of her name, the mother submerged in the darkness of the house of names.

Lutfiyya al-Dulaimi

One of Iraq's most prolific writers, Lutfiyya al-Dulaimi has published more than a dozen novels, short-story collections, plays, a half-dozen works in literary and cultural criticism, and several translations. The variety in her literary production certainly indicates a serious investment in culture consolidated through a lifetime of teaching and literary journalism. Some of her stories have been translated into Chinese, Russian, Polish, English, Italian, Swedish, and Romanian.

Dulaimi's writings deal with social, political, and historical themes and concerns prominent in Iraq and the rest of the Arabo-Islamic world, such as the relationships between men and women, love, violence, and the struggle for dignified living. But these themes are universal as well, and Dulaimi's works thus connect Iraqi realities to a wider world scene. These works urge the revisualization of the quotidian so that it becomes part of a reality that goes beyond local features. In "Lighter Than Angels," for instance, the thirteen-year embargo against Iraq after the 1990 invasion of Kuwait is central in a reality that the narrator recognizes but simultaneously refuses to make the dominant marker of her life. Similarly, the bombing of the Amiriyyah shelter during the 1991 war becomes the subject of Dhihkat al-uranium *(The Uranium Laugh, 2000).*

Dulaimi's techniques accommodate her characters' fluid movements in time and space. An obvious example appears in "Shahrazad and Her Narrators," in which the legendary storyteller comes back through the ages to reveal the inconsistencies of those who retold her stories. In this story and several others, Dulaimi celebrates the primacy of the act of narrating and shows its relevance to the lives of her contemporaries. Storytelling is a dynamic act, continuous and meaningful, and Dulaimi appears proud to pick it up to supplement her predecessor's tradition. The history and cultural heritage Shahrazad represents are extended in the lives of the women and men of the day. Equally important is the writer's effort to keep her writing from getting bogged down in the pressing realities she depicts. In "Lighter Than Angels," for instance, we feel the debilitating effects of the long embargo against Iraq, but the story retains poetic conciseness and allusive qualities, and it moves beyond such a troubling reality to explore the female character's effort to enjoy a life of art, music, and culture.

"Hayaat's Garden" is an excerpt from the novel Hadiqat Hayaat *(Hayaat's Garden; Baghdad: Dar al-Shu'un-al-thaqafiyya, 2004). The short stories "Shahrazad and Her Narrators" and "Lighter Than Angels" are translations of "Maalam yaqulho al-ruwaat" and "Akhaf min al-mala'ika" from* Maalam yaqulho al-ruwaat *(What the Storytellers Did Not Tell; Amman, Jordan: Dar Azmina, 1999).*

Hayaat's Garden

Like soft drizzle on the face that refreshes the whole body, violin music energized the warm evening. Maysaa's tunes made the world safe enough for women to crave for genuine living where they could find real love and real men. The moving tunes banished Hayaat's fatigue and wiped away the sting of her perpetual tears. They opened up the scenery in front of her, where she could bond once more with her old friend in the garden, the massive fig tree, as it whined with the moves of the violin bow across the strings. Maysaa had been taking music lessons twice a week in an effort to fulfill the dream of her missing father that she become a celebrated violin player performing in one of Baghdad's big concert halls.

The tunes extended into the night air and modified its colors, then leaped up to touch the lower extremities of the clouds. All Hayaat's senses took in the music, a condition of Sufi elevation she had acquired with Ghalib's help. He had introduced her to pieces by the Baghdadi Ghanim Haddad, the Turk Orhan Murad, and the Italian Paganini. In that musical condition in which the soul soars she had loved Ghalib even more. Or deeper, and the two of them had become one and discovered the rays of light leading to heaven.

For Maysaa's fourteenth birthday, Hayaat had got her the violin. She had sold some gold earrings and a chain with a fish that had colorful enameled scales. She had asked Ghada, the music teacher, to pick a suitable violin. Hayaat would listen to Maysaa practice, and a world brimming with cruelty and blood would gain a few bright spots. Maysaa was now twenty-four, and she had six students of her own. After enrolling in the evening program at the Conservatory, she was good enough now to play a Mendelssohn violin concerto. She also tried her hand at a piece she wanted to dedicate to her father for his dream of seeing her perform at a concert hall in Baghdad.

Women saw Hayaat and her daughter as an odd pair.

"A vain woman. She works day and night so that her daughter can study music."

"She wants her to become a player at the telephonic orchestra."

"No, no. The symphony orchestra."

"And who is going to marry a woman like her?"

"If my son ever dares a thing like that, I'll banish him to the end of the world. A woman who plays music, ha!"

"She's destroying her daughter's domestic future. She'll have to put up with a spinster."

Hayaat knew they would always find something to criticize. She would not be able to match their skill at deliberate misunderstanding and condemnation, but she knew well what she wanted, and she pursued it because she believed in it. What a waste of time it was to try to explain to relatives her views of herself and of women in general. The good thing was that she always confronted them, and they had no choice but to whisper behind her back.

"Her in-laws have boycotted her because of her daughter's music."

"None of her relatives visit her."

"They all dumped her when she turned down a marriage proposal from a relative."

"How can she remarry before she's sure of her husband's death?"

"And how can she remain with her daughter with no guardian around?"

"But where are the guardians? Her brother-in-law who's unemployed and living off his wife and mother?"

"Or her own brother who took everything, even her share of the inheritance?"

Hayaat knew, perhaps intuitively through her senses, that what grew in her garden woke like her at dawn to spread the secrets and aroma of reproduction with the first ray of the sun. Things have lives of their own and creatures have souls; she knew because when she had gone out at dawn during the days of air raids to get some weeds, she had felt then that the soul of the weeds had embraced her own and liberated in her that unstoppable force we call woman's eternal being. That night and the one after it there were no air raids on Baghdad or other cities. An undeclared truce of sorts for the people to get more drinking water and canned food and beans and tea and dates in preparation for the following round.

Charmed by the natural world and by living things, she muttered something like a prayer in praise of this overpowering heavenly bounty that binds humans to other creatures. The language she whispered was one that plants and birds shared. Her trances enabled her to rein in time and lead it wherever she wanted it to go. Challenges like these pleased her and enabled her to be what she wanted every morning. She could be the sum of things and needed no help from others. The self she saw in the mirrors of her dreams was the self she would stand by.

She bent and cut a weed with yellow fragrant flowers. She didn't know the name of the flower, but its scent gave away its secret. Then she heard a woman's voice.

"Good morning, Sitt Hayaat."

Her neighbor Ruwayda had taken her away from this union with weeds and fragrance. Her head had been sticking over the hedge separating the two gardens.

"Good morning, Umm Ziad. I thought I was the only one who woke up before dawn."

"The raids. We couldn't sleep all these nights. The two girls are traumatized, and Hisham and Ziad spend the nights following the news and playing chess. There's nothing we can do. We get some sleep during the day."

"Well, the past two days the raids stopped. Perhaps . . ."

"Hisham says news analysts predict they're preparing for a bigger assault."

"Perhaps the bombardment will stop."

"Who knows! You and we are the only people now left on the street. I suppose we're expected to guard the neighbors' houses."

"More people have left?"

"All of them have left. Left Baghdad altogether. They left at night. Amal and her three children and her husband went north, and Basma's family went to Najaf. They left the house keys with us, Sitt Hayaat. You're staying, right?"

"We're staying no matter what happens. Where would we go and why?"

"Suaad told me we must be crazy. She wondered what kept us from running away to save ourselves."

"We all are crazy, and staying is our brand of craziness."

That conversation had taken place twelve years earlier. Hayaat also remembered the column of cars leaving Baghdad when the bombardment started. People sought refuge in schools and mosques and shrines. Some even joined Bedouin camps in the desert. Hayaat used to watch them leave, merely moving in time but stuck in place. All places were alike under the rain and wind and fear, and they moved without a goal or compass. "Can somebody leave and never return?" Hayaat used to wonder. Some were willing to surrender half their years just to get away from death. What would they do with the other half? Nobody knew or wanted to know, and all they cared about was what was going to happen next. They vanished in all directions, flickering lights bound to extinguish as they went deeper into their escape.

They went to unknown villages, unfamiliar houses, and they had to change their habits and language and the way they wore their clothes, perhaps even their names, to fit in these places. Labyrinths of place that they would have to keep changing because their souls would keep denying them. Battalions of travelers exchanging hunger and fears and information. A woman gave birth on the road, another suffered an asthma attack, an old man succumbed to a heart attack. One of their companions was death; another was the anxiety growing with every step they took.

Fields of barley, ripe for harvesting, surrounded the roads, and behind them rows of trees that disappeared into the wilderness. Some women were crying silently in the cars. One wanted to go back because she had left her future hanging on a window, and another because she had not said good-bye to her beloved. A third because she had forgotten her diary, full of scandalous confessions and the secrets of the heart. What if her brother found it?

Suzanne thinks her birth was doomed by some unlucky star. Among her family members, only her sister Bouran had any luck. She left to go to Jordan and then married a Lebanese businessman. They put their capital together and invested it in tourism. Her brother Sinan had just found a job teaching architecture at the University of Kuala Lumpur in Malaysia. She was the only one who kept missing opportunities. She frittered away the fortune she had inherited from her father, a carpet and real estate businessman, and shackled herself further with ill-advised choices. Three years ago she had become engaged to Abdul Maqsud al-Ghannam. They had made the marriage contract, but Abdul Maqsud kept postponing consummation of the marriage in order to blackmail and humiliate her. When she asked for a divorce, he refused and, regardless of every legal recourse she tried, left her hanging. To add insult to injury, he married his cousin and continued to torture her. He would let her go only if she gave him half her house.

She had broken up with Ghassan after she met Abdul Maqsud, who had mesmerized her with his lies, and now she lay in this lonely bed with no hand caressing her arms or lips. She opened the bedroom window overlooking the Tigris, and the sun invaded the room. The breeze from the river was refreshing, but when the wind picked up, the house and the surrounding orange orchards were engulfed in the smell of burning gas from the oil refinery across the river. She closed the window and started up an air freshener that flooded the house with the exotic scent she had picked up that day. Luxury was her one weapon of defense against hazards that could come her way any time, especially from that man who had poisoned her existence.

To fight her troubled nights and days, she took baths in her marble jacuzzi. She scented the water with revitalizing mineral crystals and tried to forget. The body went under water, but her agony rose with the steam and spoiled the bliss of the water. That jacuzzi was a tiny borrowed sea bought with her fortune, but it was a fake sea like so many of the objects around her. Mere substitutes for real things that no longer existed. Everything in her life seemed to be an image borrowed from other, more real lives. Only the mirrors around her were able to penetrate her soul. "Do I have a soul left?" she wondered. Mirrors told her what she did not hear from people. They mocked her and possibly deceived her.

"Who am I?" she asked the mirrors.

"You're the plush silk sofas, the marble table, and the flower vase. The still-life painting, the statue that continues to stand there, and the curtains heavy with the dust of years. You're the female in her charming ascendancy and a woman in her descent into humiliating compromise."

Suzanne laughed and then wept.

Her laughter and weeping reached Umm Tomas, and she came up, her steps laboring from her heavy weight. She always carried her rosary beads with a small silver cross hanging at its end.

"You all right, may the Virgin Mary protect you?"

"I'm fine. Can I have my breakfast in the balcony?"

Two women—one thirty-five, the other in her seventies—gave support to each other in a world that was collapsing. Tomas had been sending invitations to his mother to visit him in Detroit. Before 9/11. Several invitations, with phone calls to coax her.

"Mother, go to Jordan. I'll arrange everything for you. You'll get the green card after you get here. And they'll give you citizenship. You need to hurry up before it's too late."

"Tomas, listen, you and your wife, Rita. I don't want citizenship. I have citizenship. And I don't want a green card, OK? Are you listening, Tomas? I don't want to travel. I'm staying here with Suzanne in the house of Bahjat, may Allah have mercy on his soul."

Umm Tomas had lived in this house for the past forty years, taking care of it and cooking Baghdadi and Mosuli dishes for the family. She stayed around while the family itself went in all directions. She witnessed the slow erosion of both the family and the house, and the dispersal of its descendants into graves and exile.

"They want me to leave home and go there."

"All your relatives left years ago," Suzanne would tell her. "You don't have anyone left here."

"Listen, Suzanne. My people are here in Baghdad and Telkief. My father and my mother, and my priest uncle Behnam, and my aunt Josephine and my aunt Victoria, and my cousin Joseph, and my cousin Matti. And Tomas's father. They all are here."

"But they're all dead.

"No, Suzanne, they're not. They are more alive to me than those who left me. Those who went away. I mean alive, you know, they come to me every night in dreams. I saw them when they went to the mountain on the day of the Assumption. I wish I could hear again one of uncle Behnam's sweet sermons. We don't hear them anymore. Aunt Victoria used to make *lawash* bread for the winter, and mother used to make the *kushki*. I used to go with other children to the orchards to collect the sumac and terebinth berries. Believe me, I see them every night. I don't see Tomas," she said. Then she added in her Mosul dialect, "but my prayers are with him wherever he is. May Allah give him happiness with the Virgin's blessings."

Umm Tomas wiped her tears away with one end of her black headscarf. Two braids of gray hair stuck from under its edges, the remains of her youth. The two women had tried to reinvent a family long lost, with Suzanne playing the daughter, Umm Tomas the mother. There was, of course, an allowance for the difference in social status. Suzanne was becoming drained in a strange and suspended marriage, and Umm Tomas had seen her only son leave her to live in exile. He was there and he wasn't, and she saw him and did not see him.

She visualized him at his baptism at the church of St. Yusuf, the guardian saint of workers, among children wearing white dresses with gold and purple ribbons. The deacon was going round with the incense burner. She saw the roses she placed at the altar and remembered the twenty dinars she donated for the soul of Tomas's father. The priest began singing the hymns. Tomas's beauty set him apart from everybody, including his father and me. May Allah make him happy and may the Virgin guard him.

Suzanne found an e-mail from her sister Bouran. Suzanne, do anything. There must be a way. Give him what he wants to let you go. Get out of the country with a temporary marriage contract. Come to Amman. I'm waiting for your reply. Bouran.

Dear Bouran, I can't, she wrote. Do you understand? There's no end to Abdul Maqsud's blackmail. He has refused to divorce me unless he becomes a co-owner of my house. I don't know how he knew the siblings had given up their shares to me. He has an arm everywhere, like an octopus. I went to check on your house. The guard had to go to Kut for a few days because his uncle had died. Anyway, I found the bedroom window broken and the alarm system disabled. I brought somebody to fix it. The thieves stole electronics—television, video players, and tape recorders. Bronze artifacts and clothes, and I think they took your black coat because it looked like real fur. The good thing is that the paintings are secure because they were in the basement. Your real fortune is in those paintings, the other things can be replaced. Brother Sinan told me you have been thinking of selling the house and furniture and farm. Will you be coming sometime in the near future to sell off your property? The gardenia bushes and the mango tree and the rubber trees are all dying. I cannot find a gardener who will agree to take care of the garden. It's a farm, they say, not a garden. Greetings to Walid, and congratulations on getting Lebanese citizenship. Let me know ahead of time if you'll be coming to Baghdad. Kisses, Suzanne.

Umm Tomas went to church on Assumption Day and brought an olive branch that she hung on her door. Suzanne bought a white dog, a pedigree with a birth certificate and ancestry in Switzerland and Lebanon. She also went with Abu Hussein, the night guard, and bought a large fish tank and cages for numerous parrots.

Suzanne had been trying a number of things. Japanese flower arrangement, French lessons, dieting, colored contact lenses, false nails, plastic surgery. The fissure between self and self widened. The body was becoming perfect while the soul eroded in a life of fear. One nightmare gave birth to another. She hired a night guard to protect her in case Abdul Maqsud tried to break in, and then she reported to the police assault attempts that had not happened. Dr. Salaam told her she was suffering from another bout of depression and wanted her to continue taking her medication and to see him every week.

"Finally, I'm leaving," Shirmeen al-Azmiri called and told her.

"How?"

"I found a young man interested in emigrating. For three thousand dollars he's agreed to a temporary marriage contract. The price of my freedom. We got the contract today. Aren't you going to congratulate me?"

"Are you planning to stay with him?"

"Well, if I find him likeable during the trip. Why not?"

"And if he refuses?"

"Why would he refuse? No, he wouldn't. Many would love the opportunity. What more could he want? Emigration? I'll help with that. Money? I have a lot of it. Charm? You know your Shirmeen. What about you?"

"You know how complicated it is. I'm really being held hostage now."

"You haven't persuaded Abdul Maqsud? Give him what he wants. Bail yourself out."

"No, I won't. I'll keep trying."

Shahrazad and Her Narrators

A man's captivating pursuits, his dreams, those doses of intoxicating poison, his energy, leaping emotions, power, oscillating temper, intuition, driving spirit, loneliness, and his times all converge and dissolve in a single maddening passion for a woman from another time.

Many women crossed paths with his, and in the midst of his longing they glowed then fizzled, leaving behind fallen mementos from which he made a wax monument for that coveted woman. The deep passion, confused but solid, began with a painful obsession with a female he called

Shahrazad, the one perpetually beyond reach. His infatuation gave way to slavish resignation that came with the expected pleasures, but drained the soul in a series of attachments to women in whom he sought some of Shahrazad's glamour.

The reigning woman captures his soul, showering his prime years with tales, mythology, secrets, and surprises, and sends him, body and soul, into a clash with today's discontents. In complete passivity the man celebrates this passionate bondage, for he's nothing without it. Lonely and reclusive, steeped in music and literature and art and the genealogies of solitude and hunger, his captivating pursuits override his everyday reality. He seeks refuge in her imagined times and scribbles something, adding a book or two to the hundreds that have already appeared about her.

Inside the confines of the passion enslaving him, the man nurtures the fragile emotion and surrenders to the mechanism of love. His desires are stirred and rebuffed, his dreams shattered and once more revived with a fresh and larger illusion that sweeps away his history, his job, his memories and women and pains, and carries him to a hypothetical time where he abandons all other events, passions, desires. He writes and reads and studies and compares what others wrote and said about her, feeding his craving with new discoveries and conclusions, including trivial ones. In this cycle of bondage he rejects all faces and names and possibilities; he frees his body and soul from what captivates them and disappears in an endless carnival.

A friend told me the man had taken a quotation from one of my stories and had it cast in gold Kufic calligraphy on a marble slab in his house. "Life entices, and when it entices, it enslaves, and when it enslaves, it obliterates, and when it obliterates, it produces its miracle of realizing endless beauty in the bliss of dying." When I happened to meet that man, I knew him without introduction. His lust for dying transpired like sweat from mortal bodies. He had a precarious presence, vulnerable to a dominating ghost that destroys all his attempts to break away. I saw his hypnotized walk, his eyes fixed at the emptiness, his body more like a moving agony spreading the smell of approaching sunset.

Everything around him leads nowhere but to the *One Thousand and One Nights,* and he has eliminated all possibilities of escape or departure.

Times that were once luxurious for him have turned to visible ruin, and what remains of his life are days fraught with dark possibilities. He tries to reenter the furious festivities of daylight, but can come only as a stranger shackled with synopses of books and decadent ideologies and trends. He enters daylight, but the legacy of Shahrazad besieges his world, filling it with her tales and deeds and wiles. Her artful language and seduction, her lows and highs, her wisdom, piety, vanity. From all this and from what storytellers had related of her, he creates a living idea, a celestial female body that takes form in successive rhythms. Stunned infatuation devoid of the mundane surrounding. Replicas of her celestial body invade the mirrors of his imagination and form all the scenery he can behold.

He's positive it would be a lethal mistake to give up the long painstaking pursuit of her trail in the writings about her. Through correspondence and intermediaries all over the world he has approached universities, theaters, music institutions, opera and fashion houses and collected all relevant monographs and dissertations, not to mention drama and opera and music scripts and sets. His obsession entices him to buy perfumes merely because their designers claim they have been inspired by her sensational and exotic scents.

He's devoted himself to the study of what he has collected about the talented beloved who achieved through cunning what an entire people failed to achieve, even when the heads of their daughters were at stake, and who tamed lust for blood with the artfulness of storytelling. In her endeavor to postpone her foretold destiny she overrode the king's era with an era derived from her imagination, and, infatuated with her narratives, the king had no choice but to wish secretly for her survival. She gave him three sons.

This man has knowingly fallen in love with her for one reason: that she might offer her last miracle for his own sake and in his own time. His passion has entailed a particular lifestyle that postpones living to a fantasy tomorrow that might not come. In abandoning the women of his times, he invents alternative pleasure in a vacuum and seeks refuge in Rimsky-Korsakov's music to redeem the temporal gap stretching between him and Shahrazad.

That escape route extinguishes the noise of the world of the living around him and unites him with her reigning voice as she unlocks the secrets of love. Intoxicating verbal pleasures embodying the power of love and lust, the waywardness of promiscuity and abstinence, superstitions and magic and metamorphoses, the feats of genies. Love stories of a man and a dove, a duck and an emir, a monkey and a queen, a youth and a deer, and love for him becomes not an experience of the living but an illusionary trick to breach the distance between humans and other creatures. An impossible gap that Shahrazad's tales bridge with chronicles and possibilities.

Discarding the passions of the possible, the man becomes a believer in a fantasy love. No worldly woman has ever satisfied the maddening passion for Shahrazad—hence his continued forays into the world of despotic monarchs and lustful princesses and vain old men and virile slaves. Endless scenes of rolling severed heads, spilled blood, drawn swords, conspiracies and poisonous potions, and lurking shadows possessed by the pursuits of flesh and power.

The man gives up the sense of awe for a moment and soberly traces Shahrazad's journey; he starts with reading about her risky venture of marrying a murderer for whom the pleasures of love and bloodshed were inseparable. He's horrified by the possibility that the king might have beheaded her, but is nevertheless tempted by imagining the scenes of that hypothesis, fast-forwarding to her foretold demise, the pending bloodshed that feeds the king's pleasures with intoxicating nectar.

But he also imagines a destiny for Shahrazad other than the one he finds in the books. A death that puts an end to everything. Had she died, then the whole myth would have died, and with it all the tales and tomes and the musicals and operas, not to mention decades of enchantment and slavish passion. He would have lost everything.

So what? He would have been liberated and joined the world of the living, worked, done things. In a spell of dazed pleasure he examines the outside world, finds a job, has fun, queues in a long line to get bread loaves, loiters on the streets, and courts pretty women, relishing their ringing laughs and copying the contours of their femininity onto his blank slates. And when he comes home, he eliminates their shadows one after the other, cleanly breaking with the world and its noises and dirt to preside on a throne of tormenting purity. But does he want to part with that sweet misery he almost sacrificed with the hypothetical slaughter of Shahrazad?

The curtains flutter, their fabric moving with soft touches. A beam of light explodes; a dawn the color of fiery oranges brings with it a form veiled like a giant bud emerging to embrace the light. Oh, no! This must be an illusion—a vision or a reverie. The form approaches him, and what he beholds burns him. As Rimsky-Korsakov's music dies out, he almost whispers, "Who are you?" But instead of committing the folly of utterance, he blesses the moment with silence.

Another step toward him would have brought her face to face with him, but she stops. Again he tries to say something; she moves, and his lips make the effort, but only ashes of a voice materialize. The invisible woman moves, or, rather, her right hand does. The hand gets close to him, covered by a delicate net of gold threads, almost one with the skin. An incomparable ornament that becomes her. Her first words emerge out of the orange body like flashes of lightening.

"I've come."

The man staggers, holding onto a table in front of him for support. For a split second he wishes that everything would disappear; he longs for a sudden melting into the night and tries the trick of fainting, but the brain doesn't cooperate.

"Shouldn't you welcome me?"

Her voice electrocutes him, traps him like a tiny lab rat that has been given doses of fantasy and shots of exotic love.

"What, you don't recognize me, after all these years' worth of books and music and passion?"

"Yes, . . . you, . . . but," he tries to speak, but his words just drop like frozen liquid.

"You don't recognize me, of course, because your image of me is not quite what you see now. Your image is one shaped by storytellers, cut out of their fantasies of a woman desired by starved multitudes. You're one of them. You failed to break away from the multitudes' shackles of imaginary pleasure."

"No, . . . I, . . . no—"

Her hand motions him to silence. "What do you know about me, then? My body? Voice? Words? Or your lust for me?"

"I know everything, everything about you."

"True, all that has been said and written, but you do not know me. You deceive yourself, and the more you think you know, the less you really do. Like the others, you misrepresent me. Nobody knows me."

"Yes, I do. I know your virtues, wisdom, skills. Your dignity and piety and industry. I know your family—your father the king's vizier and your sister Dunyazad—and I know you bore the king three sons. And I know more."

"You say I gave the king three sons?"

"Yes, am I not right? Didn't you bring the three of them to the king's assembly the eve you concluded the tale of King Maarouf and begged him to release you of the threat of death for the kids' sake?"

"Nonsense. Preposterous lies. I bore him no child because he, . . . well, he never touched me."

"All those one thousand and one nights?"

"This is a secret no teller has ever known, and I'm revealing it to expose a lie that has deformed the entire text."

"That changes everything then. Will you tell me what happened to your—"

"Voice?"

"You're reading my mind."

"Have you forgotten who I am? Listen, man. It was that voice that I lived on all those one thousand and one nights, and it was the one thing that breached the distance between my survival and the executioner's sword. And it was the contours of that voice that gave life to those tales of wonder and miracles about monarchs and lands and jinns and love and lust and levity. That voice carried the world to a mesmerized and avid king from dusk till silence fell when the cockerel of truce broke the night. My sister Dunyazad then would nourish the broken voice with drinks and potions and extracts, boiled or soaked, and would put on my throat bandages soaked in medicines and balms and ambergris and wines, and leave me to sleep shrouded in fear and silence. That voice was a heavenly gift that brought me miraculous survival. What remained of it after three trying years was the shadow of a voice."

"I have to apologize for stirring up the past. Please forgive me. But why this smoky veil that keeps me from seeing your face?"

"Wait, I'm not finished. I'll venture that your image of my face is also derived from what those liars wrote. Those books you cherish are worthless, and the secret I revealed to you proves that. You read all those books?"

"I spent a fortune on those countless books about you."

"What a pity! A life wasted on a falsehood—these books."

"You can't judge all books so harshly! Many taught me a lot."

"Judging from what I see, they only make you what you are not."

"How much do you see?"

"I walked around a number of times and saw a bunch of cities. Your twentieth century is closing on a depressing note."

"How long have you been here?"

"Long enough to read a lot of your books, and you know what an avid reader I am. All sorts of books, all sorts of lies. Worthless sheets and ink."

"What books did you like?"

"Those by creative and imaginative minds. Tales that go beyond your familiar world."

"Just like yours?"

"Perhaps. The ones whose events pour out of the imagination at the moment of telling. This was what I did in those one thousand and one nights, creating as I narrated. During the day I recalled what I had read and heard, but when night fell, I forgot everything and could tell only new tales."

"I'm not sure I understand."

"It's a matter of true creativity versus falsehood. In all ages history books don't tell things as they happen; they tell what powerful people want them to tell. And the result? A mountain of books that blunt mind and soul."

"I think this is too sweeping, but tell me one thing. Why did you go through that grueling labor of storytelling for a king who, you know, wasn't quite manly?"

"Life deserves narration."

"Your life?"

"And the lives of other women had I not put mine on the line."

"So yours was a salvation mission?"

"Not that. You aren't even close to sensing my intentions. In preserving myself, I paid tribute to the love of life. Postponing my death was a bloody duel that lasted for a thousand and one nights, and my resilience was a form of madness. Perhaps accepting the challenge of marrying a murderous monarch was lunacy itself. But—"

"But we all have our own brand of madness. They call me the Shahrazad lunatic, for example, and when you think of this infatuation with you, all these books, music, paintings, statues—isn't this madness?"

"Or, rather, an inexplicable postponement of life. I dodged my demise; you dodge your life in a march toward death. How many years do you have left to make your life worthwhile?"

"That depends on you."

"On me?"

"Right. You were pardoned after a thousand and one nights, a reward for your travails. You came to the end of narration and crowned your work with the saving of your life. I, too, wonder what I'll be rewarded for my perpetual passion for you."

"Look at my hand. What do you see?"

"A net of gold threads, transparent luxury that shrouds the blessed hand. What a truly royal ornament! Is it of your own creation?"

"Do you think I am immortal?"

"Is there one more deserving of immortality?"

"This is just a hand, and whatever ornament it possesses is the labor of tens of thousands of nights and days and events. It's a tale more than a thousand years old woven by the sun and the moon and the stars— the tragedies and catastrophes, loss and tears, suppression and deprivation, arms and blood, fear and unquenched desire, love and joy and pleasure and intimacy, the quiver of locked bodies, their promises and bounty. Water and air and dust and heat and nectar and perfumes and rain and gazes and touches, the longing of males and the scribbling of females and the imagination of storytellers. This net, woven of time's tested gold, is my current identity as my voice was my past identity. The hand is me."

"You blessed woman, I'm your final destination, and your hand's tribute will be my caresses and tears."

"Endless illusions. That's what you are, an embodiment of male illusions. I won't be your—"

"No, don't judge—"

"You're interrupting me. My work is only half done. A few women were saved when I mobilized my voice against one murderer a long time ago. What about all those killers in your own time? Who's going to tell stories to postpone human demise?"

"The world has changed, Princess, changed beyond the redemption of storytelling."

"And murder is on the loose, mapping with blood the entire world."

"There you go again. Is it the salvation mission that brought you here?"

"You have not and will never know me."

"Yes, I do. Then and now."

"Ignorant self-importance. I came here to—"

"Aren't you going to lift the veil and let me see your face?"

"Is it my face that dominates your thinking so much? Hasn't my talk so far revealed enough of my features? Eyesight continues to master your faculties, rather than insight, intuition, or the imagination."

"What is it that inhibits you?"

"Perhaps your tendency to judge beauty according to your habitual standards."

"That you won't dazzle me?"

"Or that you won't be able to handle the truth. Do you think I'm the same after all those centuries and their horrid metamorphoses?"

"Why not? With all your talents and wisdom?"

"Aren't you tired of all this nonsense? I certainly am. All the ones I knew through all these centuries reiterated it. No one asked me who I was or what I wanted. What got them were the masks, not my fragile humanity, anguish, deprivations, or fears. You haven't asked me why I have come, and all you ask for is to see my face. Do you know what the veil hides?"

"Shahrazad's glory and its many manifestations. Feminine beauty and the charm of immortal women."

"Good-bye, then. You can't see my point. I'm tired of what I have seen and heard from men."

"What? I won't let you go now that you came to my time. Bless me with the sight of your face. I beg you. I want you."

"Good-bye. You never asked me what brought me here."

"Your arrival has put an end to all questions."

"No use, no use."

"No, please don't go. You won't abandon me. I beg you; no, I order you! I'll leave you no choice. I'll lock all outlets and keep you from going away."

"I told you that you know nothing and you'll never learn. You'll never grow or know what you want to be. Haven't I told you that?"

"Don't leave me to this emptiness, out of time and out of place."

"Adieu, adieu."

His hand, feverish and trembling, reaches toward hers. The hand that rebelled and betrayed barely touches her hand, but enough to spread for a split second the gold threads over the dark earth. Night turns into specks of gold and ashes, and a long, tortured sigh quietly withdraws through the window over a whiff of smoke. Invisible quiver that dies in the darkness of the city.

Lighter Than Angels

Just before midnight an unexpected wave of mirth swept through me and overwhelmed me with penetrating lightness. My heart intimated a power potent enough to overcome what has paralyzed for so long my choices and movements. The power of darkness versus a daytime burdened by prohibitions and regulations and etiquette. I had little time to examine the sources of this passion to break away from earth, and I uncharacteristically embarked on counting the guarantees for tomorrow's livelihood. I opened my handbag and counted what remained of the money I got for

selling history and philosophy books and from auctioning a painting by a
dead painter, only to realize that for the history and philosophy and art I
let go, I got a pair of poorly made leather shoes for two thousand dinars
and a half kilo of coffee for three thousand dinars.

What a foolish trade; no shoes came with the power to take me away
anywhere, and coffee could only make me more alert to my daily trials.
When I actually tasted the coffee, it was exceptionally heavy, as if it had
somehow acquired the nectar of those minds I sold on the book market
and at the auction site. To escape this philosophical guilt, I watched a concert on television. It was Beethoven's Piano Concerto no. 4, and the Japanese pianist glowed and soared and then in some heavenly ecstasy
became one with the piano keys. White flesh blended with the black keys,
and the black dress with the white, and the screen emitted two streaks of
black and white pearls that drowned the pianist. The orchestra continued
to play unfazed by the woman who vanished into thin air.

From the southern window overlooking the garden a whiff of hot and
humid wind assailed my body, covering my face and neck and shirt with
stick dampness. I thought of writing a letter to him, but finding my pen
had no ink left, I hoped telepathy might reach him in his distant land and
give him a feel of my body. But when I reached to touch my body, lonely
and sticky, I had a feeling my hand roamed in a vacuum. The skin wasn't
there, and for a moment I thought perhaps my fingers had lost their ability to feel. I wondered if his fingers would find the same vacuum if he
reached to touch my body. I wished he would emerge at such moments of
longing, negating distances and seas just to assure me I exist through the
existence of my body.

But he wouldn't hear me from this rugged terrain of oblivion and catastrophe. All discourse here became a conspiracy of sorts, inscrutable
and lethal nonsense that blocks the heart's signals to those I wanted to
reach. In this part of the world my voice vanished with the vanishing
body, but I didn't give up and tried one more time to locate my body, still
lost in the ripples of the southern wind and the piano concerto. I went for
the arm and face and chest and leg, only to find more of the ghastly emptiness. The long night and the abrasive wind had eliminated my mass and
blood and being. The body without which I cease to exist itself no longer

existed, and the only thing that would stop my slide into nothingness, I told myself, was his miraculous coming. But if he came, how would he recognize me in this nothingness?

Perhaps he'd be amused by my disorientation and illusions of loss and of being in this terrain of catastrophe. But I had no illusions. Would he catch my voice, one revelation of my being? And one more time I looked for affirmations of my existence, but again found nothing. Frightened, I jumped and sneaked into my room, put all the lights on, and paused in front of the closet big mirror. There was nothing on the beaming glass but the wall and a reproduction of Goya's *The Duchess of Alba* I had bought from a penniless fine arts student. I stared at the duchess, relaxed in her luxuriously royal nudity, a stunned ecstasy that chronicles a whole period. The duchess' immoveable indifference gave me the feeling that she mocked me because I faltered in finding myself while she could see me with her metaphorical eyes. Alas, I extended my hands, and they stumbled on no hands or mouth or hair and felt no curve or bump.

I wanted to test my other senses, so I turned the radio on. I was flooded by the noise of mixed signals and voices, a jarring war of languages and voices that manipulated tunes and pitches and shrieks. When I turned to the television screen, I realized that the piano concerto had ended and was followed by scenes of shriveled and decapitated corpses, the outcome of torture where plucked limbs left blood flowing in colors becoming all races; purple, green, black, red, blue, yellow. The beautiful, lush grass gulped the blood with insatiable greed, and the camera stacked close-up images of the faces of the dying in swarms of bright blue flies ready for the feast. Birds of prey flew low and close in the spectacular sunlight. Praise be to Allah for sparing me such an end by turning me into a bloodless nothing.

I switched the television off and rushed to the garden, deliberately brushing against the lantana shrubs, but not feeling the sting of the rough and pointed leaves. Nothing but cars were darting on the street, and I returned to the house and carefully bolted and locked its main wooden door. I flung myself onto my bed, expecting but not finding the refreshing cool touch of the sheets or the pain in my neck as the pillows felt more like bubbles of silk. I passed my hand over what were the spaces and contours of my body and quickly fell asleep. I must have slept long because when I finally awoke, I was flooded in bright sunlight that crept from between the Indian lemon and the vine trees and bounced off the bedroom window. I had forgotten what had happened to me the night before and was naturally baffled by my shocking physical absence—my bed was neat as if no one had slept in it. It was also cold, and it seemed my body had left no trace of its heat on it.

I started to cry, and when I saw no actual tears or a face, it seemed that it was my soul I was crying out. I went out into the garden and into the street and could hear the clamor of cars and voices, but I couldn't see human faces. I hurried back into the house and dialed my friend's number and woke her up to tell her I couldn't feel my existence. Look around, I said, and tell me if you exist. I heard her laugh, in the stupor of sudden wakefulness, at what must have sounded to her like one of my . . . , but I shouted, Go on feel your body and tell me if you find anything! She laughed again and wondered if this was the gestation of a new story and begged me to let her go back to sleep. I begged her not to leave me to face alone those horrid metamorphoses. I struggled to make myself clear to her, or perhaps she was not quite awake yet. She was baffled by my repeated requests to feel and look at herself just to ascertain that she existed, and then I heard her frightened shriek and her words, No, I can't feel myself. Perhaps no one else here in the house can.

I told her that unlike in the old days I felt no hunger or thirst and that I was fully liberated from all materialistic obligations, including the potentials of violence or worse hunger. I could use my nonexistence to do splendid things and let out the songs long imprisoned in my heart. You mean that? she asked. Yes, nonexistence was synonymous with the resurrection of meaningfulness, I said, and I wondered where all this new greed was taking us. I assured her that our voices will remain, and so will the passions and joys of writing. I hung up before she could embark on depressing objections.

I ran again to the street, and again I saw only buses and cars rushing without drivers, and on the roads and sidewalks throngs of shadows seemed to exist apart from bodies to cast them. Voices were criss-crossing and bumping into one another, laughing and blending. In that pang of despair a moment of cruel joy came out of the certainty of escaping the pressures of physical presence and perils. Freedom from a demanding body, from its desires and limitations and taboos. Freedom from hunger and clothing and pain and diseases and destructive weapons and the rest of the silly and horrific concerns that occupy our entire human history. No longer fettered to a body, I glided among the numerous shadows on the sidewalks. Fleeing and floating energy in perpetual nonexistence.

My heart intimated what I suspected all along: that the aim of human existence in its most intense condition was to achieve the mythological disappearance, and now we all reached that aim and became a nation of charming angels, without bodies or fears or destinies. Their shadows cherish nothing other than their own secrets, not exactly something to which we had aspired. Humans had never before gone beyond the quivers of flesh and blood, the way they had now, to experience the pleasures of thin air and to vanish into infinite space.

Mahdi Isa al-Saqr

For about fifty years, Mahdi Isa al-Saqr quietly put out one volume of fiction after another to consolidate his stature as one of Iraq's key writers. His first collection of short stories, Mujrimun tayyibun *(Decent Criminals), appeared in 1954, to be followed by two other collections in 1960 and 1986. Several stories in all three volumes are among the best in modern Arabic fiction, and some have been translated into English, French, German, Russian, Spanish, and Serbo-Croatian. It is remarkable that in a little more than ten years between 1987 and 1998, al-Saqr published five novels, an explosion of creative energy at a time when many thought he was ready to sit at home and reread the brilliant oeuvre of his earlier years. Of these recent works, two stand out as worthy of wider audiences:* Al-shahida wa al-zinji *(The Witness and the Negro, 1987) and* Al-shati᾿ al-thani *(The Opposite Bank, 1998). A timely and well-deserved gesture came in 2001 when al-Aqlam, Iraq's premier literary magazine, devoted a generous section of its May–June issue to celebrating al-Saqr's rejuvenated career.*

The short stories "Breaking Away," "Waiting," and "Morning Exercises" represent major themes in his most recent works. The first deals with the obsessive longing his characters feel for remote histories and places. "Waiting" and "Morning Exercises" demonstrate their characters' refusal to accept defeat. Al-Saqr skillfully deploys imagery to embody resistance to assaulting forces. In both stories, date palms, bright daylight, music, and open skies provide the relief denied individuals in their potentially oppressive environment.

The last selection here, "A Dreamer in Dark Times," is from The Witness and the Negro, *a novel that depicts U.S. armed forces in a southern Iraqi seaport near the end of World War II. Although the place is unidentified, many details suggest the writer's native city of Basra. The book, however, quickly transcends the overarching problem of invasion and focuses on a universal* issue—men's and women's willingness and ability to break away from prejudice to embrace common human values. The central character, Najat, is a victim of one crime and a witness to another. She is raped one night in an orchard by a black GI, who then shoots and kills a white MP when the latter stumbles on the incident in the orchard. The shooting is an accident and has nothing to do with race.

"Breaking Away," "Waiting," and "Morning Exercises" are translations of "In'itaq," "'Uyoon adhnaha al-intidhar," and "Tamrinat Sabahiyya" from al-Saqr's Shawati' al-shawq (*The Banks of Longing; Baghdad: Dar al-shu'un al-thaqafiyya, 2001*). "The Returnee" is a translation of "Al-'awda" from Shita' bila matar (*Winter Without Rain; Damascus: Manshurat itihad al-kuttab al-arab, 2000*). "A Dreamer in Dark Times" consists of excerpts translated from al-Saqr's novel Al-shahida wa al-zinji (*The Witness and the Negro; Baghdad: Dar Afaq Arabiyya, 1988*).

Waiting

Her eyes on the road, the woman says, "I have a feeling we'll get something from them today."

The man turns his gray-haired head toward her. "May Allah hear you." He shouts his words into her ear.

The elderly couple sit close to each other on two old cane chairs in the shade of a palm tree just outside their house. They have been doing this every day—the ritual of hopeful waiting. The man lays both hands on top of the walking stick between his legs; the woman leaves hers in her lap, dormant like two tiny pets.

From the houses on both sides of the street, children and young teenagers take off for school, followed by hurrying men. Almost all action dies away in the alley.

"Last night in a dream . . ." She does not look at her husband as she speaks. He is lost in thought. "I saw our little son."

The man's silence puzzles her. She looks at him. "Do you hear me?"

"Yes, yes. You had a dream, and our little son was in it."

"Do you know what he said to me?"

"What did he say?"

"He said he's dying for . . ." She narrates the dream and falls silent. Time hardly passes as the elderly couple watch the road in silence. The palm tree shade shrinks on the alley's asphalt. The woman fidgets, and the man reaches for her knee. "It's still early."

"What do you say?"

He raises his voice. "I say he might still come."

The woman moves her jaws as if chewing food and says nothing. Her eyes are on the road searching for a glimpse of him coming into the alley on his old bicycle, a small leather mailbag hanging on the bicycle rod. The mailman has seen them there every day, patiently waiting for him. Dogged by their anxious expectation, they stand up as soon as he turns into the alley, well before he approaches them. He stops in front of them, leans on his bicycle, and greets them politely. Their eyes follow his movements, almost willing his hand to go into the bag, the adroit fingers flipping through envelopes to pull out a letter, perhaps two. Smiling, he would say, "They arrived today." But it has been a long time since the mailman has done that. All he offers is an apologetic explanation. "Sorry, nothing today. Maybe they're on their way," as if their mail came separately on the back of a camel. His apology, so often repeated, stalls the delicious waiting. Painful as it is, waiting has its own little pleasures, the tinkling of hope, the daydreaming, and the imaginary recitation of letters yet to be written.

"I have a firm feeling we will . . ." The woman repeats her hopeful words. The shade recedes unnoticed, exposing them to the searing sun. The children and workers come home.

The man looks into his wife's tranquil face and says, "Let's go inside." His despair makes him shout rather than speak.

"You go in."

"The sun will hurt you."

She does not answer. The man picks up his chair and goes into the house, supporting himself on his stick. The woman remains outside, surrounded by the alley's emptiness. Flooded by sunlight, she relaxes and relishes the sweet numbness creeping into her head.

A transparent wave engulfs her, tossing her up and down in swift motions. Then it flings her on a vast coast, its gold sand twinkling under the sun. She squeezes her dress to dry it, only to find it untouched by water. Not a single drop there. She looks around, dazzled. She tries to recognize the place.

There and then she sees him on that ancient bicycle, speeding toward her. He stops in front of her, gets down, and starts to reproach her, breathlessly, "You sit here enjoying the sea breeze while I rove around looking for you!" He pulls up his mailbag and lets the bicycle drop onto the sand. "Here, take this!" He gives her a letter. "And this!" His hand goes into the bag again. "And a third one!" He laughs. "All the letters in this bag are for you. They arrived today. All the boys and girls wrote—all of them. The mail has been delayed."

He holds his leather bag up and turns it upside down, shaking its contents into her lap. A cataract of colored envelopes covers her body. She turns into a tiny hill of letters, still falling on top of one another. Her head emerges, the gray hair all but gone. She giggles like a child, and the mailman bursts into a laugh, dancing around her. His bag is still up there, envelopes pouring down till they cover the sand around her with lovely colors. They fall and fall, endlessly.

The Returnee

He sat there staring at the emptiness in front of him. Her sudden absence had confounded him. Out of the loudspeaker the voice of the *muqri* reciting the Qur'an invaded the surrounding space and buzzed in his ears. It subdued the polite, intermittent whispers of the funeral guests assembled in his house's front yard. His eyes picked up and dropped the men's polished shoes as they changed positions on the grass under the lawn chairs. A day such as this had been coming, of course. He knew that. She would go before him, or he would, but he didn't know the separation would take such a toll on him. "What tortures me is the idea that once we leave this world, we never return." These were her words as they were having tea one day. He told her that no human being or object ever leaves this world as long as the world continues going around and that living things simply keep returning, only changing their outward appearance.

She felt a little better then. "So, I'll be back once I'm dead?" She waited impatiently for his reply. "You'll be back like the rest of us. Perhaps as a tree blessing the ground with a dense shade or as a bird filling the sky with happiness." She looked content and said she'd return in the form of a sparrow that endlessly circles the house and lives in the trees of its garden. "No, no. Let me think. I don't want things to stand between you and me. I'll come back like a cat and go places with you. Scratch my body against your legs as you read or sit absent-minded." He laughed and said she'd outlive him.

"Father!" His oldest son, seated next to him, touched his arm and brought him out of his reverie. He stood up and pressed the outstretched hand of one of the mourners. He said a few words and then sat down. Numerous faces passed in front of him today. Too many to look into carefully. Some were with him at the cemetery. Darkness had fallen then, and a boy had brought a lantern that shed some light on the silent faces. They were standing around the graveside as the gravedigger worked hard at deepening the dark hole in the ground. One of the faces hanging over the grave separated itself from the others, and a little later the sound of water trickling to the ground in the dark behind him shocked his ears. A jarring sound in the midst of silent sleepers. He didn't turn his head, and a minute later the face returned to join the other grim faces. As they piled the wet dirt over the shrouded body, city lights gleamed in the distance. One pair after another, car lights pierced the darkness on the road going downtown, like torches carried by ghosts into the throbbing city.

This is how a companion who had filled his life with mirth turned into a mere memory. For others, her departure was just a social occasion. They'd linger a while, but eventually would leave the funeral gathering, each heading off in his own direction. He wished they had never come because this endless movement was wearing him down. His legs ached, but he had to observe the conventions; otherwise they would say he had showed no respect for her memory. These rituals, they say, keep the be-reaved preoccupied and shield them from the pain of loss. But nothing so far was lessening the pain of her loss. An abyss had yawned open in his soul and brought him endless desolation. They had lived together long enough to know what the other thought without uttering so much as a word.

Words stopped being a necessity.

Their looks alone were enough.

"Take heart. We all are on this road." He stood up and shook the hand that the man extended. No one would argue with this simple fact, but fragile human emotions rarely take notice of hard facts. He heard some of the low, cautious conversations among those around him. Some talked of the latest news, and others finalized business deals. Bitterness crept into him. How tired and forlorn he felt. His son noticed that and stopped re-minding him to stand up to receive callers or bid them farewell. He apolo-gized for him, mentioning his weak heart. That was true enough—his was a weak heart.

He kept staring in front of him refusing to accept her absence. Then he saw her coming. He hadn't seen her in the neighborhood before—a small white cat strolling quietly over the green grass, between the chairs' and men's legs. His face lightened up as she approached, and his heart came to life when she stopped under his chair. She sat on the grass, and a little later she scratched herself against his leg. He smiled and bent to pick her up. Unfazed by the looks in the mourners' eyes or the concern in his son's, he left the funeral assembly. His back was turned to them all as he walked toward the house, his arms around the cat.

Breaking Away

Only a few patrons were at the café that early in the day. An elderly lady from the nursing home sat by herself eating the cherry pie I usually brought her with the coffee. She would cut a piece and pick it up with her fork and chew at it with her shiny dentures. Through the window her eyes followed the people going into and out of the bazaar. In the other corner of the café sat a man by himself sipping his coffee slowly as he looked at a newspaper spread on the table. My coworker, Mary, stood behind the partition washing dishes and glasses, her plump body swaying with the music coming from a tape recorder on a shelf behind her. The café owner was away depositing money from the previous day's takings.

I stood close to the front window panel watching the old painter pegging up his work on a rope he had tied between two poles. His was a corner of the roofed part of the bazaar next to a wooden bench and not far from the café. Mary came and stopped right behind me, her hand on my right shoulder and her chin on my left. Her thick blond hair was all over me, and one of her breasts pressed against my back. I was engulfed in her overpowering femininity.

"What are you looking at?"

I moved away from the lure of her maddening body, her head falling off my shoulder. She approached again:

"What is it you're staring at? I don't see a thing out of the usual."

"I'm looking at the old painter displaying his art."

"You must be delirious!"

"I know he's not there . . . . I know he's been bedridden since he fell sick, but I can't help visualizing him right there. A thin body topped by a bright, graying head."

"Leave the old man alone and try to get something done before the boss comes back."

Two days before he was taken ill, I had given him a postcard I had received from home. It pictured a scenic date palm orchard that he had promised to paint for me. But sickness was faster.

"Do you want me to call the nursing home and see if you can visit him?" asked Mary.

"Yes, please do."

A man and a woman entered the café and sat at a table. "You take care of them," I said.

"Why, aren't you working today?"

"Do it now, will you?"

I continued to stare through the window. I saw the old man approach, pushing his ancient bicycle. He used to ride that thing before he became too old to bike. But why bother now about the bicycle? Mary said the old man was a little crazy, but I didn't think he was.

The old painter leaned the bike against the wall, untied his big bag, and laid it on the bench. He then carefully emptied its contents: a bundle of papers, a square board, color pens, a plastic mug for the pens, a piece of cloth stained with all sorts of colors, a small container with clear liquid, a brush, pegs—ordinary clothes-pegs. The old man lined up his stuff on the bench and from the bundle of papers began to pick the painted ones. He would pick one and fasten it to the line with two pegs, then pick another and another. When all the paintings were on the line, he would sit on the edge of the bench, put the board on his knees, take a blank sheet of paper, and clip it to the board with four small tacks. He would then start sketching.

"The boss will be here any time now, and you're still standing there staring through the window." Again, Mary came closer and stood right behind me.

"Did you ask the home if I can visit him?"

"Yes, you can go if you don't stay long."

"I'll go this evening. Do you want to come?"

"I can't stand sick people, especially the elderly. They depress me. I'll wait for you in your room."

The old man used to take a break from painting at ten in the morning. He would wave to us, and Mary would pour his tea and put a slice of apple pie on a small plate. Then I would take it to him. If I didn't have much to do at the café, I'd linger a few minutes and look at the paintings spread out on the line.

"This one is so lovely," I once said of one of his paintings. "All this harmony of color, and these rays of sunshine trying to break through thick foliage."

"You like *The Forest*?"

"Very much."

"Do you want to get into *The Forest*?"

I looked at him in disbelief. He wasn't joking. Was he really crazy, as Mary thought?

"Get into what?" I asked him.

"Into the painting . . . into *The Forest*."

"And how would I do that?"

"Come back during your next break and I'll show you. We'll enter *The Forest* together."

He stopped painting when I returned and stood up. He took my hand and led me to the picture. "Now. Concentrate all your being in your eyes and just look at the colors."

We stood there together contemplating the forest—its trees, its dim roads, and the glimpse of a distant sea. We were silent as if in prayer. A moment later the branches quivered, the leaves fluttered, and the wind blew among the trees. I found myself there with him inside the forest. We walked on ground covered by withering, falling foliage that kept cracking beneath out feet.

"Look at that huge tree on your right." A colossal tree stood there, its thick and overlapping roots were sunk deep into the soil but were still smooth and glistening with raindrops, as if dirt had never covered them.

"Do you know how old that tree is? More than two hundred years," the old man said. We marched into the heart of the forest, with the old man still holding my hand. Birds were chirping, and those that weren't were busy digging among the fallen leaves. We watched them fly away and disappear into the trees.

"Excuse us," the old man whispered to the fleeing birds. "We didn't mean to disturb you." We continued our walk between rows of trees. A gusty breeze from the sea refreshed us and set the branches swaying, sending more leaves to the ground.

"If you're tired, we can sit on one of those benches," he said.

"I hope you're not tired."

"When I walk among the forest trees, I regain my youth."

The waves of the sea were glistening with sunlight now, and a vast sandy beach came into view behind the trees. Seagulls shrieked as they flew over the shallow water close to the coast. "Let's sit over there," the old man said, pointing to a concrete bench next to a garbage can fastened to the ground not far from the water. I sat, but he didn't. He stood facing the ocean, then one of his hands delved into a pocket and came out with a handful of bread crumbs, which he peppered on the sands. A flock of seagulls dived onto the crumbs. We silently watched the gulls fight for the food and tuned into the hubbub of the waves as they hurried, bright edged, only to break upon the beach in undying whispers. The breeze had a little bite now, so I raised my jacket collar a little.

"Let's go," the aged painter said.

In the evening I went to visit him. From the entrance to the nursing home an elderly woman led me to his room. The woman interrupted her conversation with a colleague of hers to say she was his friend. Like a loyal dog, his deserted bicycle remained on the balcony, next to the door to his room. I patted its cold handlebars consolingly. The old woman knocked with a bony finger, then put her head through the door. I heard her say, "Quit playing sick. Look here—you have a visitor," and then she pushed the door open.

"Go in," she said and went away.

I stepped into the silent room. His bed, the central piece of furniture, looked vacant as if there were nothing under the nearly flat cover. A waxen face bereft of all light, however, was visible from a tiny space on the pillow. His eyes sparkled when he saw me. "I'm glad you've come."

I pressed the hand he extended—fragile and cold. I sat on a bedside chair close to a table adjacent to the wall on which he had a water pitcher, a glass, a container of dark medicine, and a book. A spoon was balanced horizontally over the glass.

"How are you?" he asked.

"I'm a little worried about you."

"I'm fine." He pointed to scores of paintings hanging from ropes running across the room. "I did all those in my old age," he said with a touch of pride.

"A magnificent achievement."

I started looking at the first row of pictures and was thrilled with the one that immediately caught my eye. I got up and went around the bed to look at it closely.

"Those date orchards of yours I painted . . . just before . . ."

"As if you lived there."

"Take it." I pulled the painting from the rope and rolled it up. "Take any other painting you want."

"If you don't mind, I'll take *The Forest* we entered together."

"That one is on the next rope."

I unpegged it and rolled it up over the date palm painting and came back to sit by his bedside.

"Your postcard . . . that's in the Bible—on the table," he said almost out of breath.

I took the postcard. "I'll let you rest now—my stay must have exhausted you."

"I'll have a long rest pretty soon."

"No, you'll be up in a few days."

"Death doesn't scare me—it's just another way to delve into a painting."

I stood up and bent to kiss his white forehead. I pressed his arm a little and left.

When I arrived back at the pension, I found the door to my room ajar. I pushed it open and saw Mary lying on the bed. Her short dress revealed a generous portion of white thigh. She didn't stir, but merely turned her head and smiled.

"You're late."

"I didn't stay for long."

"How is he?"

"I'm afraid he's going down."

"Nothing unusual there. He's an old man." She sounded indifferent.

"There are a lot who are older than he is."

I stood there in the middle of the room holding the rolled-up paintings, looking at her bare skin.

"Leave the old man alone. Come and lie down beside me."

"Mary, please leave. I'm tired and depressed and would like to be alone." She couldn't see why I was avoiding her. She sat on the bed.

"You must be kidding."

"I'm not."

"Don't be silly. You don't want to spoil the night because of that crazy old man."

"Not just that."

Getting off the bed, she said disappointedly, "It was stupid of me to waste my time waiting for some nice time together."

"Perhaps another time."

"You think I'll ever set foot again in your damned place?" She picked up her bag and left, angry.

I closed the door and sat on the edge of the bed for a while, then I got up and unrolled the two pictures. I spread the old man's *Forest* on the table, pinned the date palm orchards on the wall, and stood there contemplating them the way he had taught me. My eyes devoured the orchards until I was enveloped in the greenery of the date palms. Hissing fronds fluttered in the air over my head; doves cooed and sparrows chirped on the branches and in the tops of trees. All these years I had missed the smell of wet, cultivated land, of the irrigation channels, and the aromas of fruits in the trees and herb bushes lining the roads. And leaves warmed by sunshine, smoke curling from chimneys in the tiny villages scattered among those orchards, and the smell of bread baked in *tannur*s.

I walked among palm trees and branching vines in sunny and shady spots, caressed by a succession of warm and cool breezes. I stepped over arches of date palm trunks that were caked in dry mud from the feet of those who had crossed during winter. Green frogs croaked in the shiny waters below, and schools of tiny fish darted away as my shadow approached. From a distance I heard the voice of a man singing, sweet sad singing echoing among the trees. I passed a mud hut where a woman was baking bread in a *tannur*, its round top blackened by years of use. I greeted her, and she beckoned me to approach. She handed me a warm, round loaf of bread and said: "Son, eat it for your good health." I took the bread and walked toward the river, savoring small pieces of warm bread and big chunks of my bygone childhood. The river swarmed with ships bound for the gulf and big, rectangular ferries pushing against the water toward the city's ports.

The other bank was covered with a dark, endless stretch of orchards. I sat on the ground in the shade of a date palm and rested my back against its sturdy trunk. Basking in the moist river breeze, I took off my shoes and stretched out my legs. I closed my eyes, surrendering to a spell of delicious drowsiness. The water flowing in the river carried me away from under that date palm, on its eternal course between endless stretches of palm tree orchards.

Morning Exercises

Our little boy was playing by himself in the front garden when the siren shook the morning's quiet.

He rolled his colorful rubber ball on the grass and ran after it, then sent it in the opposite direction. He looked happy, and his mother and I contentedly watched him through the big window. We had no pressing matter to attend to.

The ominous shriek shook our lethargy. We sprang to our feet and ran toward him, bumping into each other. He was standing there, bewildered. I snatched him, and we all ran back into the house.

He fidgeted under my arm and cried, "I want my ball."

"Later."

My wife drew the curtain, blocking the daylight, and turned the radio off. The music had no chance against the wailing siren, anyway.

"Why did you turn it off?"

She sat next to me and said, "We need to hear what goes on outside when the siren goes off." She gave our kid a tentative smile. He had settled quietly on my lap, my arms around his little body, as the stubborn siren terrorized the air around us. Under my arm I felt his heart racing.

"Don't be scared—it's just an exercise," I said.

"An exercise?"

"Yes, all this noise comes from a small thing. They're just testing it."

I raised my voice a little to make sure he heard me. The siren finally went off. For a few minutes we could hear only the frenzied traffic on the nearby streets. Then silence fell as the roads emptied themselves. We waited. The boy was uneasy, so I sat him beside his mother and headed toward the radio. I turned it on, and music flooded the room with soft tunes. My wife didn't miss the incongruity.

"You are crazy."

"Perhaps."

The sweet music mysteriously touched the place. An absurdity under that trying atmosphere. I had the kid in my lap again and heard my wife's trembling voice.

"There's a plane up there."

"I want to see it," the boy said.

"You can't see it," I said. "It flies too high."

The boy sat miserably under my arms, listening to that intruding sound vibrating in the sky. It sounded distant but unique, unadulterated by other sounds. Much like the night buzzing of a lonely insect. That did not last for long. The air around us roared with the antiaircraft artillery. The little body shrank. He asked me:

"And this is an exercise, too?"

"Yes. They fire in the air to test the artillery."

I evaded his questioning stares. He turned to his mother, who gave a smile too wan to assure him. I went to the radio again and turned it up. An odd mix of artillery fire and string instruments. My wife shot a hopeless look at me. A few seconds later we heard a heavy but distant explosion, and the collapse of a large structure, as if a torrent of boulders were suddenly let loose.

"*Ya satir!*" my wife gasped.

I gave her a cautioning stare.

"Why not make us some tea?"

"Now?"

"Will you please keep quiet then!"

The boy moved to his mother's lap, consolingly. My wife looked at me and said, "Shouldn't we sit in a more secure place?"

I said, "Every place is the same at a time like this."

Outside, heavy artillery fire continued to roar. Then a deafening explosion nearby. The ground under us shook, the doors and windows rattled. A large glass panel came crashing to the floor, barely held by the drawn curtain. The radio went dead—perhaps because of the explosion.

The child's eyes widened with fear. I saw my wife, the color of her face gone, rise with the boy and dash deeper into the house. I stood up and looked at the curtain fluttering in the wind. The artillery sounded as if they were in the next room. Glass shards pierced the curtain, and daylight sneaked in. For a moment the curtain looked laced with silver lines in all shapes and designs.

The antiaircraft fire finally fell silent. An ambulance raced on the quiet streets, then a car a little later. The heavy silence afterwards lasted only a few minutes before the siren sounded again, the wail more like a sigh this time. The city came back to life. I opened the curtain; the air blew through the broken window, loaded with smoke, dust, and other smells. There was no fire in the distance in front of me. In the pristine blue sky pigeons flew over the palm trees and houses, flirting with the bright sunshine as if nothing had happened. Except there was the smell of burning in the air and the broken glass.

"At last it's over," I heard my wife say behind me. I turned and saw the kid hanging on to her hand, his eyes still questioning.

I said, "You can go out and play in the garden."

He was hesitant, his eyes on the ball lying where it was on the grass under the brilliant sun. He let go of his mother's hand and went out.

I said to my wife, "Let's gather the glass before it hurts someone." We picked up the shards off the floor and furniture. My head was down as I carefully picked up the pieces when I heard my wife say, "Look at him!"

I turned my head. The kid stood still there, his hair glistening in the sun. The ball was in his hand, but his eyes were on the suspicious sky as if he heard distant echoes.

A Dreamer in Dark Times

Chapter One

Just before Hameed got close to the water, he saw an American MP standing arms akimbo on the bank watching the river. He recognized his white hat and white, wide belt and the big gun. A big man, too, with a flushed face topped by blond hair that stuck out of the hat. His sleeves were rolled up, exposing muscular forearms with a light suntan, unlike the locals' swarthiness. The river extended in front of him, wide and full, its tranquil surface shining with the morning sun. Close to the bank seagulls looked for small fish in the shallow waters, their shrieks adding to the noises coming from the nearby street. Owners of commuter boats at the crossing point quarreled noisily as they scrambled for clients.

Cautious and hesitant, Hameed walked toward the MP and stopped a few steps from him.

"Smoke, smoke, sahib?" he said, his hand pantomiming smoking.

The MP ignored him and kept looking at the river in front of him.

Hameed got closer to the man. Perhaps he didn't hear him.

"Smoke, sahib, please," Hameed mumbled and pantomimed smoking. "May Allah protect you."

"Fuck off," the man said as he turned an angry face.

Disappointed, Hameed retreated but kept looking resentfully from afar at the MP. He bent down and picked up a stone and looked back for a second at the massive structure in front of him, then turned his eyes away to a large seagull hovering over the river bank. He threw the stone at it, but the bird swerved away toward the river as if carried away by a strong wind. It's funny, Hameed thought, how fast it flew away.

Then he noticed the MP was leaving his spot. His eyes followed the broad back and the heaving, muscular buttocks that reminded him of the behind of a plump woman. The sparkling black butt of the gun quivered with the moving thighs. The MP joined another uniformed MP at the crossing point. They guarded the point day and night, Hameed thought with a smile, to make sure none of their soldiers crossed the river to the other side where the brothels were. But as soon as night fell, the prostitutes themselves crossed the river, with nothing but a bedspread tucked under their arms. They sneaked into the date palm orchards at the outskirts of the city, close to the barracks and depots scattered in the desert.

Hameed bent and rolled up the bottoms of his pants to start his daily work. The pants were stiff with dirt and dry mud. He stopped when he saw an American army jeep park on the other side of the street. There was the entrance to the market with the arched roof. His attention turned to the jeep. He loved these compact cars and fantasized about owning one of them. He watched its three occupants get out from a distance. Three men—an MP, a local policeman, and a good-looking, lanky young man in civilian clothes. He saw the men enter the market, led by the local policeman, who proudly held under his arm a big black official book. The sight of these men made him uncomfortable. They must have come to arrest somebody, and Hameed wondered who that might be.

His eyes then moved to the black[1] driver who stayed in the car. He was smoking and looking at what was going on in the street and the river below. He looked like a giant in a cage. A big frame squeezed into a tiny space. The driver then got out of the car and started stretching his body next to the car as he looked at the river. It was clear he was bored as he waited for the men's return. Hameed crossed the street and approached him. The driver noticed him and smiled, revealing white teeth. That was enough encouragement for Hameed.

"Smoke, smoke," he said and raised two fingers to his mouth.

Without hesitation, the Negro reached into his shirt pocket and took out a colorful pack of cigarettes and offered it to him. Hameed grabbed it and pulled a cigarette as he scrutinized the Negro's face, and when he saw his warm smile, he took another.

"Tenk you, tenk you, sahib," he said and returned the packet.

He smelled the two cigarettes and tucked them behind his ears. The Negro laughed, and Hameed looked at him for a second and laughed with him. The Negro stopped laughing, but retained a smile. Amicably,

---

1. The word *zinji,* "Negro," is used in the Arabic text. It does not have the negative sense it usually has in current American usage, so I opted to translate it as "black."

he laid a heavy hand on Hameed's shoulder. Hameed liked him immediately for his generosity and warmth. Then he heard him speak fast and lifted a baffled face to him. He had no idea what the Negro said, but decided not to offend him.

"Yes, sahib. Yes. OK," he mumbled with a positive nod.

The driver's face beamed immediately, and he gave Hameed's shoulder a gentle squeeze. He appeared delighted, and Hameed wondered where that joy came from. Then he was stunned when he saw the bawdy gesture the man was making with his other hand.

"Chicks, chicks," he said, pumping his fist sideways.

Hameed didn't like the look in the man's eye.

"No, sahib, no chicks. Not allowed. MP," he said resentfully and pointed toward the two MPs manning the crossing point. The driver's face became glum, and he pulled his hand from Hameed's shoulder.

"Oh, fuck the goddamn MPs," he said angrily and turned away from Hameed. Hameed did not know what to do for a moment and then started to check out the car. He went around it, admiring its different parts.

"OK, sahib," he said after a while, pointing to the car.

"Yeah," he said, completely indifferent, and his smile was gone.

The driver then ignored him altogether and followed with hungry looks the back of a young woman on the street. When he whistled, several passersby turned around, and the woman rushed with frightened steps. Hameed thought it was wise to get away from this reckless driver and from his car, and he went back to his spot on the bank. He was still curious about the three men, and he waited for their return. Then he saw them emerge from the market, with the MP leading the way this time. The driver went back to his seat as soon as he saw them. Hameed's heart jumped when he saw Najat. Her face reflected the bright rays of the sun as she came out of the dark market. Her mother dragged her own massive body next to Najat. He soon lost interest in the three men and devoted his eyes to the face he adored. Where would she go with her mother so early in the day? he wondered. He became even more bewildered when he saw her mother talk to the local policeman and shake her hands with obvious anger. What was going on?

The three men headed to the car, and Najat and her mother followed them. He became alarmed when it dawned on him that they had come for Najat. Why wouldn't they leave her alone? Why wouldn't they leave people alone? He crossed the street again and got close enough to see what was happening. He saw the good-looking man hold Najat's hand and help her into the back seat of the car. She was silent and quiet as if she were hypnotized.

"I will not let my daughter go alone," her mother said and continued to wave a heavy arm in front of the men's faces. "I'll go with her."

Her shouting drew in some people, and the policeman asked them to disperse. Hameed was upset and decided to follow the scene from the riverbank. Numerous questions dogged him as he kept hearing the mother's loud voice as it imposed itself on the shrieking seagulls. Najat sat quietly in the car, her head hung down, unwilling to be seen by others. The young man was translating to the resentful MP what the mother was saying, and the MP continued to shake his head and repeat "No, no, no, no" as he looked at his watch. Umm Najat then grabbed the metal of the car with her huge hands and insisted on going with her daughter. At last the MP gave in and let her get her wide body into the jeep and sit next to her daughter. Soon enough a victorious look on her face washed away the frustrated anger. The MP sat next to the driver, still shaking his head resentfully. The young man sat with the two women and the policeman walked away since his mission of locating and delivering Najat was over. He walked in the direction of the police station, hugging his record book.

Hameed's heart leaped up when Najat raised her head and looked toward the river, even though she looked dazed. Her eyes fell on him briefly, but she did not smile as she usually did when she ran into him. Her look was indifferent, or perhaps just oblivious to her surroundings. A world he knew nothing about was engulfing her; his dejected looks followed the car as it sped away. Why was she so depressed and disoriented? And where were they taking her? He wished he knew as he sank deeper in his fears.

He remembered the day when they had kicked him out of their depot outside the city. He had been leaving after work with a crowd of porters and had tried to sneak through the gate, but one of the white MPs discovered the small amount of sugar he had hid in his clothes. The MP had forced him to eat all the sugar. Then he had him take off his clothes and stand naked. He then had painted his body, including his face, with tar and had him stand there in front of the shocked porters. Then he had him stand in an empty barrel at the gate of the depot so that those passing by would see him. The barrel was hot and his stomach was upset, not to mention that the tar was burning the flesh underneath. He had felt as if his body had caught fire, and he started to vomit the wet pulps of sugar inside the barrel. He was tired but had not been allowed to sit, not even in the barrel. He had remained there till he was let free at the end of the day. He had come home after the onset of dark and had given his mother the scare of her life. She thought a black ghost had slipped into the house.

Those people might hurt Najat even though her mother went with her. What would the mother do anyway but raise a shouting hell? Hameed pulled one of the two cigarettes from behind his ear, asked for a light from a passerby, and sat on the bank smoking. His distracted look followed the direction where the jeep had vanished.

From *Chapter Three*

Najat hesitantly walked with the translator. The camp swarmed with men. Five rows of them, about six feet apart. The soldiers stood under the burning July sun separated by two feet. The colonel and his white escort were joined by a black officer at the end of the first row. A few steps away stood the four white MPs she saw a moment ago sitting in a jeep at the entrance to the camp. They all were waiting for her arrival. She felt dozens of eyes watching her as she walked and stopped out of sheer fright. The translator told her to proceed. She walked with him, still tormented with anxiety, and when they approached a group of officers, the translator told her to wait, and he went alone toward the colonel. The waiting brought trepidation. The two talked for a while, then the translator asked her to approach. She froze, and he had to encourage her again. Her baffled eyes were fixed on his face.

"The colonel says look at their faces carefully," he said with a calm voice. "Take your time and scrutinize their features. If you see the culprit or his companion, just stay in front of them. Don't move. If you identify one of them, they'll take care of the other. Let's go now."

She did not move. He spoke too slowly as if he were talking to a child. She kept looking at him not because she did not understand, but perhaps because she was waiting for some elaboration. In fact, she understood every word he said, especially his phrase "if you see the culprit." The thought that "the culprit" was among them, standing in one of these long lines, paralyzed her. She was going to see him. She was going to have a second encounter with him.

"Go ahead," the translator said, baffled by her inaction. "Don't be afraid of them. They can't do anything to you."

She moved awkwardly, then stopped in front of the man at the top of the first row. She raised her head slowly and looked at his face. The black face and broad nose and full lips look like the rapist's. No, maybe not. She was not sure. The face and neck were covered with sweat, and the man just looked straight ahead over her head and into the open space. He appeared as if he had stopped breathing, and she moved away from the frozen features and aimlessly looked at a bulging vein in his muscular neck. It looked like a tight cord along the neck, and her look lingered there to avoid looking at the face above her head. She dared not raise her eyes again, and it hit her that this was just one of many faces she would be looking at in these long rows. She wished she would disappear from the face of the earth at that moment and would not have to look at these stiff faces. And she froze again. The colonel and his men thought that this was the wanted man, and there were some quick exchanges.

"Najat, is this the man?" she heard the translator ask.

"No, no, that's not him," she managed to say.

"Move on, then," he urged her.

She heard the black soldier's sigh of relief as she moved to the next in line. Well, she almost got that man in trouble. Her unsure eyes went over the next face, and that, too, looked like him. And the third one. And the fourth. The faces covered with sweat under the scorching sun looked alike, with almost identical features. Their stern faces forced her to push her head back to be able to see them. After a few encounters she realized that they, too, feared her as much as she feared them. Those giants who had stripped her naked with their hungry looks a moment ago when she was in the car were standing there looking at the vacuum above her head in total surrender to her scrutinizing eyes. The colonel was behind all of this. He wanted to get to the culprit. He was walking along her side, his overbearing body bumping into her every once in a while, but he did not seem to feel her presence as a woman. He treated her more like one of the police dogs she heard were being used to track down criminals. His questioning looks quickly and abruptly moved from her face to the face she was looking at in an attempt to figure out responses and reactions. The men looked past him the way they looked past her.

She was very careful not to make a mistake. Every face she approached looked like the face of the wanted man. Her heart would sink for a second, and then she would realize it was not him. The lines seemed an endless succession of faces, and she wanted to be done with looking at them. Sometimes she would linger for a second and move on quickly, but at one point she felt the colonel's firm hand clamp her arm.

"Don't rush! Don't rush, you bitch!" he shouted above her head.

She lifted a frightened face to his. She had no idea what he had said or what he wanted. The translator told her that the colonel wanted her to look more carefully at the faces. The colonel pushed her arm angrily, and she moved, but she struggled to slow down.

That colonel despised her and treated her like a slut, she thought. She was not surprised, given the place where they had found her. She could not but recall the events of that miserable night in the date palms orchard. And the frightened face she saw in a split second in the MP's torchlight. She prayed to Allah that she might not see that face again. She forced herself to proceed slowly in front of the long lines of faces. Even the air surrounding those erect men's bodies was charged with anxiety and tension, and it suffocated her like a thick, sticky liquid. What if she closed her eyes and opened them and found that she was done with the whole business?

What if all this was a dream she could forget someday? The body odor coming from those sweating bodies under the burning sun and the colonel's towering and threatening presence left little room for wishful thinking. When she got to the last face in the line, she felt some relief as if she had just emerged from a long, dark tunnel. Her sigh of relief did not last long, though, for she had to examine the faces in the other rows.

It took an eternity to go through those tense faces, and when she was done, the colonel and his men surrounded her. The translator was passing on their questions.

"Have you seen him?"

"As I said before, it was nighttime and dark," she tried to justify her hesitation.

As soon as the translator rendered her words, the colonel exploded.

"Look here, you fucking bitch, you whore," he said, pointing his long finger at her face and showering her with curses she did not understand in front of all those people.

"It's better to just answer the questions," the translator intervened.

She realized she could not get away with indecision any longer. That colonel was not someone who would settle for half truths, and she did not want to aggravate him any further. He could send her to prison.

"I didn't see him," she said, defeated.

The colonel said something to the translator and continued to wiggle his finger in her direction.

"The colonel wants you to look him in the eye when you answer his questions," he told her.

She raised her eyes to the colonel and said with a quivering voice, "I didn't see him among them."

His cruel gray eyes penetrated hers in an attempt to read her thoughts and feelings, and she shook out of fear. But she struggled not to let him stare her down in case he would think she was lying. His aggressive attitude had gradually created in her a desire to challenge him. He would not see through her. If she chose, no one would find out from looking into her eyes what she wanted to keep secret. But would she benefit from keeping those secrets? The white officer whispered something to the colonel, who then talked to the translator.

"The colonel says maybe you saw him, but you were afraid to speak in front of him?"

The colonel could not believe she did not see him. She knew he was trying to get her to talk, and she was getting firmer and firmer.

"I didn't see him in any row," she said as she looked at the colonel.

"And not his companion?"

"No, not his companion either," she said. She wanted to say that she never saw his companion's face because at the time of the incident he was in the dark all the time and the MP's torchlight had not fallen on him, but she did not want to see the colonel explode again.

"How about anyone who looked like them?

"No one."

The colonel watched her for a while, then turned to the two officers and talked for some time. The alien words added to her bewilderment. The soldiers were still standing in the line looking steadily ahead. The colonel turned to the translator, and her anxious looks turned in that direction as well.

"The colonel says that's enough for today."

She could not withhold her sigh of relief.

Mayselun Hadi

One of the most promising talents to appear on the Iraqi literary scene in the past two decades, Mayselun Hadi has received well-deserved popular and critical acclaim. She grew up in Baghdad, where she was born in 1954, and has continued to live there even during the harshest times in recent years. Her extensive experience of the Iraqi reality has enabled her to produce some of the best Iraqi writing on the events of the past two decades. In two of the stories selected here, she deals with two such events, the eight-year-long Iraq-Iran War in "Her Realm of the Real" and the stifling embargo against Iraq in "Outage." Her novel Al-alam naqis wahid *(The World Minus One), published in 1996, is among the best on the psychological fissures of the Iraqi society during the Iraq-Iran War. A similar engaged position is also evident in her ten publications for young readers. Like Lutfiyya al-Dulaimi and many other Iraqi writers, Hadi has worked much of her life for literary and cultural magazines.*

A predilection for playfulness in both subject matter and style sets Hadi apart from many of the writers of her generation, but without making her fiction mere adventures in writing. The dictating mouse of "Realm" offers an intriguing version of the travails of writing and perhaps reveals some of the writer's notions on engaging a dismal reality with elaborate escapist designs. The writer who seems comfortable in the presence of an inspiring mouse does not budge from her position on an appropriate ending for a story. In "Calendars," it becomes futile to sort out today from yesterday, hence the mutating father-son figure consolidates the story's reflections on time as a dominant force.

"Her Realm of the Real" is a translation of "Zeinab ala ardh al-waqiʻ," and "Calendars" is a translation of "Taqaweem"—both from the collection Rajul khalfa al-baab *(A Man behind the Door; Baghdad: Dar al-Shuʾun al-thaqafiyya,*

1994). *"Outage" is a translation of "Inqita'" from* Laa tandhur ila al-saaʻa *(Do Not Look at Your Watch; Baghdad: Dar al-Shu'un al-thaqafiyya, 1999).*

Her Realm of the Real

Funny things happen to us fiction writers during the night. To the living, darkness brings sleep and quiet, but to our heads it brings commotion not unlike that of a hungry mouse when the house residents are fast asleep.

The mouse begins scrawling on the walls in a disorderly fashion. It runs over there, hits a wall, then comes back and hits another, and soon all that running turns into faces, characters, thoughts pushing against one another, but in a manner gentler than the mouse's running. Of all those thoughts only one might materialize. It walks out of the mess and takes the writer's hand and brings her to the writing desk to be dictated to by that unruly mouse.

He sits in front of me, and as soon as he sees I'm a fiction writer, he asks: "Will you write my story?"

"Do you mean something that happened to you?"

"Yes."

"I'm sorry, I don't write factual stories."

"What do you write, then? Fantasy stories?"

"I write about the zone that straddles reality and the imagination." Then, with a touch of condescension, I add: "Archeological excavators don't come across gold bars. They find bracelets and necklaces and rings. In a manner of speaking, this is what I do, change bars into rings and necklaces and bracelets."

"Beautiful. What my story needs is a golden touch of this type." He falls silent for a few seconds, then says: "It's been only a few months since my return from captivity."

"Nobody comes back from captivity. Once you're a prisoner of war, you're a captive the rest of your life."

"Before I went, all the relatives I had were my mother and my cousin Zeinab. We used to live together in a small house in one of the narrow alleys of Bab al-Sheikh."

"Go on. Names of places and people don't interest me."

"But I want to talk to you about Zeinab."

"I'm not stopping you."

"Zeinab isn't your typical beautiful girl, but whoever knows her inevitably loves her. She's an angel."

"Oh, please! Spare me the clichés."

"But really she's an angel."

"Do you know what an angel is? Tell me something else. How about calling her a woman?"

"But she's more than that. Her kind heart has place enough for the entire world. At sundown her hands would make combs rove in all directions so that the tangled hair of the alley's women and girls would turn into smooth braids, and when she washed our front yard, she would leave little puddles of water for the birds and stray cats to drink from. One day she saw me sprinkle hot water on a cat that kept stalking the kitchen, and she sat and cried silently as if I'd hurt someone she loved. She wouldn't even reproach me for that. In fact, she never reproached anyone for whatever craziness they came up with. She was just a healer."

"That's nice," I say.

"The last thing I remember before I left was my bedridden mother kissing me, and Zeinab standing at the door, her head down so that I wouldn't see her tears. At the time I wanted to lift her head up and wipe away the tears with my fingers. My heart, I thought, would then caress her coy, soft face. But I didn't. My heart was coarse—like my fingers. I left, and she stood at the door, eyes on the ground.

A refreshing breeze comes through the window, and the curtain flutters a little. He turns to me and says after a heavy sigh: "Our home was benches draped with clean, white covers, and cooked rice being drizzled with sizzling oil. Old women endlessly asking for rugs to pray on. That was the home I left nine years ago. I think of it, and my chest fills with the smell of risen dough, and my feet yearn for a walk on the cool, wet tiles.

Oh, to hear again the noon *athan* coming down to us from the nearby minaret and filling the courtyard with joy."

"But you've come back to it, right?"

"No, not a real return. My mother is dead, and Zeinab is gone. The house is now like lumps of dry dough on the rim of a bowl, and stray cats take refuge in the *tannur.*"

"Is Zeinab dead?"

"No!" he explodes like a bullet.

"She got married?"

"I don't know. No one in the alley knows where she went. She just disappeared."

"No trail whatsoever?"

"No. Like the proverbial drop of water turning into vapor. No word or trail."

"So?"

"Oh, I've been looking for her everywhere since my return. If I hear her name, my head spins, and a trace of her scent maddens me. Strange, I can't confidently recall her features, but I see her in everything around me. In the aroma coming out of the cupboard when I open it and in the scent of the soap when I bathe. In the folds of the shirt I wear, the braids of little girls, the squeaks of the kitchen door. I feel she's out there surrounding me every minute and going places with me, but I can't see her or touch her. A few days ago I overheard two women walking behind me talking about a woman named Zeinab who had gotten married and had a daughter. They should go and see her, they were saying. For a moment I was almost sure this must be my Zeinab, but I dared not ask them about her."

His head drops, and he adds: "I didn't dare. The following day the same two women were on the street talking about Zeinab again. Can you believe such a coincidence? Can you? Wouldn't you say fate had sent them my way to lead me to Zeinab? But I hesitated and missed the chance. I should have turned to them and simply asked about what I've lost. I was busy working out what to say to the women, wondering how to begin as I looked into the faces of the passersby. The moment I turned to pose the question, the women were gone. Vanished—as if they had descended unnoticed into the underworld. For months now, I've been going around looking for Zeinab, turning with agony when I cross paths with the mirage that has become her name."

He looks at the blank sheet on my desk and says: "Do you think it's a painful story?"

"Yes, but one I've heard many times before."

"I know this will sound strange, but my wish is that you give it a happy ending."

I put the pen away and say: "I don't like happy endings. I can't grant your wish."

He gives the pen a baffled look and says: "But I came for this reason. To tell you my story so that you'll give it a happy ending."

"I'm sorry to disappoint you, but happy endings are not my line of work. And a happy ending won't fit such a story in the first place. The whole thing will sound forced when you give it the ending you want. The critics will jump on me if I do."

He lays his head on his left hand and says: "Do you write for—?"

"Listen. There's a bunch of storytellers in this neighborhood. Go to my next-door neighbor Abdul Baqi Maqsud and tell him to give you the ending you desire. I'm sure he'll oblige you because he loves that type of ending."

He looks reproachfully and says, "Will he be awake now?"

"You'll find him fast asleep, but wake him up. I'll write you a nice note."

He doesn't look convinced, but he rises and just before he reaches the door turns and asks: "How would you have ended the story?"

"Do you really want to know?" I say, trying to be kind.

"Yes, I do," he whispers.

"All right, I would have Zeinab one day sit on a bus behind you, with less than a meter between the two of you."

"But I'll turn and see her," he thunders, nearly waking up the entire house.

The curtain flutters again, and a gust of air threatens to blow away the sheets of paper. I spread my hands over them and say: "No, you won't turn and see her. You won't even feel her presence. You'll watch the road, unaware of her smell and the hissing of her dress. She, too, will be distracted by her memories and won't see the turn of your head or hear your characteristic sneezes. She'll get up, her breasts over your head, and her blouse brushing against your hair. You'll fidget and tilt your head forward, but you'll not turn. She'll get off, neither of you seeing the other."

His angry eyes tell me: "You can't do this." He's about to slam the door behind him, but his hands suddenly let go of the doorknob. He becomes quiet and contemplates the curtain as it stops fluttering.

"Aren't you going to see Abdul Baqi Maqsud?"

"No," he says, his eyes starting to water. He collapses into the chair next to the door and cries out in torment, as if he realizes for the first time since his release from captivity that he has lost Zeinab forever.

Calendars

I see him every day. The old man who owns the newspaper kiosk at the corner. A pile of morning newspapers is forever in front of him and next to them piles of thick dictionaries and old and new tomes.

In the car I catch a glimpse of him as I turn left. Because I see him every day, I don't see any signs of aging in him. The face as wrinkled and the hair as white as when I saw him for the first time twenty years ago. Now that I think about it, even the piles of books and magazines on the counter look unchanged, as if they go off with those who buy them but then return a little later to that same counter to wait for new customers.

Two days ago something happened that made me think the man had grown younger, or perhaps older, than I thought. His hands had been shaking as he gave me the dictionary I had asked for some time ago. A small, yellowish cricket had leaped from the stacks of books and landed on his bloodless hand. I had taken the book and given him a large banknote, the only one I had at the time, but he had handed it back to me and said I could pay later. He had neither seen the cricket nor seemed aware of its forays on his hand.

I turned left the way I do every day and saw him sitting as usual behind the morning papers. He was fiddling with his tiny radio in search of newcasts from distant stations. The pointed little frequency indicator inside the radio, its tip showing marks of decay, still seemed to bring him the same station he'd been listening to for the past twenty years.

As I approached him, I noticed a much younger man sitting in his place. Thin, sullen, and bored, but looking so much like the old man. I assumed he was his son.

"Where's your father?" I asked.

"My father?"

"Yes. Isn't he the man who used to sit here every day?"

"I'm the one who sits here every day," he said and turned his eyes to his radio.

"Two days ago I bought a dictionary but couldn't pay him."

"I was here two days ago."

"Perhaps. But I came early in the morning."

"Who did you buy it from?" he said, still fiddling with the radio.

"Your father. He sits here every day. You look very much like him."

He stopped tinkering with the radio, and his face suddenly beamed. "You bought it from me," he said.

"No," I said. "I bought it from your father."

"I know you," he replied. "You used to come by when my father was here. But my father stopped coming to the kiosk years ago."

"No," I affirmed. "He was here just two days ago; and I still have the dictionary I got from him." I walked to the car to fetch it, ignoring the young man's call to come back. When I placed it in front of him, he said: "Oh, yes, I remember. I sold it to you two days ago. You didn't pay then."

Determined not to miss this lead, I said, "So, just two days ago?"

"Yes, two days ago."

"Then where's your father?"

"He's incapacitated and hasn't left the house in years. I stand in for him now."

"Wait a second," I said, remembering something that might contradict his strange persistence.

I went back to the car again, thinking of the calendar I had bought from his father two months ago. He had himself circled the date of his granddaughter's birthday and had asked me to bring him that day a roll of color film for his son's Polaroid camera. I work at a photo lab, and they couldn't find a roll. I opened the car door, but why would the calendar be in the car? It was at home. I returned to the kiosk, upset at letting this new obsession take hold of my mind. No, I shouldn't let it. I opened my handbag and searched for the money to pay the young man. The father's tired voice startled me, "What's the hurry?" he said, chuckling. When I looked up, I saw the old man sitting behind the counter and fiddling with the radio dial.

"Where's your son?" I tried to laugh.

"My son?" he said as he lowered the radio's volume.

"He was here a moment ago," I said.

He muted the radio and asked: "A moment ago?"

"Yes. I was going to pay him."

"Him or me, what's the difference?" he said and took the money and handed me the dictionary.

"Wasn't he here?" I said, the dictionary still between us.

"No way! He's been abroad for years," he chuckled incredulously.

"He said he took over from you years ago because you were unable . . ."

"I told you that," he waved a fly away and added, "when you asked about the old man who used to sit here behind the counter years ago."

"What old man?" I asked.

"My father," he said, waving away another fly. "He's at home paralyzed and has absolutely stopped manning the kiosk."

I remembered the calendar again and asked him: "Was it he or you who circled the date on the calendar?"

"Oh, yes, I remember. Yes, he was the one who did, and the birthday girl is my daughter."

All the strings I tried to follow vanished. I was about to put the dictionary in my handbag and leave. "Do you remember when that was?" I asked.

"You buy a calendar every year. I forgot on which one my father wrote." Then he added, yawning, "Today or yesterday. My daughter is married now. It must have been many years ago."

He picked up the radio again. A yellowish cricket leaped from behind it and raced on the bloodless hand before it disappeared between the books.

Outage

The man brought the kerosene lantern closer to his face. *"Shubayk, Lubayk,"* he whispered, trying to sound dramatic.

The woman pretended to be startled and said: "Bring us the power back."

The man began counting to ten very slowly, an ancient game of inscrutable hope that he occasionally played during electricity outages. Though the game was dominated by chance, his talent was in giving it a magical touch and the semblance of credibility as the house sometimes did get the power back.

His face showed how seriously he performed the role of the genie, and when he reached number eight, his counting became even slower. "Eight and a half, eight and three-quarters," and at nine and a half he wondered if he should continue.

She said nothing for a while, enjoying the playfulness in his voice. Then she ventured: "You know, the reflection of the lantern on your face makes it look magical."

He gave a broken, nasal laugh and put down the lantern next to her. He relaxed in the dark, lying back to watch the pattern that the lantern made on the ceiling. She put out her hand and slowly felt his features. It was late at night, and she wondered why the power cut happened. She touched the rim of his prescription glasses and then his unshaven face. She almost asked him something, but she didn't.

"Your beard is growing."

"I haven't shaved it since the *maquilleur* told me not to."

Had she heard right? What a strange thing to say! It sounded like a remark from a book or play. And she remembered the first time she had seen him shave five years ago. Exactly forty days after their marriage. The collar of his shirt was turned inwards so as not to be stained by the shaving lather. She had brought her nose closer to his face and smelled it. That lather was still there hidden under the thorny black stubs that he let grow because the *maquilleur* had asked him to, as he said.

She went back to the open book on her lap. Suddenly she remembered the silver bracelet she had left at the goldsmith's five months ago. She looked at things in the room as they started to become recognizable with the spreading lantern light. She wondered why she had left the bracelet at the shop for so long. The smell of kerosene from the lantern reminded her of a thick black cloud that had hovered over Baghdad one day, then dumped its black rain over the city. Black streaks could still be seen on the roofs and fences.

"The smell of the lantern is like the smell of war," she said.

"There's hardly any kerosene left in it," he said.

"Was it Hesse who described our age as the age of black fear?" she asked.

"No," he replied, forming a shadow on the wall with his fingers.

"Was it also him who said that a deferred hope brings ailment to something?"

"No, that was Samuel Beckett, too," he said.

She noticed that he used "too" unnecessarily. She waited for the fingers to leave the wall, but they didn't. She went back to her book and flipped back to the previous page, rereading what she had read a moment before.

Their neighbor's Volkswagen suddenly roared into life, and the sound reminded her of low-flying helicopters. Her heart raced, the doors of the house rattled, and the lantern gave out. She closed her book and sat in total silence. The man grumbled a little, then reluctantly got up and went to the yard to bring kerosene for the lantern.

She heard the kitchen door open and then the sound of something hitting the ground. She felt a harsh and powerful hand squeezing her heart, and the darkness became more oppressive.

"What fell?" she asked.

"I don't see anything," he said. After a while he added: "A plastic container."

He closed the kitchen door and came back to the living room. She held the candle he had taken with him when he had left the room, and he poured kerosene into the bowl of the lantern. In winter a few years back she had lit a candle in the bathroom and gotten ready for a bath. The pot of hot water had been quickly cooling down, and the candle had kept flickering because of the poor quality of the wax. As she closed the bathroom door, the siren had gone off, and she had felt trapped, like prey. The flickering shadows had seemed like Death's massive and pointed fingers pursuing her soul in that enclosed space.

She pushed her book aside and said impatiently: "When is the power coming back?"

The man gave the same broken laugh and continued his counting: "Nine and three-quarters." A few seconds later he thrust his hands in the air and leaned back against the sofa before shouting: "Ten!"

His hands remained outstretched but then fell back into the darkness. Outside, the night was becoming saturated with a black liquid spilling from an invisible and inexhaustible bowl. The neighborhood houses were drowned in that dark deluge, and her soul was banished to the void more harshly than ever before.

Abdul Rahman Majeed al-Rubaie

Abdul Rahman Majeed al-Rubaie was born in Nasiriyya in the southern part of the country, and he has paid the finest tribute to his roots through themes and characters drawn from that area. If cities could choose those who portray them, Nasiriyya could not have found a keener son.

But Rubaie's work and life also point to a writer doggedly aware of his place in the larger Arab and world scenes. His literary output and journalistic career span dozens of countries, cultures, and languages, from the Far East to Western Europe and the Americas. This might also explain his fondness for experimenting with forms and his responses to other writers' experimentations. No wonder, then, that he is one of the better-known Iraqi writers, perhaps better known outside Iraq than inside it. One of the myriad ironies of Iraqi culture under the decadent Saddam regime, this status might explain why Rubaie's novel Al-Washm *(The Tattoo), which went into a sixth printing in Morocco in 2002, has never been published in Iraq.*

A prolific writer who has produced collections of short stories, novels, volumes of poetry, books of literary criticism, and at least one autobiographical volume, Rubaie has received deserved critical attention. A bibliographic volume recently published in Arabic about him lists numerous books and scores of articles and studies. A docile and generous person who sends his books to students and critics, Rubaie has facilitated and promoted this critical interest in his work.

Rubaie's firsthand knowledge of Baghdad and other Arab and foreign metropolitan areas creates in his oeuvre a striking tension between the city and the countryside—between urban burdens and the relaxed pace of life among lush fields and open spaces. His fiction swarms with characters who inhabit both terrains and who continuously negotiate the fluid or constricted flow one into the other. In the chapter excerpted here from The Tattoo, *for instance, the main character, Karim al-Nasiri, straddles the two worlds and seeks refuge in one when he disgraces the other.*

The first selection, "The Tattoo," consists of excerpts from chapter 10 of the novel Al-Washm (The Tattoo; Susa, Tunisia: Dar al-maʿarif, 1996). The second selection, "A Man and a Woman," is a translation of "Thalika al-rajul . . . tilka al-marʾa" from Rubaie's short-story collection Sirrul Maaʾ *(Susa, Tunisia: Dar al-maʿarif, 1993).*

The Tattoo

Night was falling on the ravished houses of al-Nasiriyya and on the bodies of the prisoners, placid and robbed of all energy. Trivial talk, repeated ad nauseam, was weighing heavily on me. Tired and depressed by the overwhelming uncertainty that was lashing all of us, I couldn't fake any emotion.

Two nights ago questioning of detainees began at the camp, and the number of those present gradually declined. Detainees to be questioned would be taken to an undisclosed location; each departure was shrouded with silence, mystery, and endless speculation.

"They're being killed."

"Buried alive."

"Transported to the desert."

And the endless rumors. "The sheikh's dead."

"I won't hesitate to give my life for him," said Riadh Qasim.

"Is this a time for heroism?" one detainee shouted.

"Saving our own skin is what matters now," another added.

Mohsin Khalil then said, "Those who confess will save themselves."

"Manliness here means putting up with our private ordeals," I said to Hassoun.

I moved away from them, wishing to clear my chest with a puff of breeze from the distant Euphrates. Time is getting heavier, burying us under layers of rocks and sand. Bored, I blew my nose and wiped it.

I fetched the shaving gear, and before I lathered my face, I looked at my weathering features. A scary, dead face, like an autumn leaf, with no trace of the life that had once emanated from the swarthy complexion. I wished I could shed this face and don the younger one.

I scoured the emptiness around me and missed the sheikh's face. And Adil's and Mahmoud's and Fadhil's. They all were gone, taken to a far-away and horrid place, and we were left with pain and sadness too big for any action to overcome.

What would I leave behind? What medals would adorn this collapsing chest? The dwindling aspirations of a forsaken, extinguished face. A bullet in the head in a real battle would have been a fulfilling end, good enough for my name to be added to the battalions of martyrs. But this lackluster end was harsher than the stings of a python or scorpion. If only I could slash my wrist with this cutthroat blade!

"Mahmoud, how will you avenge the cause of your wretchedness?"

"If it is a human being, I'd kill it, and if it is an ideology, I'd devote the rest of my life to its destruction."

Hassoun, if this goes on, I'll be driven deep into the abyss of madness. Will killing Mariam Abdulla bring an end to my anguish? Will it end with my breaking away from the party's bondage? Can I change my name, color, and history and walk around like everyone else? I have a feeling my love for Mariam has mutated into a subconscious hatred that's breaking and enslaving me. My melancholic figure has become a fixture in bars—silent intoxication and a descent into filth. But I carry in my pocket a long knife that sparkles like raindrops, and I seriously think of planting it in her ungrateful chest.

Riadh Qasim was pacing the hall of the detention camp when he saw I was by myself. He approached and greeted me.

"How are you?" I said.

"I miss my mother's face," he whined.

"What about fear?"

"What fear?"

"You're right," I dodged my own question. "Why would we be afraid?"

"Ustath Karim, I've always thought of you as a man of courage."

"I still am, Riadh," I said, my head hanging low. "The circumstances are no longer hospitable."

We walked around in the spaces vacated by the detainees who had been taken away.

"Have you written a poem lately?"

"I've written other things."

"But you've never shared any?"

"Seeing the state you're in, I didn't want to add to your trouble."

I see in his face glimpses of my vanished face. If he's fortunate enough to stay alive, the histories ahead will scar this face and deform his soul. His head will be swinging right and left.

"Come now. Read me a poem, will you?"

I pulled the knife from my pocket and laid it in front of me. Its terrifying shine will pierce her chest in no time. Her eyes will turn white, and she'll drop at my feet. I'll pull the knife, then, and plunge it into my own chest. A romantic death and a fitting end to a grim tragedy. But I'm paralyzed, Hassoun, my hollow figure crushed by nonstop drinking.

Their talk was getting louder and charged with heated cursing. At first they had thought my being reclusive was a gesture of disdain, but long months together had taught them a lot about themselves and others. Among them, Hassoun al-Salman underwent a transformation. He lost his jovial sarcasm, and his face looked ghastly pale behind a red, grisly beard.

Riadh Qasim was reciting his own poems when Hamid al-Shalan's voice thundered with the Qur'anic verse, "For those who desire this worldly life, We hasten to them therein what We please, then We assign Hell for them where they shall enter it despised and defeated."

"True words of Allah the Magnificent," Hamid al-Shalan whispered.

"Yusra, please listen."

She started to lengthen her steps on the road. He couldn't find the words to stay her rebellion and make her listen.

"Why are you avoiding me?"

"Do you think it's appropriate for us to behave like this?"

"Mine are the purest intentions, I swear."

She stopped and turned to him, composed. Her face met his. A radiant composite of wine, honey, and splendor. Locks of her short, straight hair caressed her high forehead. "Why are you doing this?"

"I want to marry you."

"But if that's what you want, why are you behaving like this?"

"What else can I do when you keep shunning me?"

Their pace slowed. Their steps moved on the empty street in unison. "Aren't you tired of chasing me?"

"Nothing could stop me from getting to you."

"I realized you had a thing for me when I saw you the first time. Your hungry eyes promised a relentless chase. But that's not enough. What do you know about me?"

"It's enough that I love you."

"You love me as an image, not as a human being."

"Listen, Yusra. I'm an artist, and my intuition about people will never let me down. You're the soul mate I've been looking for in women's faces for years. Now that I'm almost hopeless, I have found you. I'll hang on to you with all the power I have."

Oh, Hassoun, she's the only one who'll help me shake off my defeat. And wipe out our disgrace. And the saga of Mariam Abdulla. And the disappearance of Aseel Omran. Your mouth will drop open in awe when you see her. I just wonder how Aseel and Mariam will compare to this magnificent Spartan figure.

A Man and a Woman

A Daily Routine

Every day Mustafa sits in his wicker chair in the middle of the roofless courtyard. His *dishdasha* is white and clean, his *egal* atop his head. His leather sandals are on the floor, for he likes to raise his legs and rest them on the edge of the chair he sits on, while pushing his shriveled body back.

He coughs a lot, turning his head to spit behind him every now and then. His pigeons coo and flutter in the big cages around him. He would sit there all day, from dawn to nightfall, when he has the pigeons safely inside the cages and away from stray cats. His wife, Sabriya, tall and ghastly slim and wrapped in a worn white *futa*, helps all day.

As soon as it gets dark, Mustafa starts receiving his visitors in the courtyard, now lit by a single bulb. All the talk is about pigeons and their types, and about those who own them in town or the dignitaries who come to town because they love pigeons. Mustafa would elaborate on his meetings with them.

"Here sat Police Chief So-and-so. Yes, he himself came, stopped his car in front of the house and came in." Then, boasting, he would add: "Governor So-and-so, may Allah have mercy on his soul, used to love birds. He knew of me even before he came to the district. On the third day in office he came and bought ten pairs and gave twenty dinars for them. He was generous, may Allah rest his soul."

Then he would clap his hands and tell of a reverse character. "But Governor _____, his name need not be mentioned, took fifty pigeons and paid not a single fils for them, and on top of that he signed the municipal order to seize part of my house on the pretext of widening the street. Why widen it when horses can race on it as it is? They just want to annoy people."

He would then wipe his mouth and moustache with his hand or lower one or the other leg and put it on his sandals. One of the visitors would tease him and say: "Zahi brought ten pairs of yellow pigeons from Baghdad."

Mustafa would explode, saying: "He knows nothing about the yellows, and, frankly, no one does but me! In all of Nasiriyya there are only three pairs of real yellow pigeons, and they are the ones I have. Zahi himself offered me five dinars a pair, but I didn't accept. By the Prophet's name I wouldn't accept fifty."

Then somebody would say something about another kind and about the Basri civil servant who liked that sort.

"These are crows, not pigeons," Mustafa would say, laughing. "What use are they? They just eat and drop."

The conversation goes on like this for hours, without Mustafa bothering to offer his visitors anything. Not even water. Thirsty visitors help themselves to water from the clay ewer standing in a shady corner. But to his more prominent visitors he offers a bottle of soda that Sabriya buys at the store at the top of the street.

At about eleven the men know that the visit is approaching its end, and they start leaving. Mustafa then gets up and collects a small wheelbarrow and pushes it to where the main restaurants are. He fills it with leftovers, sometimes with rice and bread—his favorite. When he comes home exhausted, Sabriya helps him heave the wheelbarrow through the door and unload it into a basin. She then soaks the leftovers in water all night and feeds the pigeons the following day. It is well known that the grease in the food has taken the luster out of the pigeons' feathers, which has driven down their prices. Those who buy them prefer the chicks, whose feathers will have time enough to flourish. Mustafa becomes defensive about it. "I have about five hundred pigeons, and it would cost me two dinars to feed them corn. Feathers are less important than the breed. These are the fruit of a lifetime."

Sabriya

Sabriya was content to help with errands. She knew Mustafa when he was a policeman with a big moustache. His toughness kept the neighborhood in order, and his baton had made its mark on the limbs of many, especially thugs and thieves. She had converted to Islam to marry him when she was still very young, and no one in her family could do anything other than stop talking to her. Mustafa was discharged from the force when he was accused of conspiracy to rob a goldsmith's shop. He then just stayed at home fully devoted to his old hobby.

The poor life she led with him was not any cause for discontent, for she still saw him as the man with the intimidating moustache and firm walk who occupied her memories. She used to see him every day when she took a big load of dishes to wash in the river.

The splendor of youth was long gone, and she languished now in solitude and menial work, her only solace the cooing of the pigeons and the chit-chat of those obsessed with their different types and the problems they brought with them. In the beginning she often wondered about those who were so consumed by the birds that they seemed unaware of the outside world, but habit extinguished all wonder, and she became part of the scene. Only when she was hospitalized with pneumonia for five weeks was she able to get away. Mustafa then visited her once only, and he was uncomfortable. He said good-bye to her, explaining: "I'm concerned about the pigeons. A lot of people have their eyes on them. Not to speak of all those cats."

When he left, she started crying, bemoaning the years she had wasted. She thought of running away and working as a maid, and even of throwing herself in the river. She often thought of the river, but then life is precious, and Mustafa had no one to fall back on.

"Who's going to die first, him or me?" she once wondered, and her heart-felt wish was that he would. "He's older, and he has asthma and lately has started complaining of numbness in his extremities." Sometimes he would wake her up in the middle of the night and ask her to massage his arms. "I'll sell all the pigeons when he dies and get rid of the droppings and the smell of leftovers. This is what's killing me slowly." She gave in to these thoughts, imagining the money she would then have. The government would also compensate her for the piece of land they had taken from them to widen the street. "One room will be enough for me," she would think. "I'll get a new bed with fresh sheets, and eat fish and meat and oranges and rice soaked in oil." Her mouth would start to water at these thoughts.

Another Daily Routine

Mustafa wakes up at dawn and lets the pigeons out of the cages. With a thin stick that has a black cloth tied to one end he ushers the birds to the flat roof of the house. He then climbs the stairs barefoot as if he were in his twenties. With a wave of the stick the pigeons take off together, and at the sharp whistle he makes with his thumb and index finger the birds soar in the air. His asthma and coughing have had no effect on his whistling.

Sabriya watches the scene every day and regrets the life she has chosen because of this man. One day she has a thought.

Trouble

Mustafa was following the soaring birds with sleepy eyes. He was standing on the edge of the roof some four meters above the ground. Sabriya got up and approached him and pretended she was looking at the pigeons. A shiver ran through her, but she overcame it before she nudged him with her elbow.

A Final Condition

Night guards and those living close to the street where the restaurants are have seen a tall woman wrapped in her black *abaya* pushing a small wheelbarrow at around eleven o'clock every evening. She gets all the leftovers she can before the restaurants close. Some take pity on her and push the wheelbarrow for her. A forlorn widow is what many would think. Sabriya, as a matter of fact, has heard this a lot and has also heard those who compare her to the deceased, may Allah have mercy on his soul.

One evening a night guard asked her what seemed like a rhetorical question, "Why are you doing this? What for?"

Samira Al-Mana

In the past three decades, Samira Al-Mana has chronicled the lives of Iraqis in exile, especially women. Herself an expatriate, Al-Mana liberally draws on personal experiences both to depict Arab life in the diaspora and to comment on the larger scene at home and in the Arab world. Women, then, naturally preside over her narratives about men and women perpetually struggling to understand themselves, their interrelations, the homeland, and the adjustments they have to make in their host countries. These themes have been in Al-Mana's work since her very first novel. Al-Mana was born in Basra, Iraq, and was educated in Iraq and Britain. She has been residing in Britain since 1965. With her husband, Salah Niazi, she edited and published Al-Ightirab al-adabi, *a ground-breaking journal on Arabic literature in exile.*

Cultural interactions are among Al-Mana's favorite subjects. Her first novel, Al-sabiqun wa al-lahiqun *(The Forerunners and the Newcomers, 1972), is about its Arab characters' ability to relate to Western influences and values, and she pursues the theme in the novel* Al-thuna'yya al-landaniyya *(A London Sequel, 1979) and in* Habl al-surra *(1998), published in English as* The Umbilical Cord *(2005).*

The stories included here feature Al-Mana's playful and immensely interested narrator, a modern-day Shahrazad intrigued by storytelling, but mindful of the risks it involves. "Sexual Complacency," for instance, presents a woman's consciousness as it outgrows squabbles with her husband and slowly wakes up to the pleasures of sexual contact. "A Dormant Alphabet" brings in the world of Iraqi émigrés with its levity, tensions, and the ever-present threat of an oppressive and ubiquitous regime. In all four stories presented here, the economy in language and structure is evident. A complex moment is caught in swift strokes in "That

Thing We Call Age," and the lives of its four characters emerge to claim our understanding and sympathy. In "The Soul," a longer story, Al-Mana employs a similar economy to provide us with other aspects of life in exile. Her main characters now are a couple shuttling between places, memories, and histories. An argument they have over a dead hen reveals the point at which their different cultural backgrounds clash and meet. Again, Al-Mana is at her best in manipulating a relatively trivial incident to enable her readers to view the complexity of experience in her characters.

The following stories are, respectively, translations of "Al-ruh," "Shay' ismuhu al-'umr," "TbaGat," and "Tawatu' fi al-jinis" from Al-Mana's collection Al-ruh wa ghayruha: Qisas qasira (The Soul and Other Stories; Beirut and London: Arab Diffusion, 1999).

The Soul

"Where did Carmen go, leaving all these animals? Perhaps she's out on an errand." He leaped out of his bed to see what all the commotion was down in the garden.

He saw the rooster at the top of one of the highest trees, far from the battle below, its eyes glittering like diamonds and as if watching intensely the scene of confusion. Was it possible for a dog to prey on a hen? The rooster's traumatized neck was twisting like a question mark. All creatures, it seems, are the same, the strong victimizing the weak.

The hen's ceaseless clucking was a cry for help. When Adam first heard it, he thought she was laying an egg, an enterprise that was always accompanied by that clamorous prologue. But he couldn't tolerate it when it went beyond that, so he hurriedly jumped out of his warm bed and in his pajamas and slippers went through the closed doors like an unannounced tornado. He came upon that wild dog assaulting the poor creature. It clucked and leaped in all directions and tried to fly into the tree to join the rooster, but fell helplessly short of that—the dog didn't leave her alone for long. Her helplessness must have incited his appetite, and he seemed determined to finish her off. That finally happened when he got her behind one of the bushes.

The man loathed that display of the law of the jungle and grabbed a stick from the ground thinking of hitting the dog with it. Instead, he swished it and lashed out uselessly at the dog in all the languages he knew. He searched for a rock to throw at it, but found none. It outraged him that the garden at that time had flowers and shrubs in bloom. He had to rattle the only weapon then available, the stick, and the dog finally gave up. As it left the bush, it dropped the hen, withdrew toward the neighbor's fence, and jumped over it to disappear in that direction.

The hen was dying, feathers scattered all around it. A last breath violently shook its breast. He bent over it, tenderly stroking it as he recalled what one of his vegetarian friends had once said, "I can't eat a soul." Yes, it certainly had a soul. Suddenly, it opened its eyes and revealed their light pink color. It stood up and tried to move a little, and Adam stepped away to let it go where it wanted. He convinced himself that he had tried to save it and felt relieved.

Life went back to normal, and peace descended on the place again. Adam heard the rooster crowing as if calling the time for sunset prayers, leave its safe place up the tree, and nonchalantly go to its den.

Anyway, we need not go any further into this sentimental little drama. Adam won't fool anyone by appearing kind-hearted. His hypocrisy was transparent. Yes, the hen's apparent demise aggravated and touched him, but if it were to come to him on a dish, well roasted, he wouldn't hesitate to devour it.

He was going to tell the anecdote of the vicious dog, of course, to Carmen, his Spanish girlfriend, and he was going to try to be as detached and casual as he could be. She, too, was considerate—you could tell from her behavior that day, when she left the house quietly so as not to disturb his nap. And he couldn't really be sensational, anyway, since at the time they were absorbed with arranging his visit to Spain.

After Carmen had met Adam in London and found out that he had not seen the Alhambra, she had invited him to visit her in Spain. It was in her native city of Granada, and it was part of his Arab heritage, as he used to say. She enthusiastically promised all kinds of trips to introduce him to Spain's pluralistic culture.

It was his third day in Spain, and they were still drawing up and revising travel plans. Should they start with Cordoba, the ancient Roman city, and later the first capital of Muslim Spain? They would go to the mosque there, with its spectacular marble pillars and to the Muslim and Jewish quarters. Or should they begin with Toledo? Or the Muslim castle overlooking Malaga? They both were must see places, even though they were hundreds of miles apart. These endless considerations only whetted his curiosity and excitement.

He felt divided most of the time—between intimate places he didn't want to leave and a promising itinerary that was inviting him to other places. Generous sunshine despite January's bitterness and skies filled with stars that quivered every night like lovers' hearts. He nostalgically remembered the Arab cities he had unwillingly abandoned to go and live in Europe: the glories of Damascus or Baghdad before all those wars and hatred.

Seven days among plains and hills and farms and palaces and mosques and churches and castles no longer fortified. Passionate verses written on walls in his native tongue more than rewarded him for his trouble in deciphering the characters. Reliefs of wise sayings in Arabic calligraphy embodied power and humility and compassion and humaneness and tolerance. On one of them letters appeared like spirits bonding on the walls and in the air: "No victor but Allah." There were countless olive and lemon and almond and orange trees. Carmen playfully suggested that some must have been planted by his ancestors, and she would tease him by wondering what he would bring to the landscape. "I'm here to admire and love you."

On the last day they returned to her house in Granada, a place that straddled the city and the countryside. Her mother had left to spend the Christmas holidays with her married sister in Madrid. Perhaps she had thought of possible marriage plans and had wanted to give the couple some privacy. Carmen insisted on taking him to see the house in the city's suburbs where Lorca had lived, and in Malaga she took him to the place where Picasso was born. She was thrilled to find more connections with her lover since her native geniuses were also Andalusians.

Now, at the end of this superb trip and the pleasures of intimacy with a beautiful girlfriend, would he remember the hen episode? He tried hard to forget it, even though the hen was still pecking at his subconscious and in the garden as it used to do. Anyway, Carmen was absorbed in her personal affairs, and her mother had left the animals enough food in the garden before she left for Madrid.

Adam found great pleasure in the cock crowing, much more entertaining than a concert at a celebrated music or opera hall. With the crowing he almost forgot the pressures of his stressful urban life where computers, speed, and modern technology ruled. The relaxed life here in Granada was like a basket full of scrumptious fruit. He sat back and enjoyed the offerings of a city that chose not to dwell on pain and catastrophe. Its people reflected on its history through songs and music and dancing. If they protested, they did so through the tapping of dancing feet, and if they rebelled, they did so through the pounding of their hands and chests to the tunes of guitars and the clashing of cymbals. They were not interested in past discords, and they saw themselves as the descendants of all races and cultures. No wonder people flocked to this place from all over the world.

The hen was completely forgotten. However, they could not fail to notice her disappearance a few days later. The cock was alone and swaggering around on his own in the garden, but the hen was nowhere to be found. They looked for her in the bushes and shrubs in vain. Perhaps she was sick or something. After a while they stumbled on her remains; black and white feathers blown in the wind, most probably her feathers. The sole remains of a rather short life. It didn't take them long to identify the culprit—that vicious dog was barking nonstop. Yes, it must have found the chance to assault the hen in their absence. This was enough to bring Adam's girlfriend close to tears; her curses rained down on it. Adam could not bring himself to say anything. Would he keep his word if he were to promise her right now that he would never eat chicken again? Should he say, "Take it easy, I won't touch a soul ever, a soul like the hen's, the soul of a defenseless creature?" But how could words help? And wouldn't they both forget about it after a few days? Man has forgotten much more serious things. After all, it was just a hen and the prey of a vicious dog. Its life came to an end. That's all. Period.

That Thing We Call Age

Yes, yes, differences in opinion won't affect intimacy. But intimacy, simple as it is, has its own intricacies. At least this is how it appeared to a youthful couple under a tree in a month that for them couldn't have been other than spring.

They had a long talk, or argument, perhaps, and each looked to be saying mostly reasonable things, occasionally punctuating them with meaningful silences. Perfectly suited for their words that came evenly from heart and head.

A less controversial and a more temperate and obvious scene included two elderly women who sat close to the couple. The women were quite shaken when they first became aware of the lovers nearby. Their anxiety soon gave way to a vague, diabolical joy. As the argument between the two reached its peak, the women pretended they were watching the ducks on the pond in front of them. Then the argument subsided, and reasonable talk overshadowed the heated exchanges and the silences. The ducks went on with their carefree chores, and one of the lovers unnoticeably moved from the language of differences into one of reconciliation. The lover found in a passionate kiss the eternal expression of that complex thing we call intimacy. A dramatic and romantic scene, almost one on a film set, but without cameras and director. Differences in opinion as well as reasonable talk floated up in the air. All talk became meaningless.

The two women were ready to move.

"Oh, we've sat too long."

"And the bench is rather low," said the other.

A Dormant Alphabet

"Nadim, you need to do something. Ashour is telling everybody you discouraged him from visiting the homeland. And that for his personal safety he should keep away from the land's pharaoh, who imprisons, terrorizes, and kills people at will."

"You must be kidding! Is that what he says? He's certainly *tbaGat*."

Those present exploded in laughter at hearing that word. Nadim didn't say that Ashour's head "has stray lines," a phrase Iraqis would normally use to describe deficient judgment.

Nadim's friend, however, used the anecdote to advise him. "You certainly know how things are these days," he added. "Wherever you go, spies from the internal security and the secret police take notice of what you say and simply report to their higher ups. And then you get yourself in trouble."

"What a moron this Ashour is! That was said between the two of us. He's definitely *tbaGat*."

Laughter roared again. It had to be the outlandish word or, perhaps, the rage with which Nadim pronounced it to embody Ashour's lack of common sense. He couldn't pick from his discarded vocabulary a better word to convey his frustration at a stupid move. Its repetition, however, was an occasion for the company's light-hearted giggles. Nadim's British wife wanted to know the reason behind the sudden commotion.

"What did you say? What's going on? I missed the whole thing."

She knew a few spoken Arabic words, and in her early married life she had studied formal Arabic at a specialized school. She would use it sometimes to produce well-structured sentences and to express herself reasonably well. Also, almost all their friends knew English, and they would usually use it to accommodate her. Today, they insisted on their native tongue, and the wife was lost.

Outside, a light drizzle continued, and darkness was spreading in the room. Unnerved, she got up to turn the lights on. "What's he saying?" she asked again, scrutinizing the faces of those present, the Arab émigrés in London.

Her husband knew she could be impatient, and he kindly turned to her. His eyes were red from all the excitement and laughter. He had forgotten all about spies and the secret police. Perhaps they, too, would be secretly choking with laughter.

"I said Ashour is 'layers,'" Nadim said, literally translating *tbaGat.*

"What does that mean?" she turned her head right and left at the company. "What's all this nonsense about 'layers'?" She didn't know if she should laugh like them, but she certainly didn't get it.

All the time, though, the Iraqi word floated around the room, gliding like a bright meteor. Its music sprang from the friction of the sonorous *t* with the soft and coy *b*, and the twisted *a*, like a camel's neck, with the abrasive *g*. The alphabet of an open wilderness orchestra, mixed with the dirt of those distant lands that produced it. Added to that were the trials and the pleasures of its speakers, who showed their artistry in the ambiguities and precisions of their expressions. It was the past for those Arab exiles, uprooted for reasons beyond their control. *TbaGat* was most likely a word that went back to ancient times, perhaps pre-Islamic, lurking for centuries under layers of dust. Nadim reawakened it that day in London, and it rolled over his tongue like a new discovery. He dug it up elegantly from his memory, loaded with all that lost past. The cute word suddenly came to life on his tongue, as if descending from the heavens. Was it a candle in the dark or the proverbial fingernail scratching one's own skin?[1]

Sexual Complacency

Was she going to call somebody today? Certainly, the telephone had been one way to break her isolation. Then it dawned on her that it cost more to call during the day now, thanks to Mrs. Thatcher's free-market policies, and she squelched the urge to dial. Calls were much cheaper at night, but

1. The reference here is to an old Arab proverb, "Nothing scratches your skin better than your own fingernail."

when a truly understanding husband or the kids came home at night, who would bother about calling? Had she tried to explain that to Mrs. Thatcher, she might have convinced her to change that particular policy. Self-deprecating humor was her way of evading her helplessness.

When she had come to London thirty years ago, other women could talk on the phone for hours. Not she. For her, then, the phone was a dead machine as she took care of the kids, not to mention adjust to a new city and learn English. Socializing was not for her. She used to watch television only after dinner with the children, contentedly—cartoons or soap operas to pick up conversational English. The acting, however, was often superior to what she sometimes saw in Baghdad, the city they came from, where a turban alone was supposed to invoke the revelry of a Haroun al-Rasheed or the righteousness of one of the Prophet's companions, Abu Dharr al-Ghifari.

But that was an entirely different thing. What was important for her now was that she had ended, just yesterday, all physical ties with her husband. Completely. Wait, don't rush me. Yes, she simply had told him she wanted to sleep that night in the other room. Why? If you bear with me a moment, I'll tell you. She was determined about that when she saw how rigid he was, shutting her up all the time. That was something she wouldn't accept. She'd just sleep in another bed. I don't want you to get close to me or hug me; I don't want you or need you. Not at all. I need someone who'll listen to me when I explode or complain or argue or reproach. Someone who accepts me with all my faults, for I'm not always sweet and smooth like candy. Not without blemishes and lines and sagging flesh. It comes with the territory. I have a lot of scratches, and the heavy legacy of centuries. I need to groan. What should I do, the way you see it? Go on the street and scream at the people? Somebody has advised a British magazine's female readers to go to a remote train station and vent their frustration by screaming as the train passes, the noises becoming indistinguishable. That's because their companions won't listen to them. Should I do that, too?

This whole thing really began yesterday after she read a harsh book review in the *Guardian*. The book, by a wealthy and beautiful Arab widow, had been recently translated into English, and the reviewer berated both the original and the translation. She completely agreed with the reviewer, but perhaps not with his sarcasm. It was his awareness of the current sympathy with Arab women's harsh realities, he wrote, that brought him to review such a trashy book. Well, at least he didn't fall under the widow's ravishing influence and wasn't seduced by the delicacies of Middle Eastern cuisine. His review didn't smell of oil, either.

Banished to a London suburb, our woman wanted to share with someone her humble opinion on the book and the review. Her children were no longer with her, and the only one present when she finished reading the article was her husband. She leaped on him, only to be baffled by his nonchalant, lukewarm response. He silenced her by his brief and discouraging reply, "Why bother about them, may their fortunes plunge into the mud," which he half-heartedly said as he slowly rose from his seat. What? What did you say? Is that all? Is that how you end the whole issue? You won't even let me voice my opinion and expose a depressingly fake woman? At the moment she felt as if the dilettante was responsible for all the corruption and bribery and injustice in her country of origin and even for her own emigration and exile. She liked it that a brave person had finally exposed her.

The husband wanted to terminate the conversation and was about to leave the room, uninterested, but patronizingly touched her shoulder and repeated his sentence, "Why bother about them, may their fortunes plunge into the mud." OK, OK, all I have now is the train station; I'll go there, but not before I end all physical contact with you, once and for all. Don't touch me, and stay away from me. Enough!

Ignoring her protestations, the husband left the room and started getting ready to leave for work. She was pleased with the determination she showed on the spur of the moment. She'd spend the night in the other room. She felt comfortable with that, and she took her sleepwear and brown slippers so that she had no excuse to run into him. From now on she'd sleep there, and she felt more secure as she made him her nemesis. That was it. She doesn't need him anymore. That'd do for now, and she could go and scream at the train station later.

She was an ordinary woman in exile who couldn't but see and hear what went on around her. No close friend, neighbor, family members.

Nothing but Allah's mercifulness, as the native saying goes. The Brits in their homes—or castles, rather—and she with her loneliness. She became an avid reader and found in the nearby public-library books of all sorts with which she bonded jealously, as if a good book were family and home. She got but faint echoes of home from London's Arab community, and that was how she met the rich widow who spent a few months in London. At one of her many homes in glamorous capitals. And she found out how the widow writes and how much she pays to get a book of hers published in Arabic, and then pays again to get it translated. The publishers who visit her and the journalists, reviewers, translators, and cover designers who suck up to her. She memorized all this, pained at the damage that that woman could do to her latest passion for books. The Filipina maid who opens the door, always in a white lace skirt, and the big desk where she stacks pens and papers were visible to all. And the neatness everywhere. And the party when the book is finally released, and the cronies filing in for their signed copies. If people only really knew.

She was alone most of the time, and her husband wouldn't even listen to her. Sometimes she'd like to protest the falsehood around her. She turned to herself. "In a civilized place the sham would be exposed someday. A writer should fill up her space, not just sit behind a desk. Will the tricksters of her native land give up their tricks? Will they feel disgusted? And why would they help cover up her doings? It must be the money, all that mythic wealth that buys silence and flattery."

The few friends she visited comforted her with their conversation, but they were often busy. And the others who only blathered about who was marrying whose daughter and the bride's dress with its fabulous, long train and the sale season in big stores and where to get cheap *halal* meat and politics, tearing to pieces those who differed with them and denigrating British democracy for not being democratic enough. The women, however, wouldn't go against their husbands (that would be unthinkable), and they settled for the role of followers. One of the men said he wouldn't pay taxes even if Mrs. Thatcher dropped dead, and another fantasized about getting a British passport and working in the United Arab Emirates. No taxes to worry about there. All they feared was ending someday in a nursing home at the mercy of others' charity and a nurse's kindness. She stared at their faces flabbergasted and felt lonelier than she was before.

So her husband spent the night by himself in their bedroom, but in the morning as he was leaving he stopped by her bedroom. She was staring at the ceiling, a library book in her hand. He bent over her apologetically and said: "Honey, forgive me. I had no idea you'd be upset like that. Come on, I didn't mean to hurt your feelings."

"Don't touch me. I don't want anything from you. It's over."

"Relax, please. I'm sorry."

"I suppose you just can't relate to me anymore. I know how limited your sympathy and understanding can be. Too selfish to care about someone else. I'd rather remain alone since your presence doesn't make any difference. The problem is that some think a man's presence makes a woman better—happier. Together for better or for worse. Downright lies. You know all this nonsense."

"Honey, I'm sorry!"

"Just leave me alone. That's it. Don't get any closer, and, please, don't touch me. At long last I'm free, liberated from your embraces and hugs."

The husband nearly gave up and cautiously brushed his fingers over her shoulder.

"Take your hand off—it feels like fire. Let me tell you a couple things you don't seem to know about a married relationship. First, when I told you one day how lonely I felt, you dismissively reminded me that Amal, your friend's wife, was like me and doesn't complain. You forgot that Amal arrived in Britain just two years ago, a young mother busy with her new life and little baby. Like me three decades ago, she doesn't have the time to be lonely. It's different now, with the kids grown and away. No English-language lessons to take. What remains for me is companionship. After thirty years of marriage a woman of my age needs not just kisses and hugs, but spiritual communication."

As the wife lectured him, the husband sneaked his hand under the bed cover. "Yes, I see, I see," he said. He seized one of her feet and started to message it the way he would when she had a cold. She'd ask him to rub her legs and would relish then the pleasures of his comforting squeezes. "Here? Here?" he'd say. "How about here?" Today he kept quiet, for fear she'd see his intent, but suddenly she freed her leg, annoyed, and continued lecturing him. She wanted him to see why she was upset, to understand her loneliness and her need to connect and be heard.

"Second," she hastened to say, "our relationship, you need to know, I should say . . ."

The husband found the leg again and went on rubbing it.

"Oh, what was the second point? I knew it a moment ago, an important one. What was it? I'm sure I'll remember it." The leg felt good, and soon the other sought the hands. The husband took care of that, too. The pinky toe was reveling, and the big toe couldn't wait to get to the hand. The wife, distracted, struggled to remember her second point. "Where did it go? It was crystal clear just a moment ago. Wait, I'll remember it."

The husband couldn't care less for that second point. The legs relaxed at the sweet massage and shook off their lethargy. He laughed now as he sat on the bed gleeful like a naughty boy who'd just gotten his favorite toy. The laughter verged on gloating as he saw her complacency.

The wife realized that, too, and attempted to explain. "Wait, don't gloat. Wait, I'll remember the second point. In a minute, it'll come of its own accord . . . when I'm not thinking about it."

But the rubbing went on.

Abdul Sattar Nasir

Many in Iraq and the Arab world remember Abdul Sattar Nasir as a writer who suffered a year of solitary confinement soon after the publication in 1975 of his short story parodying the absolute power of a dictatorial figure like Saddam Hussein. When "Sayyidna al-khalifa" (Our Master, the Caliph) was published, Hussein was not even the president. Remembering Nasir in only this way is somehow unfair to him because he has more than two dozen other publications, but the event was such a traumatic experience that it imposed itself on many of his works. It is certainly present in "Good-bye, Hippopotamus," which he published after he left Iraq in 1999. Nasir was born in Baghdad, in a quarter that became the setting of his controversial novel **Tattran** *(2002). Much of the controversy lies in the harsh light Nasir casts on the squalor of the slum where he was born, in particular the prostitution there.*

In "Good-bye, Hippopotamus," a theme common in Iraqi fiction is given a powerful treatment. The narrator is not only thrilled to leave the homeland, but motivated enough to make the severing of all ties public and official. Although it is tempting to read the story as autobiographical owing to the writer's suffering in Iraq during Baathist rule, one would be mistaken to interpret it as expressing loathing of the homeland. Nasir has retained interest in Iraq and has written moving pieces about its troubles in the past twenty years. In this interest, he seems close to James Joyce, for whom Ireland remained a central concern even though he wrote about shaking off the homeland's hold. Perhaps comparing this story with Ibrahim Ahmed's "The Arctic Refugee" will illustrate the point here. Whereas Ahmed's narrator expresses nostalgia for Iraq, Nasir's story seems to suggest a stronger bond with the homeland even without naming it. The narrator's dramatic gesture of making a public break with the country left behind testifies to what binds the two more than to what separates them.

"Good-bye, Hippopotamus" is a translation of "Wada'an ayuha al-kharteet,"
written in 1989 and originally published in the collection Ba'da khrab al-Basra
(After the Ruining of Basra; Beirut: Almu'asasa al-arabiyya, 2000).

Good-bye, Hippopotamus

First of all, he needed to believe the bounty that perched in his hands
this morning. A bounty that he had awaited for ten years and that brought
him the blue passport that could take him anywhere. He wouldn't think
of the past—a handful of wasted years and a poisonous, slow ordeal.
His fortieth birthday was only a month away, and this was the first time
he was leaving the country. If only the days of humiliation could be
dumped in the water to be carried away to oblivion. The past had robbed
him of his ideals and left him with a gaping wound. No remedy but
emigration to cool, cloudy lands where drizzle washed open streets and
sidewalks.

His wife and three children and the blue passport told him that the
way to the world was open, but the claws of the past might still hold him
back from embracing Paris or Rome or Madrid. He was departing on a
plane that was anxious like him, that could hardly wait to land in London. He was taking his wife and kids without luggage. Just the clothes
they wore to get them to a land with no torturing memories. He didn't
want to remember, and his buzzing head would soon cool down when
the plane took off toward mountains and lush grass.

Could a little passport be such a lifesaver? He needed to believe what
was happening because the distance between dream and adventure was
as wide as the distance between him and a type of people he couldn't relate to for the past forty years.

A dungeon as deep as memory, grass on fire, and an iron throat were
the lifelong nightmares of this suffocating body. Even though no actual
figures had appeared on the gates, the dungeons had numbers that the
guards had memorized, and the guards' hands of steel had lashed out for

no reason. Whoever entered these dungeons had lost his features to the guards, who in the darkness beat faceless bodies soaked with sweat and urine and tears.

Would these nightmares end? Would he be able to sleep a single night under a forgiving sky? The blue passport in his hands had all the places in the world written all over it. This page smelled of Austria, and the characters here revealed the legs of dancing women in Copenhagen. Were these Parisian streets on page nine? Perhaps with a bit of brazenness he could make love to a woman in a bar in Casablanca.

The blue passport he cherished was a grant from illusion. He was going to migrate—no; he'd say he was going on a short trip to Beirut, the sea, Cyprus, Istanbul, or Buckhurst. Anywhere, just in case a heartless thug was within earshot of him. A short trip for the wife and kids, he would say. For ten days.

Even his own head and thoughts had become sources of fear. Who knows, someone might read his thoughts and block his departure forever. He looked at his wife, who understood his agony and who like him indulged in this strange, luxurious dream. His three kids were rejoicing in a tight circle of fantasy, tethered by a thin cord to the head of this tired father who smiled only today, after years of damaging depression.

That Thursday was the milestone that separated past from future, the sword that cut his life into two parts, one worthy of the dumpster, the other of adventure. That same sword could have severed his whole being and destroyed everything.

Under the protection of darkness he had sold his furniture piece by piece. He had to leave Thursday night without luggage so that the neighbors wouldn't notice anything.

The passport officer at the airport smiled at the family and said: "You're traveling without luggage? That's the weirdest thing I've ever seen." But he stamped the passports and pronounced the father's name, Shafiq Ahmed Yunis. Shafiq smiled and turned to his youngest son to hide the pounding of his heart. That horrible man was not going to end this humiliating inquisition.

Shafiq looked at the massive structure on the tarmac. It was going to take him away from the land of his ancestors to the land of his heart's desire. He sat with his family in the waiting area and waited for the moment of release from an ordeal that had spread across his body like weeds. In less than thirty minutes he went to pee three times.

"Shafiq, sit down, please. We don't want others to read your transparent thoughts."

But he couldn't sit down. He took his youngest child and paced the hall for an eternity before he heard the miraculous call for the flight to London. An inexplicable paralysis seized his legs, and when he tried to move his body, it seemed like trying to lift a cow with one finger.

"What's the matter, Shafiq?" his terrified wife whispered. "It's only a few seconds before we get to the plane."

The wife and three kids walked up the stairs of the plane, but, with genuine humility, Shafiq had to invoke Allah's name and had to lift his leg with his arm. He was the last passenger to enter the plane, and dreaming of that was the last thing to pass through his head. The golden clouds up there from here to London will send their rain for him, he thought. For five hours he didn't say a word. Two tears trickling down his face said what he wanted to say.

At the first clothes shop in the heart of London, before the day was out, the family bought new clothes and shed the old ones. His wife looked much more beautiful than before. Shafiq flashed a smile at the three kids. He rolled up all the old clothes and put them in a bag, then started looking for the nearest post office. For an address he put the police station close to his house. He left this note with the clothes: "I am citizen Shafiq Ahmed Yunis, currently residing in London. I'm sending you the remains of our last connection with you—my and my family's clothes. As long as I lived among you, I didn't kill, rape, steal, lie, or commit even a minor felony. You killed my senses, usurped my mind, robbed me, and lied to me, and on top of that threw me in prisons, detention camps, and slavish jobs. Let bygones be bygones, and may Allah forgive you and me. I'm severing all ties with you, and all I'm asking of you is to strike my name from all your records of citizenship, conscription, taxation, and sharia courts. I owe you nothing, for I gave all I had, and I forgive you your too many debts. It was you who taught me that one's lot is a mincing machine that one has to put up with.

"Now, I, Shafiq Ahmed Yunis, shout for the first time in my life, in the harshest and most liberated voice, and say to you: You are repudiated once, twice, and thrice from this day to the day of judgment."

Jalil al-Qaisi

Jalil al-Qaisi was a central figure in the "Kirkuk Group," a literary movement formed by Arab, Turkmen, Kurdish, and Chaldean-Assyrian writers in the 1960s that energized cultural life in the city for the next two decades. The group re-flected Kirkuk's diverse ethnic makeup, which created what Qaisi described in a recent interview (August 2005) as "a symphony of languages."[1] Several of the group's members, however, also knew English well, and their writings reflect as-similated Western influences. Born in Kirkuk in 1937, Qaisi still resides in the city in a life-long commitment to his belief that home is a source of nourishment for writers. Although the place is not called Kirkuk in his story "Zulaikha," this city seems the favorite setting for many of Qaisi's works, even when it is not named.

"Zulaikha" presents a prominent theme in Iraqi fiction: political suppression and the role played by the enlightened in fighting it. The female character, though not visible, exemplifies a typical feature of the writer's works: women are usually the source of constructive visions. For the two detainees, Zulaikha is the beauty worth living or dying for. Qaisi's skill in portraying the horrors of confinement, torture, and possible physical demise in a dreamlike atmosphere testifies to an ar-tistic maturity noticeable in the majority of his work. Sentimental moments, such as when the two detainees bond or the crowd encircles them at the end, are com-mon in Qaisi's work.

"Zulaikha" was originally published in the collection Zulaikha al-buʿdu yaqtarib *(Zulaikha: The Remote Converges; Baghdad: Matbaʿat Al-Adeeb, 1974).*

---

1. The interview was conducted by Nozad Ahmed Aswad. It is worth noting that Qaisi's personal life reflects such diversity: his father is Arab, his mother a Kurd, and his wife Armenian. See http://www.sardam.info/Sardam%20Al%20Arabi/6/14.htm.

Zulaikha

When confined, what else but memories to soothe us? In the midst of such solitude they make the present more coherent. For a person locked up in a tight cell, the present flows out there, in the streets, markets, houses, valleys, caves, and the endless whistling of bullets. A buzzing sound snapped me out of my recollections, and in the faint yellow cell light I saw a spider trapping a big fly. Flies like that feasted on rotting flesh like mine in this solitary confinement. So why did time matter? The fly was buzzing as the spider wound its sticky gray threads around the wings. I looked closely at the fly. The fine sticky threads were squeezing its body, and its eyes were bulging. It struggled in vain, continuing to buzz. A demise I couldn't care less about. But was this life?

Once upon a time my friend playfully threw handfuls of wet sand at me as she ran around on the beach we went to every summer. She used to swim and laugh and then lie down next to me and shout, "This is life," as she tried to catch her breath. Captivated by the sun, she used to tell me unbelievable stories and repeat, "This is life." But then we were young and innocent. The beach and the wet sand and the sea were now gone, and we had learned the ways of bullets to try and bring about happiness. Happiness seemed no longer an illusion; *and* it seemed close, as close as the shot from an old rifle. Ah, baby, our futile attempt to evade our collective shame—the shame we saw in the faces of others and in our blaming of fate or some other factor for our misery. Did we reach for those handfuls of sand to relieve ourselves of what weighed us down?

The fly was still buzzing. I looked closely at it as it struggled to free itself from that impossible siege. Why was it hanging on so dearly to life? What was all this buzzing for? The spider carefully dragged it up the wall, and I could see the fly's green eyes as its head dangled down. What a striking color! I had no idea why I became so upset, but I shrieked out uncontrollably, and, soon enough, heavy boots shook the corridor leading to my cell.

I was taken to an opening that overlooked a wide concrete courtyard, with scattered figures I could hardly make out. As the cool morning sun bathed me, its rays stung my eyes like needles. How long had I been shut away from the daylight? My insides started to boil, and I was gulping air continuously. More light fell on me, and I felt I was expanding into a strange mass of light. I couldn't tell how long the days had felt more like black ink, with no real nighttime or real daytime. I couldn't open my eyes, but I felt it was morning because of the cool sun. Perhaps it was spring. I froze there and then, an uncertain silence all around me, until I felt a sharp pain piercing my head. I instinctively shielded my eyes with my hands and longed for something I could lean on. Betrayed by light and sunshine, my body swung like a sunflower. A body devastated by torture and by the humidity and stale air in the cell. Somebody grabbed my arm and squeezed it till it hurt. I leaned against something, and suddenly the fly's green eyes popped up in front of my eyes. Were they pleading? As the man squeezed, the fly's face swelled, and I could see its tiny body dripping fluid. The man started to shake me. Dizzy, I uncovered my eyes and tried to see. Chalky saliva dribbled from my mouth. Shame helped me pull myself together for a moment, but my body was collapsing. The yard below showed signs of life, and blurred khaki figures appeared next to a vehicle.

Someone in uniform pulled me toward a stairwell, and we descended slowly. Then I was taken into a large iron cage on a carriage drawn by a white cart horse. What! A cage? I was stunned. Through the cage bars I became aware of grim faces and closed green doors and green walls and bayonets gleaming in the sun. Heavy military boots and a rapid guttural language. When I looked at the carriage, I could see only the head and neck of the horse. Then the cage door was opened, and a tall thin man was pushed in. His face was covered with blood. He kept looking at me and after a long silence said: "Wipe the blood off your face."

Blood? I wondered. Did they beat me? Possibly. I felt my face with my hand a few times, but couldn't find any.

"There's no blood on my face. They didn't beat me today."

"But your face is covered with blood," he said kindly.

"I'm telling you, there's nothing."

With my hand I wiped the blood from his face and eyes and asked: "Do you see any blood on my face now?"

"Oh, no. There's none now," he said after a quick look.

"Were you in solitary confinement all the time?"

"Well, it was hard . . . and rewarding," he said in a resigned tone. After a period of silence, his warm voice was back: "Oh Lord, I wonder where they are now?"

"Everywhere," I said.

He was quiet for a long time, then looked through the bars and said: "Then everything has been arranged."

"What do you mean?"

"They're taking us to the arena." And he added: "We won't give up now that the remote draws near."

"I don't understand."

"Have you ever contemplated an honorable death?"

"Isn't that what led us to our current situation?"

"Dogs!" he said angrily. "They're holding back the masses who want to come and honor us. They don't want them to find the hidden key to all those issues."

"What issues?"

He was silent again. Then he bent down and gave me a closer look. "We'll see."

His silence encouraged me to speak again. "This cage. Where are they parading us?"

"In the streets. The city streets."

"Why in the streets?"

"So that . . . so that . . . oh, we'll soon see why." Then, whispering, he asked: "Where did they arrest you?"

"In the hills overlooking the city."

"Oh, Lord, a cage!" he sighed. "Lusting after the truth *can* be your undoing. We'll see."

I heard many voices around the carriage and lifted my head. As the horse moved, the cage shook. The sun brought us delicious warmth as we approached a long street lined with patches of khaki and shining bayonets. Scattered, slumbering houses adorned the background.

"It's so quiet in the city," I said.

"They're playing tricks on us. They want to scare us. But to tell you the truth, we are the real scare now. And only now do I feel a sense of relief."

"But why is it so quiet here?"

"We are breaking down the siege of fear consuming *the* people, my friend. Perhaps complete satisfaction will come all in one day. The remote draws near." Then he lowered his head and looked at the distant houses. "We'll be killed today. Yes, we will be killed." He stared at me for some time and patted me on the back. "It had better be the demise of this world, if I or anyone else is to believe their cheap tricks." He cleared his throat and added: "She used to tell me that life is courage."

"Who used to say that?"

"Zulaikha." A contrite smile spread over his face. "A beautiful name, 'Zulaikha,' isn't it?"

"Very beautiful."

"She's here in the city. And you, do you have a Zulaikha?"

I smiled back at him, and he patted me on the back again.

"It's OK to talk a little about Zulaikha. We've been too hard on ourselves, and I see no harm in thinking about Zulaikha when we're surrounded by death."

We'll be killed today, I kept thinking. What an enticing dream. It's beautiful and thrilling and frightening to tell oneself, "This is my last day."

"I don't think death scares you," he said in a voice choking with kindness.

I didn't say anything. My ordeal had cured me of the fear of death. In the midst of the most terrifying experiences death seemed like just another natural happening. Part of the cycle of life. Like sleep. Or food and drink.

"What are you saying?" he prompted me.

"Is there really death when all senses are almost dead already?"

He embraced me. "Man is destined to suffer." After a considerable silence, he added, "We're turning into another street. As I told you, they're barring the people from coming to see us."

"But why?"

"Our presence here in this iron cobweb would have opened their eyes."

I had nothing to say to that. Without thinking, I recalled the entrapment of the fly and somehow felt guilty for not helping it out. For some reason, I revisualized the movements of its fragile legs scrabbling in desperate attempts to break away. Perhaps the clear green eyes were appealing to me for help. I could not stop visualizing the fly, and I screamed again. I was brought back to reality when a sharp metal thing pierced my thigh. An uproar of human voices was coming from the distant houses and fell on the desolate streets and the facades of closed shops.

"Stop screaming," my companion said.

"I ignored all its appeals for help."

"Try to be quiet," he said in a firmer tone.

"I was indifferent to all those appeals."

"Wake up, do you hear me?" His tone was dry and commanding. "They're coming to bid us farewell. If only they could get closer."

"They will, certainly."

"And if only you could see Zulaikha."

I started shivering as the pain worsened. My companion was startled: "Your clothes are covered with blood!"

When I looked, I could see a wound five centimeters deep on the lower part of my right thigh. "That soldier must have stabbed me when I screamed," I said.

"I saw him thrust his bayonet through the bars," he said, and then he leaped like an injured animal and screamed at the soldier and spit on him several times. "You dog . . . dog! Scoundrel!"

The soldier pushed his rifle through the bars until its barrel touched my companion's neck. I struggled on one leg to push him away from the rifle. He was still spitting at the soldier. The soldier pulled his rifle away after a superior dealt him a few punches. The soldier was furious.

"Leave him alone," I said to my companion as I struggled to stand. "What's the use of trying anything with these degenerates?"

"No one should stab a defenseless person!" he kept shouting at the soldier.

"Let's think about those who are coming," I said when he became quiet. "Don't you think our last hour will be more wonderful if they are here?"

He nudged my shoulder. "Those cowards are keeping them away from us," he bristled. "This hardship will be so much more bearable if they come."

"They'll come for certain, and we might even have an opportunity to say a few fiery words."

The carriage turned into a more desolate street. My thigh was still bleeding profusely and blood covered the wooden floor of the cage. The pain seemed less, perhaps because my future was now determined or because the long months in that damp cell had destroyed all concept of pain. We realize the limits of our stamina only when we put it to the test.

My companion was lost in thought, probably remembering Zulaikha. I wonder if Zulaikha was ever closer to him than she was on that day. It was probably for her sake that he took up arms to overthrow that hollow system. A child, or a pair of eyes, is worth fighting for.

Then we passed by a side street that made me suddenly very emotional. How many times had I walked it on my way to school! And then as a young man as I waited for comrades. Or as we planned together and replanned and argued. Impetuous youth clueless about aim or destination. The street fell far behind, but it brought to the carriage the smell of spring and sweet memories.

"Was it Zulaikha who told you life means courage?" I asked my companion.

"Oh, you took me out of my reminiscing," he said, annoyed. He apologetically flicked his fingers through his dusty hair.

"Never mind," he said. "Listen, try and recall some of your memories."

"That's all I ever did in the cell."

"Sometimes you can go on doing that infinitely. Especially in a slow carriage like this and when we still have time. Come on, try!"

"It's not easy," I mumbled.

"Don't you have your Zulaikha? Zulaikhas rise like the phoenix." Again, he bent down, but this time he looked at the sky. "This spring is sauntering," he said ruefully.

The voices were getting closer, and the soldiers' faces were becoming more sullen. They could have shot us right there and then. My eyes moved from the street to the closed shops and to the houses. More voices seemed to be coming, followed by the tramp of heavy shoes. My companion was unsettled, and tears started to trickle down his face.

"You're crying!" I exclaimed.

"You know, not because of fear. Only the good know how to cry."

I leaned forward, and my eyes fell on the clots of congealed blood on the floor of the cage. I noticed that my companion's military uniform was burned away at the knees. And I looked at my shoes. All those valleys and hills I had walked in them. And I thought of my comrades in their homes or in the wilderness waiting for darkness to fall to launch another attack. Bullets whistling by, last good-byes, renewed meetings.

My companion was crying again, and I could no longer hold back my own tears. His solemn words consoled me: "Oh, Zulaikha, the remote grows closer and closer. Distant horizons close in on us." With his long fingers he lifted up my face. "Only the good cry."

"Who's Zulaikha?" I tried to change the conversation.

"If we don't die, we'll meet your and my Zulaikha."

The waves of voices got closer, and things around us started to shake. The carriage reached a roundabout, and the horse stopped. Soldiers were sprawled all over the place like giant lizards. The voices now seemed to be coming from a street only a hundred meters away. Then a massive crowd of angry people surged up to the roundabout and soon broke through the wall of khaki round it. There was hail after hail of shots.

"I'm afraid the children might get hurt. What a terrible price to pay!" my companion said.

"I agree. They should have let us die quietly."

"But if the barriers are torn down," he shouted as the crowd got louder, "then no force can stop the masses!" Then he added gleefully: "The barriers have been torn down!"

A bloody fight erupted with hands, teeth, stones, shrieks. A group of men and women approached the carriage and reached with their hands to touch us—our hands, legs, and even shoes—as if we were blessed. Some women touched the blood on my thigh and ululated.

"We don't deserve all this," my companion said.

Some women leaped on the cage, then a few men and children followed and quickly formed a human shield round us. The horse was soon unharnessed, and a group of men started pulling the carriage away with dizzying speed. The two of us rolled around on the floor like sacks of cotton. Bullets were still raining down. A man fell from the carriage when a bullet hit him in the back, and I had a glimpse of him writhing on the deserted street. The carriage was pulled from one street to another, and the jolting brought about more bleeding in my thigh. At the start of a dark alley a bullet hit me in the shoulder, and another hit my companion in the arm.

Eyes were still fixed passionately on us, and hands continued to touch our saintly bodies. My companion crept up to support me.

"Did you see Zulaikha?" I asked him.

"All these are Zulaikhas," he cried jubilantly.

Hands reached in to hold me steady. A woman rubbed my numb face. I tried to look at her before I passed out. I managed a faint smile and kept looking at her green eyes. The carriage stopped rocking, and I saw again the appeals of the fly's green eyes. Only then did I realize that the eyes of the fly were like the eyes of my woman. She had died when they blasted her house with dynamite.

Samir Naqqash

In a series of articles published in 2002 and 2003, Samir Naqqash gave intimate and warm portraits of Jewish life in Iraq as he knew it personally or through others. His topics ranged from food to Jewish holidays, Muslim-Jewish relations, fashionable Baghdad neighborhoods, and Muslims' efforts to protect their Jewish neighbors during the pogrom, or farhood, *of 1941. Despite the obvious nostalgic overflow of his memories, Naqqash also addressed in some of these articles the tensions between Jews and Muslims, particularly after the creation of Israel. In "Tantal," a similar complexity reveals the ups and downs of the modern Jewish experience in Iraq through a folkloric figure that both Muslims and Jews share.*

Naqqash has insisted on writing in Arabic even though he was only thirteen years old when he left Iraq during the mass exodus of the Jews in 1951. In Israel, he learned Hebrew and then spent the bulk of the years from 1958 to 1962 traveling in Iran, where he learned Persian. Naqqash's aptitude for learning languages might not be surprising, but his choice to write in Arabic has kept his work from the wide circulation it deserves and has prevented him from getting institutional support in Israel. Writing in Arabic in a state where that tongue is considered the language of the enemy might be seen as a deliberate choice on the part of Israeli writers to point to the ambivalent status of Arab Jews in their adopted country. "Tantal" indeed suggests such ambivalence, particularly in depicting discrimination against Arab Jews.

"Tantal" is from Naqqash's short-story collection Ana wa ha'ula' wa al-fisam *(Me, Them, and Schizophrenia; Jerusalem: Matba' at al-Sharq, 1978).*

Tantal

Urban development has finally become a reality in the Sa'doon neighborhood of al-Sibaq al-Qadeem. There stood our mansion on the edge of a wilderness facing a wide, unpaved street with the temporary name of Al-Ahwazi. The name actually belonged to the street with which it intersected.

On the other side of the street stood large mansions surrounded by lush gardens. Before our house was built, these mansions were the edge of the neighborhood. My family sacrificed five lambs at the gate of the house the evening we moved in. Five was also the number of its outside doors and the number of childhood years I and my brothers spent in that house.

Our room was on the second floor. The children's room—unbelievably large and with beds almost twice our number. Our relatives' and friends' children usually used the extra beds. At night you'd hardly find an empty bed. There was a bookcase, also, and tables and chairs, but I rarely spent the day there.

Something mysterious and taxing weighed heavily on me in this room. Something I might have come across in a thick book or just in my own thoughts, but when it was triggered, I'd open the door and storm along the stone stairway to my grandma's room.

The mansion had the old and the new, but it was the old that always fascinated me. Built-in oil heaters and air conditioners in the rooms had less charm than the bronze brazier during winter nights, when it glowed with red embers. The aroma of dried orange peel wafted out as it burned in the fire, and we no longer noticed the oppressive smell of burning coal. Colored hand fans were nicer and less noisy than the electric ones, which we avoided anyway, fearing for our fingers and even our lives. The tea brewed over the steaming samovar tasted better than that brewed on the electric stove, and bread from the *tannur* was incomparably better than that from the kitchen oven. Um Jamil, the baker, used to make *tannur* bread for us. She built a mud hut next to our garden fence. We ate the bread she made, especially the small rounds she baked for us kids, even though the heat burned our fingers. The kitchen oven saw action only during seasonal holidays and family occasions.

My grandma's room was a living monument to the old. In that bare room there was just a Kashan carpet and a big wooden crib. I remember the crib very well—perhaps the biggest and most elaborately decorated crib in all of Baghdad. A custom-made crib that could accommodate a breast-feeding mother. My newborn sister nearly disappeared in it between the mattress and the bright silk quilt. My grandma would sit in the corner on the carpet and rock the crib by pulling at the attached string. I'd lie down in front of her and listen to her lullabies: *delillol,* my child, *delillol.*

I liked to stare at my grandma's face. Its tranquility induced awe, and the light it radiated looked angelic to me. The adults in the house praised her goodness and infinite dedication to her children and now to her grandchildren. Her prayers included friend and foe.

When the baby fell asleep, I'd take my grandma's hand and walk out of the room. She would follow in total loyalty. If it was a summer evening, we would sit on the front doorstep overlooking the street. The doorstep would still be hot from the day's burning sun, and my behind would feel it. My grandma would soon embark on a tale. *Kan ya ma kan . . .* Once upon a time . . .

At the center of our gatherings during cold winter nights were the coal brazier and the stories. We were enchanted by the tales about wizards and male jinn and female demons,[1] and we used to ask for the story of "the woman with the picture" or the one about "witch pomegranate seeds," and my grandma would tell stories for hours. When the stories were exhausted, they were repeated, but occasionally she would come up with a new one. We kept asking for more, and she kept on narrating. She had little inclination for invention and told stories as she had heard them, and when her memory faltered, she recoiled, muttering, "No, no, my

---

1. I translated *daewat* in the original as "male jinn" and *sa'ali* as "female demons." Naqqash footnoted *daewat* as Iraqi folklore creatures close in appearance to a human being, but much hairier. They sleep with eyes wide open and close their eyes when awake. If struck once with a sword, they die; yet another strike brings them back to life.

God," and corrected herself. We couldn't care less for her convictions and scruples; all we wanted was endless storytelling.

My imagination was deeply touched when one day I heard her mention the name "Tantal." Images of all shapes floated in my mind and inspired in me emotions of all kinds—pleasure, awe, curiosity.

Tantal was not a myth, but a reality that the entire town perceived. Neither was he the jinn of the stories who always brought trouble. Tantal was fun, and with that fun came wisdom of an unusual depth.

"Tantal likes to fool around with people," my grandma said in her quiet, engaged manner. "He does not hurt really, he just likes practical jokes. He appears in all sorts of forms, now a cat or a lamb, now a piece of thread. His jokes are funny."

"You've seen him?" I interrupted her.

"No. I won't lie to you and say I have seen him, but your uncle has. Not just your uncle—a lot of people say they have."

Next to our room on the second floor was my uncle's. He lived there with his wife and three children. I left my grandma in a hurry and ran upstairs, pushing open the door to my uncle's room and going in. Before he got married and had kids, he was fond of me, but I understood when his mind shifted to his family after the marriage. He liked to talk, and he still liked me nonetheless. One needed to find him in a good mood, preferably not when his losses at the horse races had upset him.

He was having his dinner, but I longed to hear about his many adventures with the jinn. Some were pleasant, others horrifying. It was well known that he was bedridden for three months because of one of those adventures. That one I heard more than once.

"It was nighttime!" His voice quivered as it always did when he was telling the tale. "I was with a Muslim soldier, on guard in a fruit orchard. What an orchard it was—endless! After a while, we heard the rattling of shackles; then a man as tall as a palm tree sprang out in front of us. His legs were shackled, but he kept coming toward us. 'Stop!' we shouted, but he kept advancing. 'Stop or we'll shoot,' we said, but we were simply wasting our breath. We panicked—really panicked. The Muslim with me whispered: 'Haroun, help me—I've shit in my pants.'

"The shackled giant was still coming toward us. We shot at him, but nothing happened. The bullets hit his chest, but he kept walking till he towered over us. What happened next I do not know. I found myself home, and I stayed in bed three full months."

My uncle's adventures with the jinn were countless. They liked to fool around with him. Not only them, but their ravishing daughters, too. On the way home from his grocery store one midnight he had an encounter with one of the daughters. Luckily, he was with a colleague. They saw a beautiful blonde sitting on the doorstep of the celebrated Khullani mosque, combing her long hair. If my uncle had a soft spot for women, that spot grew into a yawning gap when he saw the lonely midnight blonde at the mosque door. A gap that kept widening as the two men came closer to her. My naïve uncle wanted to flirt with her, but his partner warned him.

"It is strange, right? Why would a woman of such stunning beauty sit there at such an hour? It's the dead of night."

They walked past the woman, still overwhelmed by the strangeness of the situation. They hadn't walked far when my uncle nearly dropped dead.

"She's calling my name," he said. "How does she know me?"

"I warned you, didn't I?" his frightened partner said. He wouldn't let him turn around. "If you look back, we're doomed," he told him.

Then the ravishing woman's voice called the partner's name. My uncle had no doubt then, but was torn between fear and curiosity. Soon after, their backs were bombarded with stones. Scared, they took each other by the hand and ran as fast as they could. Indeed, he was lucky that time to have had his partner by his side.

I crept closer to my uncle till I nearly disappeared into his clothes, my eyes glued to his mouth. The moments between one morsel and the next seemed like hours.

As soon as he had swallowed his last mouthful, I asked him: "Uncle, is it true you saw a Tantal?"

Perhaps he had been losing more money at the races because he gave me a nasty look. When he loses all his money, he usually walks home—an hour and a half trip. I was too curious to allow for discomforts of any nature, not even his impassioned appeal, "Will you leave me alone, for God's sake?" I begged him, and perhaps the tears in my eyes overcame the losses at the races and the day's hard work. What an impulsive man he was!

The rituals of finishing the meal intensified my curiosity. "My God," I secretly prayed, "extend his hour of peace until he tells the story of seeing the Tantal."

"Come on, Uncle," I pleaded.

"Who set you on me this time?" he resisted. He went to wash his hands and mouth, moving about warily. I kept looking at my uncle and wondering at the meeting in him of two opposites. The quiet, peaceful, and gentle person and the explosive, angry beast. Life taught me, by and by, that opposites have a harmony of their own. I had a feeling that behind all his resistance was an urge to boast about his adventures—an urge to tell. The frustrations of losing at the races were things that came and went. Tantal was something else. Tantal was his thing. Others tell stories about Tantal, but they pale in comparison to the one who has actually seen him. And when he spoke about Tantal, he did so with passion, as if he were reliving his experiences.

Yes, he saw Tantal more than once.

Once, he held him in his hands. Tantal came to him at the barracks as an old dwarf wearing Bedouin clothes and gestured to him that he was hungry. My uncle gave him a container of food that he devoured instantly. He wanted more, and my uncle handed him a second and a third and a fourth. My uncle became suspicious and asked him who he was. He wouldn't say. My uncle then picked him up and tossed him away. He vanished into thin air.

Tantal also appeared to him as a black cat. It approached him at the house door and rubbed itself against his legs. It was useless to try and get rid of it. When he knocked at the door, his hands felt like they were knocking at a wall. He stepped back and looked, and the door was there. He approached it again and knocked, and again he was knocking on a wall. His familiarity with such situations came to his aid. He pulled out his pocketknife and invoked the name of God and lunged at the wall. The knife landed on the door and made a deep mark. He became used to Tantal's practical jokes and knew that their ordeal usually left only a passing memory. "Dreams," he would say, "dreams that you remember, and that's all." I did not understand that, and my mind remained possessed by burning images and illusions that blended reality and dream.

I became obsessed with seeing Tantal, an obsession that had its share of fear. I also started to become reclusive and somehow lost interest in the tales of lesser jinn. What took hold of my imagination was the impossible. But why would seeing Tantal count as impossible?

"By God, by God, I saw it with these two eyes," my uncle asserted, and my uncle was an undisputable fact. Why would Tantal appear to some and not to others?

I started to spend hours behind a closed door in my room. One day I opened the glass door of the bookcase and picked up, with trembling hand, a book illustrated with pictures of mythical creatures. It was a book about Greek mythology. I went through it and lingered at the picture of a strange creature—lingered long enough for the creature to take hold of my imagination and to start to come to life. The snakes crowning the old man's head began to move. They all stared at me and stuck out their tongues. I had to close the book before they flattened me with their venom. Afterwards, even ordinary creatures, frozen in their ordinary places, scared me. I felt then creeping up my forearm, and they filled my insides with maddening images. I kept wondering what these mythological creatures had in common with Tantal, and when no satisfactory answer was forthcoming, I sought solace in the outside world.

And in forgetfulness. The nastiest of all human afflictions—forgetfulness. But it helps us live. Lost in the trivia of living and survival, I forgot Tantal. School and the pursuit of pleasure for the following three years buried my burning desire to see Tantal until one day when I was sitting in the courtyard overlooking the mansion garden watching fibers flying from the tool of the cotton carder. My uncle's wife sat nearby, watching and talking to him. An existence that had shrunk because of the dust and the flying cotton and the rhythmic sounds of the carding. Soon enough, that small world was pierced and nearly swallowed by an overpowering force.

The carder had put his pad away and started brushing cotton fibers from his face. He carried on the conversation he was having with my uncle's wife, the beginning of which I had missed with all the beating he was doing: "I'm telling you, there are things in this world that make the mind boggle. Those who have not seen Tantal won't believe in him. But we all heard about Tantal, and I saw him with these two eyes. Jumps at you when he likes, you know, that bag of mischief. Gives you the smooth side of the rug only to pull it from under your feet. Like everything else in this world. Sometimes he does things as if a human being is nothing to him. I'd kill him if I could. He wants to have fun, of course, but why at my expense? Why would he make me a laughingstock?

"Once I was riding a donkey, causing no offense, going somewhere, but halfway there the donkey just stopped. 'Move, you senseless beast, move!' I said, but it was rooted to the spot. Then its head started to drop down, and I had to get down and see what was going on. Its black thing was erect and getting longer by the second. So long it touched the ground. 'You shameless thing, enough!' I said, but it was useless to talk to it. That thing was like a black snake getting longer and longer and creeping along the ground. Two meters, three, four meters, and it came after me. Nearly touched me. The fucker was after me to fuck me, I tell you. Then I understood what was going on. People stopped to look, and some were scared away. Then the crowd started laughing. 'You idiot, how come you're riding this donkey?' they called out. I told them I thought it had no owner, and I needed the ride. 'You good-for-nothing,' they said, 'you wanted to ride it, and it almost rode you.' I tell you, I let the donkey go and fled home. I had no idea where the donkey ended up. They said that after I left, the donkey just disappeared—melted away like a lump of salt. They looked everywhere. That was Tantal, of course. How did I miss that?"[2]

My uncle's wife was reeling with laughter. Guileless, passionate, and sexually deprived, she fell for it, and he was all eyes. A young, beautiful woman to whom he had just narrated a salacious, bawdy tale.

---

2. The speech is given in the dialect of Baghdadi Muslims. The writer gives a standard Arabic rendering in the margins.

I was a child who nearly turned into a man then, a jealous man who wanted to silence the vulgar carder and put an end to his dirty ogling. But I did nothing—I was engulfed by a torrent of emotions, and my determination waned. It made little difference whether he was describing what had really happened to him or was simply making it up. The important thing was that Tantal had come back, and the years in between had made me more reflective and appreciative of good stories. Tantal. An elusive mischief with a thousand shapes. A truth and a lie, and the rash impulse to see him added my head to a thousand more. "I have to see it," I told myself. But once again, life and forgetfulness put a damper on that impetuous urge.

Israel, the Early 1950s

The age of speed had touched everything. Keeping up with change was becoming more daunting. One day we opened our eyes and the world had changed; we found ourselves in a new world. Al-Sibaq al-Qadeem suburb had vanished, and instead tents replaced uprooted trees. A faded, gray tent had replaced our huge mansion. The first night, I slept on the floor of the tent, feverishly tossing and turning and ceaselessly stung by nightmares and thorns. Big reddish ants feasted on my body as well. Before that night was over, I felt I had become an old man. I suppose that was what they meant by the leap. My grandma lay down in one corner of the tent, her face still glowing, although its light was now dimmed by patient silence. She had never complained before, and her pains could never bring her to her knees. Stunned and disoriented, I kept to another corner of the tent and wept.

"Come here, *ibdalak*," she said once and hugged me. "Come, I'll tell you a story."

I resisted and freed myself from her embrace. Then I laughed cynically because I had grown up—become old indeed—and stories of the jinn could no longer entertain me. It seemed only yesterday that I was reading the biographies of world celebrities and wanted to be like Madame Curie or perhaps greater than her after discovering the elixir of life. And I wanted to go to the Sorbonne where Madame Curie went.

Now at age twelve, I had become old, and the entire world was ageing with me.

The tents scattered in the wilderness looked like spooky tombstones. In fact, the smell of death was all over the place; the elixir of life was nowhere to be found. Another cynical laugh brought the realization that what we needed was water. Water itself had become that elixir and the force behind demonstrations in the camp. I joined those who shouted, "Water! Water!" The accursed leap of the early 1950s devoured people, including my father, and its aftermath hit children as well. The demonstrations were also for food and work.

"It is not our fault," one of those in power once wrote. "We are trying everything we can. The problem is that you came from poor, backward countries still living in the dark ages."

That somehow brought life back in the mansion, and Madame Curie and the elixir of life—all fell before the winds sweeping through the fragile tents. A nameless feeling drowned me until forgetfulness once more made survival possible for those in the camp. We forgot the old life and started to get used to the new, cruel routine. We stopped demonstrating and stopped asking for water, that new elixir of life.

In the camp, shops started to appear, built from bits of wood and tin, and when more of them sprang up, we had something like a village market. Behind the market and a little beyond the creek—a creek from which the bodies of dead children were collected one day—was the tent in which my uncle and his six children lived. I used to cut through the muddy space between us and cross the crumbling wooden bridge to reach my uncle's tent. I used to think that my uncle was probably the sole beneficiary of that disastrous leap—he had a separate home. A decaying tent, but a home, nonetheless.

Like most of the camp residents, my uncle was not working. He rarely came home before midnight, and I sometimes had to go to the camp café, pull him away from his playmates, and bring him home to his wife and children.

"Your hair is white," I used to tell him. "Is it not time to give up gambling?"

"It's just to pass the time. Do you think I place bets?" he retorted.

"You haven't forgotten the races, have you?" I'd joke with him. "You used to walk all the way home."

"There are no races here."

"There's a café instead."

"Do I owe anybody anything?" he would reply angrily, foaming at the mouth. "Nobody can tell me what to do."

"OK, let's move on," I'd say, and sometimes he himself would say that after a short pause.

Sometimes, I would find him in a tent in the evenings.

"How come you're here?" I'd ask. "No café gambling tonight?"

"I'm not staying late anymore. I'm not that crazy to risk my life."

"Why, what happened?" I asked.

"Do you mean you don't know? Tantal has moved from Baghdad and is just across from here. Just after the bridge when you come from the market."

"What?" I said, laughing. "This Tantal must like you so much that he had to follow you. Left Baghdad and found no other place but across from you."

"I'm telling you," he shouted, "you don't believe me? A lot of people have seen him. Abu Rahma, for instance, who sells vegetables at the market, saw a black dog planted right in front of him as he was crossing the bridge. The dog began to grow bigger and bigger till it was the size of an elephant. Now go and look at Abu Rahma—he nearly died, the poor thing. Abu Rahma and many others, I tell you."

"Are you afraid of Tantal now? You two are friends. You've met him a thousand times and even touched him with your own hands."

"What are you talking about?" he cut me short. "This is not Baghdad. Who has the courage anymore? Or the strength? Such stories are scary now. We can barely stand up, and if we see things like that now, we'll be finished."

In no time the entire camp was talking about Tantal, and many stated that they had seen him near the bridge next to my uncle's tent. I started to go to the tent at night and to leave late, hoping to see Tantal. When I approached the bridge, my heart would start pounding, and real fear would overwhelm me.

That misguided urge of mine remained unsatisfied. I often thought of my uncle's words that this was not Baghdad and that people had lost all courage, and I realized some hidden wisdom was there. More experience only bore witness to this wisdom and prompted me to get to the heart of it. The urge to see Tantal and the fear and cowardice that came with it started competing with each other—the latter always seeming to have the edge. The heart of that wisdom, though, remained intact—a mystery just like Tantal.

Israel . . . 1970

I returned to that camp after spending long years outside Israel, still looking for myself. I was a man with thirty solid years of living behind him, which now seemed just worthless memories. And six countries that seemed to be different in everything, yet very much the same. And five romantic adventures—five women I had loved and who had loved me. Five attempts and five failures and five scars, and all that remained was the bitter taste of boredom.

No job was left untried—thirteen all told, the last of which was as a porter at a huge grocery warehouse in Tehran. My back was bent, but so was my face and my spirit, and all for a trashy meal at the end of the day. I eventually decided to go back to the camp, still searching for meaning in life.

The camp had changed, and those in charge must have counted the change as improvement. The tents became boxes made of wood, then boxes of stone, in each box two rooms. The camp had become a humble but horrific suburb. The tents were gone, true, but the ugliness remained in the semblance of modernization that had replaced them. I was still searching for myself and my life, but when I entered our cubicle, I lost all hope.

My uncle was one of those to welcome me. His cubicle was next to ours.

"You came back with the booty, huh?" he said, his sarcasm overshadowing his humor.

"And you? What have you achieved? Got younger?" I challenged him.

"Well, what can we do?" He sounded defeated and apologetic. "The young grow up, and the old get older, and the very old die. This is how it has been since the start."

"So, what's the purpose of life?"

"What? You want to change the world?" he protested.

I was silent. I had been glum to start with; now all attempts to have a normal conversation were futile. Then I remembered Tantal.

"What happened to Tantal?" I asked him. "Is he still there at the bridge, or has he followed you here?"

He grew excited for a moment, but did not seem to like my sarcastic tone.

"You still don't believe in him, do you?" he said. "A school has been built there, and no one can go past it at night. Rahmeen, tell him what you saw the other night." Rahmeen was his youngest, born in the camp. When I had left, he had been a toddler.

"A friend of mine and I were walking by the school one night and we saw someone walking in our direction. He grew taller with every step till he became as tall as the electricity pole, maybe taller. Then he reached us, but he was just a little boy. Nothing."

Rahmeen stopped and then, as if embarrassed by what he had just said, continued: "Maybe because it was dark and foggy the street light made things look different, and he looked tall. What are we talking about? There is no Tantal!"

"Why not?" I protested. "He must exist, and if so many have seen him, I must, too." I sounded convinced, and my childish assertions drew some incredulous looks from those present.

Nightfall was approaching as I plowed aimlessly through the crowded streets of the city. Lack of interest was becoming second nature to me, and I walked quietly, hopelessly. Inside my head a different kind of existence was in perpetual flux. I still looked at the thirty years of my past life as a handful of ashes. Was that life? And where was that woman who wanted me to see her naked through her window? I wrote to her once, "You have an affliction—get down, where life is." Now both woman and life were disappearing. And the other woman who kept to herself in her room and danced. Danced every day as I looked on from my room. Perhaps she danced for me, too. Nonsense. Nonsense was the outcome of everything else in life. My uncle had said it—the routine of life since that start—and he was a friend of the jinn, so he knew. Now life had made him afraid of the jinn—broken him and left him for dead. What was really worthwhile were the accidental insights as life ran through one's fingers.

At a crossroads I stopped—alone, jobless, and indifferent. I crossed a street and wondered why people were hurrying. Where to? When I got to the seafront, I slumped into a chair at a café with bright, colorful lights. The previous night I had been at another café with a friend, and when the waiter asked me what I wanted to drink, I had said: "The elixir of life." Then ordered a cold drink.

"You wanted to discover that elixir," my friend said.

"I was a fool," I said. "It was a dumb human slip."

"But I believe in science," my friend interjected.

"I believe in Tantal," I answered.

My friend wouldn't listen to such talk. When the waiter brought the drink, I didn't like it.

"It's my fault," I told him. "I'm feeling sick. The drink is fine." The waiter did not seem to believe me.

"Tantal is our only certainty," I told my friend. "Everything else is an illusion."

"You haven't ever seen Tantal, and you know it."

"Perhaps I'll never see him, but I started to feel he has become part of my life."

"You seem touched by . . ."

"Madness?"

"No, delusion."

The sea breeze refreshed me, and surroundings restored my sense of being—the sunset, a child building sand castles, the tempting heart and sea. I took off my clothes and walked to the water, and soon felt lost inside a giant being. The sense of a challenge drew me away from the shore and toward the setting sun.

"Where am I heading?"

"To deep water," the waves answered.

The next wave carried me away, and I felt I was shrinking. That was a moment where combating existence became real. The sea had powerful arms, a gaping mouth, and empty bowels.

I looked back at the coastline, frightened. I wasn't quite up to the challenge and wanted to flee. The sea kept pulling me in the other direction, toward the deep waters.

"Help!" I cried and swam furiously back toward the coast.

"Don't be scared!" I heard a clear, shrill voice coming from the distant horizon that was colored by the sinking sun. "Take my hand," it urged.

I looked for the hand and saw it—a giant hand that came from the direction of the deep waters. I tried to reach for it and heard the urging voice again: "Come on, come closer and take my hand." I followed the hand toward the limitless monster. The hand beckoned, and I followed. The gap between us seemed to widen, and the hand seemed to flee, but the voice still urged me to come closer.

I saw his face in the dying light—a swarthy giant with a big smile.

"You scoundrel! You're pulling my leg!"

The giant laughed.

"Who are you?" I asked, enraged.

The giant disappeared. I was tired and scared and swam frantically toward the coastline. An inconsequential feather that the sea was toying with, but still capable of thinking and remembering.

"It's Tantal . . . I saw Tantal," I shouted with all the strength I had.

A weak echo came back, "It's Tantal . . . I saw Tantal."

Salima Salih

Salima Salih is one of a small but very important group of writers living in the West. Particularly in the work of émigré women, the Western experience seems to have enabled liberating and bold visions and given writers more freedom to depict what would have been considered controversial material in the home culture, such as female sexuality and racial and religious interaction. "Those Boys" is certainly characteristic of such writing in its representation of the challenges facing the integration of Arab and Muslim communities into Western countries. Salih was born in Mosul, northern Iraq, in 1942 and studied law and art at academic institutions in Baghdad. She went to Germany in 1978 to study journalism at the University of Leipzig and has been residing there for more than two decades. She has been active as a fiction writer and translator, and among the writers she has translated into Arabic are Ingeborg Bachmann and Christa Wolf.

"Those Boys" is a touching piece whose theme has a long history in Arab fiction—life in the West. What is new in this story is the presentation of the theme from the perspective of a parent as she reflects on children whose sensibilities are being shaped by their Western experience. Unlike traditional Arab fiction about the West in which adults have a temporary presence, the writings of émigré writers deal with settling down and integration into Western communities. Nurruddin and Ali represent two very different personalities and attitudes toward assimilating Western values. Nurruddin is well adjusted, and Germany is home to him; Ali still seems attached to the norms and values of the community he left behind.

"Those Boys" originally appeared as "Haʾulaʾ al-abnaʾ" in the magazine Al-Ightirab Al-Adabi *51 (2002): 61–65.*

Those Boys

At school the kids talk about video games, about Codam, the aquarium, and the botanic garden. And the Eiffel Tower and the Giza pyramids. There are no border crossing points in Frederickstrasse and no border guard who inspects the passport and asks about the kid. I say, he's here in Berlin. "In the capital," he corrects me.

The kids also talk about their latest purchases and about political parties and trends. They're confused, and they feel out of place. They listen to their parents at night and ask questions, but get only half-answers. Their parents are preoccupied with vanishing institutions and lost jobs, and their teachers with designing curricula and selecting textbooks and calculating their overtime hours.

When Nurruddin comes home, we usually sit down to talk. "Thomas roots for the Republicans," he says hesitantly and bashfully. This is when Nurruddin was thirteen and still capable of talking to us, his parents. He had known Thomas since the first grade, and the two had become close friends a few years ago. It is this closeness that made Thomas reveal his thinking. But wouldn't that mean the end of their friendship? Nurruddin has realized in the past few weeks that Republicans cannot be his friends. He has an Arabic name and complexion, but German manners. A bicultural boy.

Thomas's political choice confused him a little. They used to invite each other to birthday celebrations, and lately Thomas would come with his parents and take Nurruddin to their orchard in the suburbs and bring him back in the evening. Once, Nurruddin returned with a bag of cherries. Thomas's birthday comes during the cherry season.

Thomas thought Nurruddin was ambitious because his grades were good, even though he never worked hard for them. "Cheat on your tests, but don't let them catch you," he used to tell him. I had to lecture Nurruddin to stay away from that. This year Thomas is not celebrating his birthday. He is going on a bike tour and will play soccer with Nurruddin, who never has enough of it.

Around 11:00 P.M. darkness starts to spread over Rudolph Zeiwert Street. From the balcony I can hear noises from the playground. The

German children will go home around seven or eight, and the Arab boys will start another round of play. Nurruddin, Ismael, Hadi, and Khalifa won't miss dinner even if they are late. Their mothers will be waiting for them, and they will always have a hot meal. Nurruddin plays with both teams—with the Germans till they leave and with the Arabs till darkness falls.

Nurruddin no longer belongs to the select group of children who can buy whatever they want in the western side of the city. Nor will he get a "1" in math and in language and history or a "4" in self-application because he did only the assigned work, finding it unnecessary to fill out pages and pages with extra exercises. And a "3" in behavior because he touched the school fence when the pupils went with the caretaker on their daily walk. He's seventeen now, and on his way to school he smokes a mint-flavored cigarette, oblivious to outside noises and scenes. Even to exotic fish in a bowl or to a drunkard crowing like a rooster in public.

Nurruddin writes diaries I can't read or, rather, whose lousy handwriting I can't read.

"Mother keeps reminding me that she was the first person I knew when I was born, and she is therefore the person who knows me the best. Flirting with her, I'd say, But my eyes were closed, and when I opened them it was the nurse's face I saw first. The nurse, what was her name, Zahida? She was the first person I saw as I lay on the scales. Anyway, when we have an argument, she tells me I don't know you anymore, which gives me the feeling that I beat her. Then I go to my room satisfied and even forgive her her oppressiveness."

In London he writes his diaries in English, and in Paris he meets new friends. I remember all his old friends, Sacha, Nico, Matthias, Bourne, Nadine, Ulrika. Those who played with him and those who didn't, they all have changed, and I don't quite recognize them when they show up at the door with shaved faces and harsher voices. But I remember the names—Michael and Stefan.

"Do you really want to know something about Stefan? He volunteered for the army."

I hardly knew the young man, but I remember him as an ideal child. He wasn't one of Nurruddin's friends, and Nurruddin made no effort to befriend him. Now I see in him the fruit of firmness and obedience.

But Thomas has remained a true friend and never became a Republican.

Ali, who came from a distant land, tastes the cookie I offered him and then recoils in terror. "Does it contain any alcohol?" I apologize sincerely because I don't know. Who steeled these boys against the temptations of new experiences and against the influences of a new environment? Not just their mothers, who have stayed at home and think of their faraway boys and whether they heat their dinners and manage to do the laundry. They never did these things when they lived at home. Homes to which fathers would return late, lucky if they caught a meal with the family. More often, the boys would succumb to their hunger and eat early.

Ali remembers his mother, and his face contracts with anguish. He's learned the ritual of becoming a man and cries without tears. He also knows that as a man it doesn't become him to fail. These boys adore their mothers, their partners in oppression, the guardians of their secrets, their allies in the face of cruelty or lack of sympathy. They are the ones who would intercede on their behalf when fathers became unrelenting. To shield them from punishment, before the fathers returned, they would fix the windowpanes the boys had broken or simply claim the pane was hit by a stone no one knows where it came from. Sometimes the boys didn't get pocket money from their fathers, and they had to do odd chores to earn it. But they could always count on the resourcefulness and generosity of their mothers, who saved pennies here and there and hid them between layers of clothes. When the boys were sick, the mothers would rub their foreheads, and when they came home from school, the mothers would examine them just in case they were missing a body part.

Nurruddin knows that scrutiny and dodges it. He hates it because he knows that I, his mother, will see through him and discover his joys and worries and miseries. He hurries to his room when he has something to hide, and the door closes before my look can corner him and he finds himself dealing with questions he doesn't want to answer.

Ali says, "My brother called this morning and wanted to know what I have been doing in Berlin since I arrived here a year ago."

What glamorous results could he achieve within the confines of his conditional residency? He goes to school with little kids and has to be home before 10:00 P.M. He has to get a reduced-price transportation pass from the Department of Social Security and has to learn how to say, "Gestaten Sie bitte, darf ich durch, Rindfleisch, kein Schweinfleisch."[1]

In the communal kitchens of their housing complexes or in their tiny cold apartments the boys try to cook what their mothers cooked for them, but they add too much garlic or forget to add salt. The tastes they knew at home will remain beyond them. They sleep in and go late to the German-language class. They stay up until two in the morning, debating the causes of the Lebanese civil war or Emad's opinion that freedom sometimes can be dangerous. They can't sleep because their mothers' prayers are not hovering over them.

In their letters they become remarkable university students or successful professionals working for big companies and living in villas surrounded by trees. They consolidate their positions by marrying the boss's daughter. But by doing so they put themselves at a disadvantage: "Why don't you send some money, then?" And so they have to become even thriftier and save to send their mothers a first installment. Perhaps their mothers need the money or perhaps just assurances that their sons are not failing. For such gestures the boys live poor and work for little pay. Can they write to their mothers and say that they don't have the status of residency that would enable them to work legally?

Working in the civil service, Nurruddin has a chance to get to know these boys. They tell him stories about the routes they took to get here, the interrogations, the legislation directed at foreigners, and the types of residency. They ask him how he ended up here, and he can't answer. He has always

---

1. "Excuse me, let me through; I want beef, not pork."

been here, a baby, a little boy, a young man, simply at home here. Kids played with him at the kindergarten, invited him to their homes, and celebrated his birthday. They quickly got to know his name and not only accepted his brown skin, but coveted it when they let the summer sun bake theirs. He was here when a child snatched his toy in a doctor's waiting room. Stunned, he didn't say a word and looked to me, his mother, for help. He was two and hadn't learned the word *mine* because ours then was his. He had refused to take pocket money. "What would I do with it?"

"To learn how to take care of your needs," replied the neighbor, "how to economize." Nurruddin knew he didn't need money because he had what he wanted. But one day he realized that "ours" was not enough, and "mine" gradually became more sharply defined and more urgent. Now, he asks for pocket money and saves to pay for his trips and the cigarettes he smokes in secret. He has dumped the piggy bank and bought a safe with a lock. Approaching his rite of passage to manhood, Nurruddin has severed the umbilical cord. It's the age of the first cigarette, the first kiss.

Now, Nurruddin doesn't eat the food I cook. He buys frozen foods that only need heating and won't tell me where he goes in the evening. His friends' names have become secrets, like the secrets of where he plays soccer or the school supplies he likes most. The secrets are multiplying, and he gloats at my increasing curiosity and anxiety. He reads Hermann Hesse and Karl Krause but can't find words to say to me. He keeps changing his friends and plays "Work Is a Rotten Thing" on the guitar.

Samuel Shimon

Samuel Shimon's work offers a significant perspective on the degree to which eth-
nic and religious markers in Iraq converge and intersect. Christian by faith and
Assyrian by descent, born in Habbaniyya, west of Baghdad, in 1956, but now liv-
ing in London, Shimon comfortably deals with characters and situations that
involve diverse Iraqi groups. The selection given here presents Christian and
Muslim characters, Shia and Sunna both, even though the locale is western Iraq,
a predominantly Sunni area. In this diversity, Shimon is not an anomaly because
the majority of Iraqi writers refuse to recognize race, religion, and sect as domi-
nant factors in Iraqi society. Shimon is a journalist, poet, and cultural figure in
the Arab diaspora. He manages cybersites that cater particularly to young voices
and is assistant editor and cofounder of Banipal, *the prominent London-based*
English journal of Arab literature.

"The Street Vendor and the Movies" tells of Shimon's personal fascination
with the film industry and faithfully depicts Iraqis' attitudes toward this aspect of
Western culture. In an environment such as the one in which we live now, where
notions of clashing cultures and values are common, the piece might sound odd to
some. The narrator and Kiryakos, for instance, look at life as if it were an exten-
sion of the movies they see, and for the narrator, John Ford looms more like a shap-
ing influence than does his own father. Equally intriguing in this piece is Shimon's
blend of traditional and indigenous storytelling with a fast-paced and sharply
visual sequence of scenes.

"The Street Vendor and the Movies" is an abridged translation of "Al-baa'i'
al-mutajawil wa al-seenama" from Shimon's collection Iraqi fi Parees *(An Iraqi*
in Paris; Cologne, Germany: Dar al-jamal, 2005).

The Street Vendor and the Movies

"Joey, serve me first—I'm your brother Teddy's friend."

"Joey, may Allah spare you, give me a sorbet. Like you, I love the movies. The bell is about to go."

"Joey, one evening I brought your father back home. He was boozed up. Ask him."

The kids at the elementary school surrounded my handcart. Their tiny hands waved the money as I handed them small cups of sorbet. Nasrat Shah was by my side, satisfied with the speed of delivery. He touched his yellow headwear, imported from Tehran, and smiled as he saw the money slip into my pocket. He had told my mother that in that business I was the fastest in the world. When the bell finally rang, I had managed to serve all those kids and had even given Amir, who claimed he took my drunken dad home, an extra cup for free.

As soon as the school closed the gate, Nasrat Shah said he was going to pray at the *husainiyya*. "Listen, Joey, you should be heading to the girls' school now. They like red sherbet."

He knew what he was talking about. As soon as the girls came out, they jumped on the cart. Some swallowed two cups, and others borrowed money from friends for an extra one. The sorbet made their lips red. The school knew what we were doing, too. A teacher, Sitt Madeline, once told us, "I know you put in a lot of red coloring to lure the girls. You should be ashamed of yourselves." Nasrat Shah didn't answer her then, but lowered his headwear and kept eyeing her rear as she walked away. "Bitch," he said, "yes, we make their lips red and cool them off. What's wrong with that? She's forty years old," he added, shaking his head, "and still single."

I pushed the cart toward the mosque and waited for Nasrat Shah to come out. Meanwhile I started making more sorbet. I poured water into the big copper pot, added two kilos of sugar, two and a half spoonfuls of green coloring, a spoon and a half of vanilla, and some citric acid. Around the outside of the pot, I broke up ice with a screwdriver and covered it with coarse salt to slow down the melting, then started to spin the pot against the ice. The green liquid began to freeze on the inside.

Samson wanted to know if I did well that day. His question surprised me as I was counting the money. Yes, I said.

"You're a resilient boy," Samson said and patted my head.

"Do you want a sorbet?" I asked my elder brother.

I gave him one. His shoes and schoolbooks had mud all over them. "You didn't go to school today, Samson. Right?"

He nodded as he devoured the sorbet. "You know, I'll start school next year," I said.

"Great. You'll be able to read film magazines and the movie subtitles." He finished his cup, and I was about to give him a second, but he said he needed to go. "I need fifty fils," he said. He took off as soon as I gave him the money. He did not seem aware of my desire to talk to him. We hardly talked at home, and sometimes a month passed by before we said a few words to each other.

Samson was lanky and swarthy, handsome and athletic. He used to spend a lot of time outside, and my mother used to say that for him the house was just a place to sleep.

I gave the rest of the money to Nasrat Shah when he came from the mosque. "You're a Tarzan," he said as he pocketed the money. "Go home for a bite and get ready for the evening shift." He gave my head a kind pat with his hand. He had just three fingers on that hand.

"Mom, how long have we known Nasrat Shah's family?" Samson asked one day as he came in around noon for a piece of bread.

"Since forever. We've been together always. I breast-fed their Fatima and Ibrahim, and Sukayna breast-fed Teddy and Joey."

Nasrat Shah had built a separate room next to his house for his son Ali when he became a student at the Teachers' College. Ali hated that narrow room, however, and Ibrahim and I turned it into a play den. We dubbed it the cinema room and used it for shadow shows. The walls were covered with pictures of actors and film posters. Norman Wisdom; Roy Rogers, the king of cowboys; Alan Ladd; Randolph Scott; Gary Cooper; Cary Grant; Errol Flynn; King Kong lifting up Bob Hope; Montgomery Clift; Eleanor Powell; Frankenstein; John Wayne; Tyrone Power with a bushy beard and a sad look; several pictures of Henry Fonda; Charlie Chaplin, and one of Chaplin and little Jackie Coonan.

That particular picture spurred an argument one day between me and Khajik over silent and sound films. You like silent movies, he said, because you're the son of a deaf and mute father. That day I found a piece of rope and planned to strangle that mean Armenian boy, but Ibrahim did not think that was a good idea, especially when my dad was trying to get a job at Umm Khajik's bakery. I had also heard my mother one day tell Sukayna, "I hope Umm Khajik takes Kikah on. Those who work at her electric bakery get reasonable wages and don't work themselves to death." I also had a pang of guilt because Khajik's dad used to give me a whole dinar every Christmas. Not last Christmas, though, because he had passed away just the week before.

I was in the cinema den when Ibrahim brought the good news that the movie theater was showing a new Norman Wisdom film.

"How do you know?" I asked the elated boy.

"Walid, the owner's son, told me his dad brought a lot of movies from Baghdad, and one of them was a Norman Wisdom. The theater's manager, Hikmat al-Hindi, has given it the title *Norman Wisdom Joins the Airborne Force*." I approached the Norman Wisdom poster on the wall and dusted it over with my hand and kissed it. *"Norman in Love,"* I said. *"Norman the Milkman,"* Ibrahim said, and we went on reciting the list of Arabic titles that Hikmat al-Hindi came up with. Hikmat was a real Indian, and his father originally came to Iraq as a "babu" with the English army and decided to stay in Iraq. Shakir al-Hindi, however, was not a true Indian, and "al-Hindi" was just his family name. He came to Habbaniyya from Albu-Kamal on the Syrian border. Short, stocky, and well liked by the people, Shakir used to sell vegetables and fruits and complained that no one bought fruits after the departure of the British. He used to tell stories of how British wives sent dogs with baskets and money attached to their necks, and Shakir would send back fruits and vegetables in these baskets. The wives would write something like, "Good morning, Mister Shakir

Hindi," and he would write back, "Please enjoy your fruits, and very best wishes from Mister Shakir Hindi." Those were good days, and they were gone, he would say before he lighted a cigarette.

Kiryakos dubbed Nisreen "Audrey Hepburn" when he saw her sitting with me outside her aunt's house. I used to tell her all sorts of things about films and the town. She was thin and fair skinned, with short black hair. I kissed her delicate nose three days after her arrival in town. She had come from northern Iraq to stay with her aunt Zahra, who worked as a gardener at the British barracks. Zahra had succeeded her brother when she was just eighteen and never married despite the many suitors she had. She fascinated me, and I was delighted to do chores for her. Her niece Nisreen became a friend of mine as soon as she came visiting. Zahra introduced me as a dutiful "son" ready to help her on all occasions. Needless to say, she didn't mention that I mostly fetched her cigarettes.

"Everybody calls me 'son,'" I turned to Nisreen. "Aunt Sukayna does, Aunt Zaynab, the fava bean vendor's wife, Aunt Zahra, and even my mother. I hope you won't call me 'son.'"

"No, you're my friend," Nisreen said, sticking her hand in my long hair. Her looks to her aunt suggested she liked our town.

The following day I showed Nisreen around, especially where to buy things. When I took her to the bakery, I seized the opportunity to introduce her to my father. On our way back I told her she could buy practically everything at Yosha's. It was close by, and he sold on credit. His daughter, Victoria, had left for Detroit three years earlier.

On our way to collect salt I decided from now on not to dole out any money to Samson or to anyone else. My daily expenses had increased since Nisreen's arrival. I thought I could "put away" fifty fils before I handed over the sorbet revenue to Nasrat Shah. I needed to do that cautiously, though. Eyes were everywhere, and as Kiryakos used to say, there were watchful eyes on earth, not just in heaven. The first time I did that, I turned my eyes toward heaven, then looked right and left before I slipped the fifty-fils coin in my underwear.

At the end of the day I gave the sorbet proceeds to Nasrat Shah, but before I left, I made a confession. "Uncle Nasrat, I already took my daily allowance because I needed it," I said.

"But why did you put it inside your underwear?" His question surprised me.

"I didn't want to lose it," I blurted out.

Nisreen told me one day that her aunt would be away all afternoon and asked me to buy her a watermelon and three chunks of bread dough. I had to put in some of my own money for that.

"What's this?" she said when she saw a big watermelon and five pieces of dough.

"Oh, I get things cheap," I bragged. "People at the market love me."

"You're so sweet," she said and pressed her breasts against my chest. She kissed my cheek and got as close as you can to the lips. My heart sank.

"Do you want me to sing a song from the Indian movie *Junglee?*" I asked her.

"Yeah," she whispered and took away the warmth of her breasts.

I asked Nisreen to take the reclining pose of the woman in the song, and I started singing and humming the tunes, and moving around imitating the singer Shami Kapoor in the film. I leaned toward her and kissed her nose. No, she doesn't look like Audrey Hepburn, I thought.

"Very beautiful," she said. "You're really nice, Joey."

Kiryakos noticed that I had lost interest in the world of motion pictures and shadow cinema, and one day he asked me to accompany him to the cinema den. "I have a bunch of Hollywood nuggets," he said.

"I'll catch up with you in a minute," I said, looking at Aunt Zahra's door.

I didn't. Kiryakos had already put up about a dozen new pictures on the walls of the den. Ibrahim later told me that after a long wait, Kiryakos left, wondering what was happening to me. Five of the pictures were rare ones from *The Man Who Shot Liberty Valance.* Ibrahim said he thought Kiryakos had shed a few tears.

Kiryakos tolerated my betrayal, and one day he dropped in at the den and told me, "I just read that Jack is sick," he said in a tragic tone.

I straightened the bucket on which I used to sit and waited for more.

"Jack is really sick," he said, still pale and tragic. "So sick that he couldn't finish his new movie *Young Cassidy.* Isn't this heart-wrenching?"

I lowered my eyes. "Nisreen says she doesn't know John Ford," I said, looking up at him.

Kiryakos slapped me with such force that I was knocked down. "I talk to you about a genius, and you babble about a silly girl," he said, furious. "You know what," he added with a regretful smile, "that stupid mountain girl doesn't look a bit like Audrey Hepburn."

My mother was surprised when Kiryakos told her he did not want to see me anymore. What made things worse was that Samson hinted to my mom that I had spent some of Nasrat Shah's money on groceries for Nisreen. Ibrahim, annoyed that I was spending less time playing with him in the den, also whispered to his mom that I not only did chores for Nisreen, but also housework. His mom thought the matter too serious to overlook and had to counsel my mother. "Your son, for whom I was a midwife and a breast-feeder, must be under the spell of this bitch of a gardener who wears military boots."

"You're right," my mom said. "Otherwise, he would be splitting people's heads with his talk about the cinema and actors."

In his own way my father understood what was going on. He came to the den as I was eating rice and lentil soup, without meat because, my mother used to say, we were like Christ who did not like eating meat. My father smiled and with his left index finger communicated his thoughts to me. He knew, his finger indicated, that the tall guy with the long hair and checkered shirt did not want to see me. Then he blew a raspberry, meaning I shouldn't care. He pointed to me, then rubbed his two index fingers on his own chest. This was his way of saying we were friends.

It really got into my mother's head that Nisreen's voodoo was controlling me. "Look at him," she told Sukayna one morning. "His face is as yellow as turmeric. He's not natural."

"Gurgiyya, I told you he's under a spell. That gardener with the military boots won't leave us alone."

"Can't you break this magic spell?" my mother pleaded. "You're a mullah of sorts."

Indeed, Sukayna had some reputation as a genuine mullah with supernatural powers and knowledge of secret remedies, and her reputation was consolidated when she saved Zahra's life. Sukayna didn't like Zahra because Zahra had bragged that her father was the spiritual leader of the northern Kurdish region, with supernatural powers that even the British recognized. British civil engineers, Zahra claimed, would come to him to tell them where the best routes were in the most rugged terrain. They used to kiss his hands, too. Anyway, when Zahra was stung by a large scorpion that crept into her boots while she was napping, Sukayna sucked the poison out of her stung toe and finger and spat it out. Then she brought her own bare foot close to the scorpion and started reciting appeals to Allah and Imam Ali bin Abi Talib. When the scorpion stung her foot, it flipped over and froze in a matter of seconds. Sukayna then told Zahra to swallow the ashes of her cigarettes for a whole month as a sure remedy. Kiryakos was often quoted on Zahra's stomach as "having its own 'Tobacco Road.'"

Sukayna decided to break the spell that Zahra and her niece had cast around me and thus save the child she had breast-fed so that he could focus on working for her husband—and, more important, consolidate her genuine spiritual powers.

"As soon as he gets home from work, bring him to me," she told my mother. "Do not give him anything to eat." My mother followed this advice and dragged me by the hand to Nasrat Shah's. She made me lie on my back and wait for Sukayna's treatment. Preoccupied with my hunger,

I looked at the picture of Imam Ali on the wall and thought of the picture we had at our place of St. George mounting a horse and piercing a dragon with a lance. Kiryakos thought it was odd that saints carry swords and lances. Anyway, my mother lit the primus, and Sukayna put a piece of lead in a frying pan and placed it over the primus. Then she lifted my shirt and massaged my stomach, all the time looking at my eyes. She asked my mother to pour water in a tray, then Sukayna dumped the melting lead into the tray. "They have no fear of Allah," she said, slapping her own cheek. "They want to blind the boy, but Imam Ali will put their necks to his splitting sword."

She asked me to close my eyes, and she rubbed and kissed them and warned me not to open them. She wrapped my head with a scarf, which I guessed was black, judging from the smell of her Tehran incense. Then she began murmuring soft appeals to Allah and Imam Ali. When she was done, she asked my mother to keep me in that state till dawn.

"But I'm hungry," I cried. "May Allah keep you safe, I'm hungry."

The following day the theater was showing the new Norman Wisdom movie, and I knew the excitement would turn the town into a madhouse. Hikmat al-Hindi had his ways of advertising the Norman Wisdom movies, with promises of "one hundred minutes of nonstop laughter." After my morning shift I looked up Ibrahim, and we gathered the neighborhood kids—Jalil the Bear and Jalil the Japanese, and Gloppie, and Teddy and Mahdi and Mahmoud—and we sat in the cinema den. Ibrahim promised to buy Teddy a ticket, and the Bear complained that his mother wouldn't give him enough money. Mahmoud told him he would give him the rest of the money even though he had broken his leg once. When Ibrahim whined that we knew nothing about the movie, I rushed out and asked my mother about Kiryakos. She took that as a sign of the end of Zahra's spell and hailed Sukayna as a true mullah. Glasses of sherbet were rushed to the den, and Yosha the grocer spread the news of Sukayna's latest miracle.

Later that day I was rushing to go to my evening shift when Nisreen asked me to fetch cigarettes for her aunt.

"I can't. I don't have a minute to spare. I need to work and see the Norman Wisdom movie."

"Just five minutes," Nisreen pleaded.

"I can't. I'm already late."

Yosha reported that encounter to my mother, and she embellished it to Sukayna.

"By the blood of Christ and by the Virgin Mary, Nisreen was in tears begging him, but my son told her to leave him alone because he wanted to go to work."

On the poster Norman Wisdom was shown leaping in the air and laughing, and Hikmat al-Hindi wrote under it in Arabic, "Norman Wisdom in the Airborne Force." I was selling a lot of sorbet in front of the theater, and people were blowing onto their cups to melt the sorbet and devour it before they darted into the theater. When the bell rang, I envied them for spending a hundred minutes of laughter and looked forward to watching the second show. Nasrat Shah told me I would be able to see the movie that night and promised he would come as soon as he was done with the evening prayers or send Hussein to take over for me if he was delayed for some reason.

Well, neither Nasrat Shah nor Hussein showed up, and the laughing crowd that came out of the theater made things worse. And all my buddies were among them, even Peyous, who seemed to have quite forgotten that five army officers from the Dilaim tribe had taken his elder sister Rosa to the lake and kept fucking her all Thursday and all Friday. The kids were reenacting Norman Wisdom's antics, and their ringing laughs pinched my heart.

The bell rang for the second showing, and soon after the front lights were turned off and the gate was closed. With that died the hopes of seeing the movie that night, and I found some solace in the hope of watching it the following day.

I was rinsing the cups when I noticed the theater's caretaker removing the Norman Wisdom poster. I ran up to him and asked what he was doing.

"We're showing another movie."

"But so many people haven't seen this one yet."

"I know," he said and let the pieces of the poster fall to the ground.

I picked them up and folded them carefully. "I haven't seen it yet," I said. "Everyone's seen it but me. It's not fair. I know Norman Wisdom better than anyone, you know that," I begged.

"OK. When was he born?"

"April 4, 1920, in London," I snapped.

He agreed, and I also corrected him about Norman Wisdom's first movie, *Trouble in Store.* Kiryakos had translated it as *Trouble in the Shop.*

The caretaker approached the cart. "Don't worry, Joey," he said as he helped himself to a cup of sorbet. Then he added, "How about if I treat you to a private show of the movie?"

"Oh, yeah! May Allah prolong your life!"

"I'll let you watch it this evening if you help me clean the show room."

"I will. I'll clean the entire cinema in no time." And I filled his cup with more sorbet.

"There's one more thing."

"What is that?"

"We'll keep this our secret. I'll also give you some censored bits from other films."

"By Christ, I won't tell anybody."

"Deal," the caretaker said.

Nasrat Shah finally appeared as I approached our place. He was limping and seemed to expect my angry reaction. My calm surprised him, and he not only doubled my daily pay, but promised to double what he paid my mother as well. He knew that if I was upset with him, then nothing would make me work for him. I would leave and then come back on my own terms.

When I left home that night, I told my mother I'd go fetch my dad from the bar. I started in on the cleaning chore when the caretaker headed to the projection room. There must have been a ton of garbage under the wooden chairs, but every once in a while I'd look at the screen and hope Norman Wisdom would pop out and take me away with him. Suddenly the lights went out.

"Wait," I shouted, "I'm not done cleaning."

There was no reply.

"Hey! Switch the lights on!"

I started to panic in that quiet darkness. I dropped the sweeping brush and began to cry.

"What! Are you scared?" the caretaker said, emerging from between the rows. "I'll start the movie in a minute."

"I want to get out! I want to get out," I said, still crying.

"Calm down," he said and grabbed hold of me and reached for my pants buttons. "I'll give you a bunch of film bits and magazine pictures."

"Leave me alone, leave me alone! I want to get out."

"Think about the film bits I'm going to give you."

"Leave me alone," I shouted and lunged at his hand, biting it with all the force I had left. His pain was undoubtedly great, and he screamed and punched me. As I scrambled away between the rows, he kicked me, "You son of a dog, if ever I see you again in this cinema, I'll smash your face and the face of Kikah, your deaf and dumb father."

I ran through the hallway to the outside gate, still crying. Moonlight was falling on the posters on both sides. I knew them by heart. I was torn between going straight home and heading to the bar to fetch my dad. I lost track of time, then suddenly I saw my father next to me. He must have seen the tears in my eyes because he immediately made the sign of friendship by putting his two index fingers together. He hugged me before we headed home.

My first day in school brought a few surprises. Even though I looked familiar to everyone who knew me as a street vendor, pupils and teachers needed to see me as a pupil, too. I also was the oldest student in class, which explained why the teacher made me the class monitor. And I found out that "Joey" was not my name and that "Kikha" was not my father's name, either. "Samuel Shimon" was my name in school. I also needed a long-overdue haircut.

I was delighted to be home. On my mother's lap, I wanted to know who "Samuel" was.

"He's a prophet," she said, as she searched for lice in my hair. "I told you a thousand times to stay away from the kids of Arab peasants. Their heads are full of lice."

"Who chose that name for me?" I asked, looking at the fluttering clothes on the laundry line nearby.

"The day you were born, Kiryakos asked me if I had picked a name yet. Not yet, I said. He took the Holy Bible and opened it and asked me what I thought of the name 'Samuel.' Well, I liked it."

"Where was Dad?"

"He was at the hospital for an operation."

"Is that why you all call me the 'bad omen boy'?"

Her hands caressed my face, and she looked at my eyes. She had tears in her eyes.

"You have beautiful eyes," she said. "Like the eyes of fallen women."

She wanted me to go with Robin to Yunan's for a haircut and to Israel's for photos for both of us, and to say that Dad would pay at the end of the week. At the photographer's I recognized the pictures of some locals and those of British pilots, but I was struck by a black-and-white photo of a beautiful woman.

"Who's she?" I asked Israel.

He laughed. "Come along, you're late already and you need to go home."

"She's very beautiful," I said as I sat for the photo.

"Of course. She's a Hollywood queen."

"She is? Kiryakos never mentioned Hollywood had a queen."

"She's Marlene Dietrich. Ask him about her."

"Oh, that boring actress?" Kiryakos said dismissively when I asked him in the cinema den about Marlene Dietrich. He wanted to talk about school. He thought it was good for a genius like me to learn to read and write. He didn't believe in degrees.

"Jack Ford had no degree. Schools produce no geniuses. I learned that a long time ago." He had a box with him and asked me if I knew what it was.

"It's a magic box," he told me. "You're right about shadow cinema, it's boring, more or less like Marlene Dietrich. I've had this box for more than thirty years, and now it's yours."

It was a square box made of lightweight fiberboard, with holes on two sides. One hole had a light bulb in it. The bulb had been emptied of its contents and filled with water. The other had a film strip attached to a spool. A small handle on the side would spin the film reel. Kiryakos perched the box on the bucket and walked to the doorway. He held a mirror up to the sun and directed the reflected light through the bulb. On the wall Henry Fonda appeared in a blue scout outfit.

"Wow! This is real cinema! How can we get films for it?"

"I have plenty of them. You'll like them when you see them. If I had a camera, I would have filmed you and Kikha." He came into the room and sat down in a corner.

"I don't know why I didn't become a film director," he said in a very sad voice. "Sergeant Mike admitted I had the imagination and the knowledge. Hey, Joey! Listen up! You have to become a film director. You'll succeed, I'm sure. That's one reason I'm giving you this box."

He broke my heart. To change the subject a little, I asked him, "How's John Ford doing?"

"Oh, he's better now, and working on a new movie. *Seven Women.*" He turned to me and smiled. "Call him Jack Ford, the way his friends do."

My friend Jack Ford, I thought.

Kiryakos lived up to his word and the following week brought me several reels, each with a running time of a few minutes. They were strips from different films that Kiryakos had stuck together and composed something out of them. A Western, a musical, an action film. I showed them to the kids, and they soon became wild favorites, but when I acted on Yosha's advice and asked the kids for a small fee, they refused. "This silent cinema was made for deaf and mute people like Kikah," they said. The box made it easy to look closely at film stars on the walls of the room and at home. I stared at their features, clothes, hairdos. I wished we had sunshine at night as well.

My father liked the projections but didn't like the time I missed working for the "limping guy with three fingers," as he used to call Nasrat Shah. We couldn't make money operating our own cinema, and I had to continue with Nasrat Shah. During the winter, when we didn't sell sorbet, we made mango pickles at Nasrat Shah's, but told clients that they were imported from Bombay. One day a client asked me to swear that the product was of Indian origin, and I swore by Imam Ali. No, he said, swear by Christ, and I did. I knew that was not right, but I also knew from my mother and my friends' mothers that angels begin to take notice of human sins only after you're around fourteen years old. I had four or five more years of unregistered sinfulness.

I made mango pickles by half-filling a bucket with water and adding to it half a kilo of turmeric, five spoons of salt, a lump of citric acid, slices of eggplant and potato, and ten crushed hot peppers. Nasrat Shah would taste the mix and make necessary adjustments. Finally, he'd bring a bottle of imported mango pickles and pour it into the bucket. That was the stuff I sold to kids at the schools. Their pleading words rang in my ears. "Joey, please, a quarter of a sandwich!" "Joey, may Allah spare your life, half a sandwich!" "Samuel, a quarter of a sandwich, please!" I sold sandwiches between classes, and teachers cooperated by letting me out of class a few minutes before the bell. One teacher thought that regardless of the appetizing product I sold, I needed to get rid of its strong smell.

My father's interest in the new cinema box started to affect his job. The bakery owner complained to my mother that he was letting the bread burn and that more clients now were going to the fat Armenian lady's bakery. He also hinted that his son had completed his military service and was looking for a job. My mom reproached Kiryakos for giving me that box, but he told her that people went to the Armenian's because it was more fashionable, not because of Kikah. During lunch my parents had a sign-language argument during which my mom let him understand that Atallah the bakery owner was upset with him, and my father pointed to his behind as a reply. Sukayna tried to interfere, but my dad didn't let her. He pulled me by the hand to the den, pointing with his right index finger to his left wrist and suggesting we make good use of the daylight left.

My dad let me understand he didn't like the idea of my working. He wanted me to have fun like the other kids and to focus on school. In the den he was excited, and he kept moving the box in all directions to get the best effects. The strip was showing Victor Mature dressed in black and holding a gun in a saloon. Another frame showed a man wearing a white shirt and a black apron. He approaches Victor Mature and throws his gun on the table. Then the man's face becomes clear, Henry Fonda. My father thrust his own hand into the picture and pretended to snatch the gun and shoot at me, bang, bang, bang. I held my stomach and fell to the ground. I came back to life after I heard him clap. The pictures then disappeared, and we noticed that Teddy and Ibrahim and Beayous and Jalil the Japanese were at the door blocking the sunlight. My dad stuck his tongue out at them and went home. My father was so excited when he left for work soon after that my mom wanted to know what I did to him.

I thought about his wish that I stop working for Nasrat Shah and had no idea that my father that night was contemplating a nasty act against the man. I was awakened by a strange dream to find that he was not home. I saw myself in total darkness, and I was naked and alone. I felt thirsty and cold, but I was suddenly covered by a host of black shrouds. Then I smelled incense. "Sukayna," I screamed, then a thread of light appeared. It fluttered right and left and finally rested at my feet. I understood I was to follow it, and it led me to a pond from which a strong light came as if a powerful mirror at its bottom was reflecting the sunlight. A man was sitting on the surface of the water. A round, fair face and a black beard and sparkling eyes. His chestnut hair was half hidden under a green turban. He was holding the long line of light. I smiled. When I reached to scoop up the water, the man and the light vanished.

I wondered where my father was in the middle of the night. The bar could not be open at that time. I went out to check, for sometimes he slept on the doorstep when he did not want to awaken us or bother us with the strong smell of alcohol. Nothing was there but frogs croaking. Where did they go during the day, these frogs? I was heading back to sleep when I heard noises coming from the cinema den. It wasn't a thief, for sure. We had just one thief in the neighborhood, and when he dared steal one of Sukayna's hens, Samson gave him a good whipping with an army belt. He let him go only when the thief promised to stay away from our street.

A strong smell of kerosene slapped me as I approached the area where the den was. My father had just doused Nasrat Shah's vending cart and was holding a box of matches. I rushed to the cart and stood between it and my father. He was furious. He glared at me and then spat on the cart and put the box of matches back in his pocket. I pushed the cart in the direction of the water tap. This must have made my dad sober up again, for he rushed to bring a box of Tide and helped me wash the cart. Nasrat Shah couldn't believe his eyes the following morning, and I explained that my dad did not like its look and decided to give it a good wash. Nasrat Shah gave me a two-day break to reward my dad with as many shows as he could take. He also told me to take every Sunday off. "Like the English and Shakir al-Hindi," he said.

I put on a special shadow show for my dad that day. He brought me a picture of Queen Elizabeth, and I glued it to a piece of cardboard. I cut the excess parts and inserted tiny sticks in the corners of the picture. Then I placed it behind the transparent sheet between the two candles. Queen Elizabeth emerged in front of us. "Listen up, Queen Elizabeth," I said. "I'm Joey, Kikah's son. The son of the man you loved and gave your royal silver box to. He knows how much you love him, and I wanted to tell you he loves you very much. Your love story will finally silence my mom, who keeps telling my dad that he was sold a box that wasn't worth half a kilo of lentils. I'll make a film of your love story, I promise." My dad frowned as if he got what I was saying.

My brothers and I often wondered about the nature of my parents' relationship. Once Samson asked her why my dad was deaf and mute, and she proudly said that he was a pilot and that he was injured when his plane was hit by a shell. We would have believed that, of course, but when my mother was angry, she said something else. "Damned be the day I married that mute and deaf husband." But he was a pilot, wasn't he? we'd say. "What pilot? He was deaf and mute the day he left his mother's womb."

But they had their good moments, too. During the wedding of my sister Shmiran my dad danced at the Assyrian club with a woman other than my mother. He picked up a young woman, and after a while all the other dancers stopped and started to watch my dad and his companion. Rain began to fall, but they carried on, and they continued even when the others rushed inside the building. They continued to watch the couple from the balconies. When rain started to fall hard, my dad, we heard, pushed his companion aside and began to dance by himself. He was probably dancing to tunes he alone heard, perhaps a waltz with Queen Elizabeth and a host of princesses and princes on some royal dancing floor. He continued to dance till my mother came out and dragged him inside. "You fool," she said, "who'd feed your kids if you fell ill?"

I was selling sorbet in front of the girls school when one girl screamed, "A snake! A snake!" It was a frightening sight. The snake was more than a meter and a half long, but it looked scared. I picked up a stone and aimed at its head. A few hits and the thing froze. I dragged the snake by its tail and paraded it before the dazzled girls. If it weren't for the custodian, who came out and took it away, I might have thrust my hands in its mouth like Hercules and split it into two.

When I told my mother of that adventure, she struck her cheeks.

"You must be crazy to kill a snake in the month of May. What did you do that for?" she wailed. "Don't you know that snakes are avenging spirits?"

She was quiet for a few seconds. "Had you killed it at the end of the summer, then the hibernating period might quell the vengeful drive in its offspring or companion," she added. "But now they have all summer to plan their terrible revenge."

"I didn't know that."

"Well, movies have left nothing in that head of yours. You're dumber than your dad. Listen, from now on you'll have to lock the doors wherever you sleep."

She told me a story about her grandfather and his seven sons. The father kept a snake in the house for years, and one day one of the sons climbed up to the crack near the ceiling where it lived. He found a couple of eggs and snatched them. He and his friends played with them on the street. In the middle of the night the snake got down and crept among the sleeping sons. When it found the culprit, it bit his right foot with such force that his head exploded.

Fear of death from a snake bite became an obsession of mine after that. I would inspect the cart before I reached for something, and I'd look in all directions when I walked at night. I also slept under heavy blankets even though it was summer. I didn't just lock doors, but also used cloth to stuff the space between the door and the floor. I did schoolwork by the light of candles to make it difficult for the snake's relatives to find me.

I was scared despite Nasrat Shah's comforting words about my mother's old wives' tales. Sukayna advised me to read the Qur'anic sura for seeking refuge in Allah ten times before I went to sleep. That sounded like a good idea, and when I wasn't sure I had read it ten times, I'd throw in five more readings to be on the safe side.

One of my subsequent adventures with cinema led me to prison. The notion of enacting a story hit me on the soccer field close to the orchards, and I immediately explained it to my friends. I was the script writer and director and caster. Ibrahim was to perform the lead role; Globbie, the villain; Albert, the sheriff; and Mahdi, the lead female role. Mahdi was eight. The scenario was simple. The villain kidnaps the girl and vanishes into the orchards. Ibrahim would come on horseback, so to speak, looking for her. When he finds the villain, they have a fight, and the sheriff interferes.

"Action!" I shouted. The boys took off toward the orchards as if they were on horseback. Half an hour later Ibrahim and Albert came back with the news they couldn't find Globbie and Mahdi, and we all went to look for them. Gladys, a wild thirteen-year-old girl, came along and joined the search team. When we finally found them, Globbie was on top of Mahdi kissing his chest the way we saw in the movies. This, needless to say, had nothing to do with the scenario.

It was Gladys who told Umm Mahdi, Salima, of what she saw. The mother was upset, and she came to our place with a knife in her hand. "Allahu Akbar, Allahu Akbar!" she shrieked. "Gurgiyya's son has disgraced us! I'll kill my son in front of you all, right now. Right now!" When she saw we did not really believe her, she backed down.

"Send your son to a correction facility if you can't bring him up," she added. "I'll kill my son, I swear by Allah, I'll do it."

Some people went up to her and calmed her down, but she didn't leave our doorstep until she saw my mom leap on me and bite me. The kids, my actors, were on the roofs of their houses watching their director humiliated. Globbie later told me not to worry because my mom didn't exactly look like Dracula.

Salima launched an official complaint against me, but I was not imprisoned. Kiryakos explained to the police inspector that the kids were enacting a scene and that Joey shouldn't be held responsible for what wasn't part of the script. The police also knew that Salima's hot air about honor was not to be taken seriously. Half the town knew she strolled the streets at night with nothing but a cloak over her naked body.

In my bed that night I looked at the sky and had just one wish to make to the Lord, who somehow took the form of Mar Shimon, with his familiar black dress and white beard. Please fulfill my desire to become a film director. Teddy elbowed me and asked me to stop fidgeting so that he could sleep. I began reciting the Qur'anic sura, and to confound the snake's avengers further I stuck my right foot between Teddy's feet and the left between Robin's.

I didn't know my mother was listening to my recitations, and I heard her mumble, "I'm afraid you'll trash your own religion one day."

Mahmoud Saeed

Mahmoud Saeed, born in Mosul, northern Iraq, in 1939, is one of a number of Iraqi writers who have had firsthand experience of the brutality of dictatorial rule, especially the Saddam Hussein regime. Between 1969 and 1980, he was imprisoned or detained six times, for periods as long as one year. His novel Saddam City *(2004) presents aspects of this agonizing experience. He left Iraq for the United Arab Emirates in 1985 and has been residing in Chicago since 1999 as a political refugee. Saeed demonstrates an astonishing ability to adjust, and his latest works are novels about the Arab American experience, especially in the Chicago area.*

In opting to focus on the psychological horrors of totalitarian authority, the story "A Figure in Repose" draws on Saeed's political troubles but leaves out most graphic details. There are enough of the latter, of course: the dreaded early-morning visit, the blindfolding, the silence. At the heart of the tale, however, is an intriguing contrast between authority's immaculately professional handling of a pickup operation and its total disregard for its disruption of people's lives. Saeed displays remarkable sensitivity to the contours of political oppression, and hence the story's climatic moment comes when the picked-up individual is sent home. Totalitarianism preys on vulnerabilities and makes normalcy the exception. "Bitter Morning" offers a glimpse of Saeed's engagement with Iraqi realities on a different level—the suffering of families owing to the long and cruel international embargo against Iraq. Again, Saeed chooses suggestive rather than shocking detail when he opens the story with a scene about the giggles of a child in a crib.

"Bitter Morning" is a translation of "Sabah murr," originally published in the magazine Al-Adab, *nos. 11–12 (2002): 108–11. "A Figure in Repose" is a translation of "Al-munsadih" and was published in the London newspaper* Al-Hayaat *in 1999.*

Bitter Morning

Cock-a-doodle-do . . . cock-a-doodle-do. She was awakened by the cock's shrill calls. She giggled. She turned her eyes to the window and called out at the cock. It didn't answer. She was lying on a mattress on the floor not far from the window. The branch of a pomegranate tree studded with bright red flowers was fluttering in the wind, its tips playfully brushing against the window bars. The cock crowed again, and once more she gave that pure, enchanting giggle. She called out again and was again ignored. A nightingale landed on the window and sang for a few seconds, its tail bobbing up and down all the time. She giggled again and called to it. She stretched out her hand toward it, but it couldn't see it. The sound interrupted the nightingale's song. It turned to one side, and its round, beautiful eyes searched for the source. The window lattice must have prevented it from seeing through the window. It burst into song again, and again she called out, waving her hand in its direction, but the nightingale turned its attention to a female of its own kind, sang elegantly for her, and flew to join her.

Her father stopped snoring. His prolonged, noisy intakes of breath were followed by rather short exhalations. She noticed how different it was from her mother's snoring, which had a rhythm like light tapping on wood, and different from the lighter breathing of her sleeping brother. But her eyes were still glued to the window; the songs of the nightingale and its companion were still coming from that tree. She enjoyed the singing and waited for the birds to perch near the window even though they had ignored her repeated invitations. She turned her head when she heard her mother's words to her father, "Stay in bed. Why are you getting up so early? Misery can wait."

"I need to get ready."

"We still have a lot of time."

"When I'm awake, I can't go back to sleep."

He started to get up, but she held on to his hand. The giggle came again, like a delicious musical tune this time and with enough magnetic power to draw the father to his daughter's side. That was laughter filled with boundless happiness. She clapped her tiny hands and then stretched them as if to embrace him or perhaps to fly. Two tiny upper teeth shone like pearls, and her big black dark eyes dominated the milky surrounding. When she felt his breath close to her, she trapped the air in her mouth till her cheeks looked like small, red balls and then playfully sprayed his face. Her little victory brought the giggle back. "You little rascal, look what you've done!" and he laughed.

She was still looking at him when she raised her chubby leg and held her foot with both hands. She drew it to her mouth and sucked the big toe. She stopped for a second, looked proudly at him and lisped, "bib . . . bi . . . bib." The big toe, now a red hazelnut, went back to the mouth.

His wife pushed him aside and grumbled: "You have to torture us this morning of Our Allah! Can't we forget for a while? At least when we're asleep, we don't think. Move, let me wash her."

"Don't show her a frowning face. She understands everything. Keep her out of our troubles."

Almost immediately she saw her mother bending over her, locks of her hair completely shrouding her face. Excitement filled her eyes, and she let go of her foot. She grabbed a lock of hair and pulled it toward her mouth. The mother laughed as she unwrapped the tattered cloth round her daughter's thighs. She looked at her husband and said: "Look, she didn't wet her mattress. This is the third night in a row. I can't believe my eyes."

"Don't jinx her."

"She's only seven months old."

She put her on the potty. The baby started to tap the ground with her feet. Then her mother came back with a cup of milk and said, almost in tears, "This is our last spoonful of milk."

"I told you to smile when you talk to her. She understands everything."

The mother didn't answer.

"When are you going to realize that children understand everything?"

"Realize what? She's only seven months old and she understands everything? Isn't that crazy?"

The sparkling light in the child's eyes was gone. The father approached her and flashed a big smile. He blew air in her face. She flinched a little, then laughed. He laughed, too. She took the cup of milk from her mother and wrapped her little fingers around it. He put his open hand under it, without touching it. She took a sip and raised her head. Her upper lip had a milky stain. She looked at him as if to say, "See what I can do!"

He laughed and kissed her hand. "You're a hero. You have a milk bottle. A hero."

On the verge of crying, the mother sat on one of the mattresses on the floor, her head in her hands. He guessed she was still thinking about the baby's milk, their three-year-old son's food, and the dark future awaiting them.

"I'll make you some tea."

"I can't take anything. The doctor said so."

"You are not going to sell it."

"What? We are not playing around. I gave them my word."

"You are not selling it."

"But you agreed yesterday."

She approached him and sat on the baby's mattress. "I've been thinking all night. After you went to sleep, I cried and cried till four in the morning. How many kidneys do you have? Just two. Yes, you're young now, but who knows what will happen four, five, ten years from now. What will you do if something happens to your kidney? You'll die. A lot of people have kidney trouble. You're sacrificing yourself. And how much are you getting for the kidney, anyway? The money will last only a few months. I did the sums last night. Not more than four months. What are you going to sell next? Your eyes? We're not selling anything anymore. We've sold the refrigerator, the television set, the carpets, beds, air conditioners. We sleep on the floor. Enough!"

"We're not going to starve our kids to death, are we?"

"I'll give Raja' to Umm Ali."

"We're going to sell our baby?" he shouted in disbelief.

"No, we're not selling her. I reached an understanding with her, and she and her husband will sign official documents so that we can get her back when we want. When things change. She also said she wouldn't mind it if we all moved in with them. Their house is nearly empty after their four sons left the country. Two floors. The second is empty. Four empty bedrooms. They want some life around them."

"I won't sell my baby."

"Well, then, you'll have to choose between me and selling your kidney. If you go to the hospital, you'll never see me again."

A Figure in Repose

"Did you hear the doorbell ring?" he asked her, his eyes still closed.

"Go back to sleep—it's the *athan*."

She turned her back to him, and her head sank under the quilt as faint echoes of the *athan* reached her. "Prayer," it said, "is better than sleep."

"That's strange. It isn't even five o'clock. What *athan* is this? Somebody is messed up."

"Go back to sleep, will you? It's the Shafi'i *athan*. It's always earlier than the others. Let me get some sleep."

He groaned and pulled the quilt over his head.

The doorbell rang again. He pushed the quilt away and said, "I say the doorbell, and you say the Shafi'i *athan!*"

She turned the lights on. Who would come at such an hour? she thought. She sat up. For a while he didn't know what to do, and then he got up. His face was still showing the power of sleep.

"Don't open the door," she said, terrified. "Don't even go downstairs."

"Does this make sense?"

"Please ignore them. Stay here."

"They'll keep ringing the bell, and if they believe no one is home, they might break in and kill us."

He put on his robe and made sure it was tightly wrapped around his body. He opened a drawer and took a gun. She watched in horror.

"Do you know how to use it?"

"You just press the trigger. Abu Khalid taught us. It's not rocket science."

"I'm coming down with you. Careful when you go down, you're in your sixties."

His heavier steps made up for his lack of mobility.

"Don't open the door," she said. "They gunned down Umm Sami's household as soon as the door was opened."

"I know."

"Perhaps they have already broken in, and they are hiding around the house or in the driveway behind the car, the way they did with the jeweler Abu Amir. They slaughtered all of them."

Distracted, he felt how heavy the gun was. Couldn't Abu Khalid have found a lighter one? There are guns half this size and weight. The size of the palm, but Abu Khalid brought me one from the Ottoman era. At least two kilos. "Yes, doctor, it's heavy, but it's the sure thing," he had said.

"I'll switch the lights on," he said, "and you look at the driveway and around the house."

"But don't rush to open the door before I get down."

He switched on all the lights on the upper floor, the garage, and the driveway and went to open the door after he heard her descending steps. He went out to open the house gate. The biting January air seemed to penetrate his bones, and he pulled with his free hand the upper end of his robe to cover his neck. The gun was in his other hand. From the darkness beyond, the *athan* was still coming intermittently. His wife, glum, walked with him, whispering her wonder about who would be coming at such an hour. As they approached the gate, she separated the door key and chain-and-padlock key from the rest of the keys. His frozen fingers managed to unlock the door, but not the padlock, and he pulled the door open slightly. He could see a man in his forties in military uniform; his wide smile betrayed tired features. A black Mercedes was parked at the door.

"Don't be afraid. Open the door," he said.

"Who are you?"

"From the Presidential Office."

His heart shot fresh, hot blood through his body, and sweat banished the freezing cold. His wife leaned against him to control her shudder. She tried but could not repeat what the man just said.

"There's really no cause for fear," the military man's voice came through the frozen door. "It's nothing—just a few minutes. Just come with us."

"Where to?"

"To the Presidential Office."

"Why not wait till the morning?" she asked with a quivering voice.

The military man's smile nearly vanished, but he seemed determined to get what he came for, and the smile persisted.

"His Excellency the president himself asked for him," he said.

He looked at his wife, who struggled not to cry.

"What for?" he asked.

"It's just a matter of five minutes."

He hesitated and then was afraid that the man on the other side of the door might interpret his hesitation as unwillingness to comply. The military man facing him at this frozen hour of the night knew nothing but compliance. He wouldn't be patient for long.

"Give me some time to change," he said slowly, dogged by fear and anxiety.

"Take your time."

He walked back toward the house and suddenly felt cold again. His wife walked ahead of him, visibly upset.

"Do you want to go?" she said as soon as they were inside. "Who knows what they'll do to you? They must have been watching us. They must be aware Dr. Ibrahim was here yesterday. That's why they came for you. His cousin and the father of his eldest son's wife died while in Dr. Ibrahim's care, and you think they'll let the doctor go? You believe that? This is not Europe. Not in your wildest dreams."

"Why would they punish him? What has he done? He told me the story a number of times. The whole story. You laughed when he told it in front of you. They brought him that relative forty days after the dog bite. What could he do to save him? The viral infection had destroyed his nervous system."

He could visualize Dr. Ibrahim's face as he had told the story. He could also invoke the sympathetic face of his wife, Wadia, as she had listened.

Ibrahim said he thought the hospital turned into a war zone when the Republican Guards brought in the man. A row of armored vehicles followed by a procession of presidential automobiles. The blaring horns and the deafening sirens. The whole hospital was besieged, and soldiers with semiautomatic rifles rushed in throngs. All one could hear was "comrade Rakan Mihqan Mizban, His Excellency Rakan Mihqan Mizban, Lieutenant General Rakan Mihqan Mizban."[1] We all laughed when Ibrahim asked if we had heard of him. Rumor had it he was a herdsman who had made it to the rank of lieutenant general with surprising speed.

"The door to the examination room was kicked open," Ibrahim had told us one day, "and a special-force lieutenant colonel, armed to the teeth, forced his way in. I was examining an old lady, and for a second I didn't know what to do. He looked at me defiantly, and I left the patient and went out with him. The corridors were swarming with soldiers, and one could hardly move among them. On our way to see Rakan Mihqan Mizban I told the colonel that the soldiers should vacate the hospital. They could do what was necessary and leave so that we could do our job. Mizban was nearly gone when I saw him. Drooling, his eyes red, high fever. They said he had bitten everyone he could—his wife, two of his sons, his daughter. Then he had bitten a few animals—his dog and horse. They locked him up in a room till he collapsed. We had to quarantine him. We got the vaccine from Jordan that day via a helicopter and vaccinated his four wives, his children, his thirty-seven grandchildren, his battalion of shepherds. I went myself to the presidential estates—huge and swarming with all kinds of cattle. I told them that he might die in two days and that he should be quarantined. They insisted on taking him away and signed papers to that effect. I kept the papers with his sons' signatures."

"But they'll go after Dr. Ibrahim," my wife said. "You'll see."

"You're exaggerating. Ibrahim called me yesterday from the hospital and told me a bunch of jokes. We had a good laugh."

---

1. This name would remind Iraqis of former Iraqi president Saddam Hussein's relatives, who had prominent official and party positions, especially his two half-brothers Barzan and Watban. *Mihqan* in Iraqi Arabic means "funnel."

"Why do they send for you at such an hour then?"

"How can I know?"

"This is your problem. I have been begging you for ten years to leave and join our kids abroad. All your colleagues left. Is this life we lead here? We die a hundred times everyday. Why are we staying behind?"

He was still putting on his clothes. He picked up the pieces quietly. A silk tie with fiery red dashes on a pristine blue background. He didn't forget his favorite eau de cologne.

"What are they going to do to you?" She was crying now.

She wiped the tears away before she said good-bye. She did not feel the cold this time, but it took her quite some time to secure the chain and padlock. The lock was certainly frozen this time. The loneliness she felt then terrified her and kept her at the door for a while. The Mercedes left, followed by two military escorts. She had no idea where these two vehicles came from. She started crying again. His look and smile and wave before he disappeared into the car were still fresh in her mind. Was that wave to assure her or bid her farewell? She hoped he was as quiet as he looked because he used to think if he was quiet, then no harm could happen to him. Perhaps that was why he smiled. A signal that he would come back. She was almost sure of that.

The military man asked him to fasten his safety belt, and when he was surprised, the man said these were the orders. Then the man pulled a black blindfold from his pocket and politely asked to blindfold him. He was relieved that they did not handcuff him.

He was not as much concerned about himself as he was about her, being away from her children and now lonely and terrified. She would surely go down if he was to disappear. Life can be an inscrutable trap for this vulnerable, silly thing we call man. Only a few hours ago he was the owner and director of one of the county's best hospitals, and now he was blindfolded and as much in control of his fate as a goat on the way to the slaughterhouse. His fear increased as the car started to speed up, its brutal raw power violating the quiet of the night. He saw why the man insisted on fastening the safety belt. These official cars always darted on the streets, crushing on their way not only traffic rules, but the property and lives of those not fortunate enough to escape them. He had no idea how long the nightmarish trip took. When the man removed the blindfold, he looked at his watch and was surprised when he saw it had been merely twenty minutes.

"Don't say anything to those you come across. Live cameras are everywhere. I hope you heed this advice," the man told him before he was let out of the car.

It did not seem that he was a person guilty of something, and he felt somehow assured. He found himself in a garage surrounded by dark gray concrete and yellowish lights. What a depressing environment. A row of new cars of all models crowded the vicinity. No war or embargo even touched this place, he thought. He was there for perhaps five minutes. The freezing, blowing winds suggested that the place was in a desolate area out of town. The man motioned him to stay in front of him, and soon they stopped in front of an elevator. A sparkling, gray metal door opened as soon as the man pressed the keypad. The elevator was big, elegant, and warm, and it somehow gave him the impression that it was familiar, but he could not remember where he had seen it. Its sides were of polished hardwood and mirrors, and they bore pictures of national archaeological pieces. Was it similar to an elevator he had seen in a five-star hotel he had stayed in two years ago? What a dead memory!

The elevator descended fast, and when it stopped, its doors opened on the other side. A wide, long corridor, with beige sides on which hung copies of celebrated art pieces. Again, he had the feeling of familiarity with the place. Where? Where?

"This way, please," the military man said. In front of him was a short, bald man, heavy with no face hair. He was wearing dark glasses and the green uniform of the Popular Army.

"The doctor?" he asked—his voice sharp, his features frozen. When he saw that the man's face was fixed in one direction, he realized the man was blind.

"Yes," he said.

He was not sure how to behave with the blind man. The military man disappeared, but the blind man came to his aid when he gestured him to walk along his side. It was rather warm, so he took off his coat and carried it on his arm. They turned and soon came to another elevator. The man dexterously pressed the button, and he wondered if the man was really blind.

"Go ahead," the man said. The elevator looked like the first. Was this deliberate to give visitors the illusion they were in the same place? But that did not make sense. The elevator descended one floor, and again its door opened on the other side where another blind man was waiting for him.

Had the other man not been a little taller than his predecessor, he would have suspected his faculties. Same outfit, same clean-shaven face, same stern features. Perhaps they were brothers? That didn't really bother him, but what did was the mystery of repeating the elevator routine five more times. When he reached what would have been the seventh underground floor, he didn't find a blind man, but a slim young man in his thirties. Perhaps a nurse. He signaled him to follow him.

He dumped the thoughts that were occupying him about the blind men and the single-floor-downward rides, and somehow convinced himself that he was more like a goat. Yes, just that. The corridors again struck him as familiar, even though now they seemed circular and endless. They approached one with doors on both sides, and he had a feeling that there were people behind those doors watching. All the doors were ajar. Were there gun barrels sticking out of some of them?

"This way, please."

A door opened to his left, and he saw a lavatory over which hung a big mirror, an examination table, two closets, chairs, a desk, and a physician. A beaming smile and brown eyes, big and lively. These features were familiar, too, like the elevators and the corridors. Perhaps his mind had begun to falter. This was not a dream, was it?

"In here, please."

The nurse was standing behind him.

"Undress," the doctor said as he pushed his fingers into examination gloves.

He was silent and merely looked at the doctor.

"Undress, please," he repeated.

"Take off my clothes?" he finally managed to say.

"Yes."

The nurse took his coat and hung it on a white plastic hanger. Then he helped him out of his jacket and even smiled when he helped him with his tie and shirt and undershirt. His chest was fully exposed, covered with white hair. Well, at least the hair on his arms was still black. Then the nurse unhooked his belt. That surprised him, and his look implored the doctor who was in a world of his own watching a sea program on television. A shark ferociously attacking an unsuspecting prey. When the nurse gently pulled his underwear, he hung on to it with both hands. The doctor turned away from his sharks and said with a sweet smile: "Everything, sir."

When he heard "sir," he thought the doctor was a former student of his, but he could not remember his name or when he taught him. That was a trivial matter now, and what mattered more was his humiliation, standing there completely naked. The doctor smiled when he covered his genitalia with his hands.

What was the point behind all of this? And the military man told him it was a matter of five minutes. The doctor motioned him to lie dawn on the table. The nurse took away his watch. As he lay down, stressed, he covered his middle with both hands. He saw two cameras hanging from the ceiling. Why two? Perhaps one for him, the other for the doctor? He closed his eyes and recalled the military man's warning about the live cameras and about talking to anyone. He was about to cry when the doctor asked him to open his mouth and say "ah." He tried to avoid looking at the cameras as he wondered, Why would they examine him, and him a doctor? The doctor was doing his routine quickly as if he wanted to get it over with.

"Turn around."

What shame! Naked and flat on his belly. No problem with the doctor, but those behind the two cameras! He was able to tell the course of the stethoscope before it moved from one spot to the next. When he thought the exam was over, he wanted to get up and put on his clothes.

"One minute, sir."

He felt the doctor's finger poking at his rectum. He himself has done that to patients, but why was it done to him here?

"That's it, sir."

He leaped to the floor. He wanted to speak his mind, but remembered the military man's warning. He went for his clothes, but the doctor stopped him. In no time the nurse was helping him into a white cotton apron like the one he used to wear, and he gave him matching pants and white rubber shoes. The nurse knelt on the floor to help him put on the shoes.

They left the examination room and shortly stopped in front of a dark glass panel. When it opened, the nurse asked him to step in by himself. He did, and the glass panel closed behind him. He took a few steps in an elegant big hall and came to another glass panel. When it opened, he found himself in a massive hall. In the middle of the room a man in dark green silk pajamas was stretched out on a rocking chair. He was watching a wrestling match between two giants on a wide-screen television. The reclining figure was rocking quietly, its eyes closed. When he looked carefully at it and recognized it, he nearly froze. The reclining figure continued to rock, eyes closed, features worn out. He could see his skin color clearly—light brown with a yellowish-bluish shade. In the hall's foreground there was a massive bed and behind it a floor-to-ceiling case that had a few books on one of the top shelves, but was filled mostly with exotic artifacts. The other side of the hall had a huge fish tank with exotic fish of all colors and types.

He was becoming unsettled, and it was becoming harder and harder to control his emotions. Luckily, the reclining figure spoke without opening his eyes.

"Is rabies contagious even without contact?"

He was not sure he understood the question. The words were clear, the voice powerful, but what was he asking for exactly?

"I beg your pardon?" he blurted out.

The reclining figure's eyes remained closed, and he looked neither at him nor at the clashing giants on television nor at the nearby two purple fish that seemed to be exchanging a long passionate kiss.

"Does the flu virus travel through the air?" the figure asked, his eyes still shut.

"It depends on the distance."

"This same distance between us."

"There's a chance of possibly 10 percent."

"What about rabies?"

"What about it?"

"Is it contagious without contact?"

"No."

"Does one catch the virus because of a handshake?"

"No."

"Are you sure?"

"Absolutely."

The reclining figure opened his eyes for a second. He could see redness in the eyes, perhaps owing to some ailment or lack of sleep. One giant was dancing on the back of his opponent, raising his hands in gleeful euphoria. The two purple fish had disappeared in the massive tank.

The glass panel opened behind him, and he heard a voice from the distance.

"This way, Doctor." He had no idea how the reclining figure had communicated to his entourage that the meeting was over.

He turned around and left.

In the examination room he saw neither the physician nor the nurse. He put on his clothes in a hurry. He felt an urge to cry, but the presence of the two cameras stopped him. He was tying his shoestrings when the nurse came in.

"This way."

"Where to?"

"Home."

He stood up, elated, and stepped out of the room, the urge to cry still tormenting him.

Nasrat Mardan

Another writer from Kirkuk whose work can be seen as homage to the city is Nasrat Mardan. Indeed, one of his most recent works is a booklet on Kirkuk published in Arabic in 2005. A fiction writer, poet, and translator, Mardan was born in Kirkuk in 1948, but left Iraq during the harsh years of the 1990s and has been residing in Geneva since 1996. He writes in Arabic and in his mother tongue, Turkmen, and his translation of Yashar Kamal's novel To Crush the Serpent *into Arabic has been widely praised. Some of his poems and stories have been translated into Arabic and Kurdish.*

Both "Bar of Sweet Dreams" and "Sufi Blessings" are set in Kirkuk, and they fairly represent Mardan's work even though they are among his most recent works. "Bar" offers a more open critique of an authoritarian regime, but it does so in an imaginative manner that identifies victims of political oppression with writers. In "Sufi Blessings," the writer pits the naïveté of the public against the cunning representatives of state power. The Sufi character, the sayyid, is sympathetically drawn, but he and his followers are also shown as out of touch with reality. Their opposition to the bulldozing of a cemetery to build a new road suggests attachment to a tradition that is not particularly critical and might explain their failure to understand the regime.

"Bar of Sweet Dreams" and "Sufi Blessings" are translations of "Hanat al-ahlam al-sa'ida" and "Tilka al-ra'iha al-qadima," both from the collection Hanat al-ahlam al-sa'ida *(Bar of Sweet Dreams; Traun, Austria: Dhifaf, 2003).*

Bar of Sweet Dreams

The red flower in the pot wondered if I was actually going out at an hour like that. A reasonable question from a flower that only made my room more beautiful. It must be late, I guessed without bothering to look at my watch.

Kirkuk was dead asleep, and a stroll at such a time might not end well. My city goes to bed early, and the last to go to sleep were the drunkards after the pubs closed. But I had to go out, and I knew the dangers such as running into a police patrol—there were a lot of them. You wouldn't know where their questions might lead, for they usually took people to the nearest police station for the flimsiest of suspicions. The impulse to go out was as powerful as if an invisible hand or power were pushing me. I hurried to change my clothes and cast a quick look at my face in the mirror. I made sure to extinguish my cigarette before I left.

The woman asked where was I going so late at night.

"I have an appointment with my story's main character," I said.

"What story?" she asked.

"The one I want to write."

The woman pursed her lips. I couldn't care less because she was just a female presence in my room. I couldn't tell how long she had been there, and her opinions didn't really matter to me. I left.

Outside, the night sky was dazzling with sparkling stars, and the breeze seemed to be coming from the gardens beneath which rivers flow.[1] The streets were dead, and the windows overlooking them were shut as if in deep slumber. I was alone and fearless, and I really enjoyed my city. The sidewalks were differential and even seemed to suggest I was intoxicated tonight, but not with wine as usual. I couldn't really care for what the sidewalks thought. It pleased me, though, that I was the subject of the sidewalks' nocturnal rumination.

Rows of houses appeared like apparitions as I walked with firm steps toward the house my feet were leading me to. I didn't know where exactly

---

1. This is a common description of the Muslim paradise and occurs in a few variants in the Qur'an and in Prophet Muhammad's sayings.

I was going or to what house. A pack of stray dogs clustered around a waste barrel watched me quietly as I passed by indifferently. One dog seemed hostile, but the rest kept him under control. The biggest among them told his colleague, "Leave him alone. I see him around here every night. He doesn't want to harm us." That was true, for I intended no harm for a dog or any other creature. I was just walking, minding my own business, on the sidewalks of my city on a lovely night under a sky bustling with sparkling stars.

Suddenly I stopped at a door. Light from a window in the house spread on a large portion of the sidewalk. I reached for the door bell, but before I pressed it, the door opened, and I saw the delicate face of a woman.

"Welcome. You're a little late but come in," she said warmly. "My husband is waiting for you."

I entered without the least hesitation even though I hadn't seen that woman or house before. A man approached me with a warm smile.

"Welcome, sir. Please, let's sit down."

I sat down and looked at the room. A sofa with a flowery fabric, drapes of green velvet, and a copy of Picasso's *Guernica*.

"The children are asleep," the wife said, amicably. "My husband has been waiting for you for a few days. Would you like a cup of Turkish coffee?"

"Yes, please."

The man's face was smiling, too. Their warm welcome made me feel at home, and although I had not met this family before, I thought I might have been introduced to them somewhere. The man was nice, and I decided to be blunt.

"I'm sorry," I said as the wife brought the coffee, "but have we met before?"

The man gave such a laugh in that quiet night that I thought the children might wake up. His wife smiled in a way that somehow indicated the naïveté of my question.

"Have you forgotten, sir, that I'm the main character of your new story," he said after he stopped laughing, "the story you're writing now?"

I must have looked like someone who had just awoken from a deep sleep. I stared at him for a while. "So it's you I've been looking for all these days."

"I apologize if this surprises you," he said and laughed again. "I'm the hero of your new story, and I intuitively felt you'd visit me someday, and here you are."

His wife left the room, perhaps to go to bed since it was late and she needed to get up early to prepare the kids for school.

"Make yourself at home," he said.

I was feeling drained, in fact. True, I had been eager to get here, but I also realized that it was only to visit the main character of my story. All that was very nice, of course, like a deity meeting his creatures, but I didn't know exactly what to do after the initial introduction, not to mention the unfamiliar house at such a late hour.

The hero of my story must have guessed my bewilderment.

"You look confused still, sir," he said with a cunning smile. "What is it? Just tell me." His words somehow saved me.

I wanted to tell him, indeed, as much as I could.

"Believe me, I'm happy to meet you since you're the main character of my new story. The problem is: What are we supposed to do?"

He roared with laughter once more. I'm usually gloomy, so I was bemused by the high-spirited hero of my story. He even seemed optimistic.

"We'll go together to the Bar of Sweet Dreams," he said.

I was surprised by that suggestion, a bar in Kirkuk that would be open at that hour of the night.

"It looks like you haven't heard of it," he said as he read my bewilderment again.

I thought I knew my city better than him, and I decided not to let him have fun at my expense.

"You must be joking. Where will we find a bar open at such an hour? And, frankly, I haven't heard of such a bar."

"Trust me, sir," he said with confidence, and his smile now seemed sarcastic. "There is a bar called the Bar of Sweet Dreams, and it stays open till dawn."

This hero of my story seemed foolish and pretentious, but I decided to go along with him to expose his ignorance.

"Where's this bar?" I said.

"It's in Shaterlow, near the watermill," he said with confidence.

I knew immediately he was lying, for I was very familiar with that area. There was no bar with that name near the mill. No bar at all was there, only a Catholic church in a nearby alley.

He stood up and gave me his hand.

"Let's go my friend," he said. "You don't believe me. You'll see with your own eyes. Have you forgotten that the events of your story take place there?"

I got up and we left. I had no idea why my character claimed that bar was the locale of my story. I had not yet actually thought of a setting. All I knew of the plot was that a person was waiting for me, the narrator, in a house, in some alley in my city, and that it was not nice to keep him waiting for too long. I had to go and get to know him. But I had not decided his specific role. I just had the urge to write a story, but its events had not yet taken shape.

The two of us walked silently under the star-studded sky of Kirkuk. The strange quiet of the night magnified the sound of our steps as my character led me to a world I had not heard of. I had to go with him. The dogs were still digging in the waste barrel.

I started to hear the water flowing into the mill, and I saw the Catholic church. The icons all must be asleep now, I thought, and Baby Jesus must also be asleep in his mother's lap. Only the bells seemed on edge, waiting to call the faithful to prayers.

Then I suddenly saw a place bright with lights.

"You see now, sir," my character said. "This is the Bar of Sweet Dreams."

There was some movement in front of the bar's door. Am I dreaming? I thought. Since when had this bar been here? And why hadn't I seen it all this time? I passed by this place on my way to school every day.

My character patted my shoulder as we approached the place, and I noticed for the first time a woman of stunning beauty standing at the door. She kept looking at us. I did not need to say a word, for my character read my thoughts one more time.

The magic condition I enjoyed with my character did not last, and I was rudely and abruptly awakened by the noise of a military vehicle that stopped in front of us. Bewildered, I turned to my character and noticed that his face seemed utterly unfamiliar, inhuman. The door opened, and two armed men in uniform got out, followed by a ranking officer. The officer hugged my character. I had no idea what was going on. The bright lights disappeared, and my city regained its gloomy, tired face.

"Abu Qaed, you're sure this is the man," the officer said.

"Well, he's here," my character said with a wicked smile. "You can make sure yourself."

"Your ID card!" the officer yelled at me. "Finally, we have you in our hands," he added and scrutinized me with the kind of suspicion that had become part of his profession. "You'll soon learn in your hole the benefit of writing all these communiqués and statements."

"I'm here just to meet my character. For writing a new story," I shouted as high as I could as if hoping my city would hear me.

My character laughed. He looked the most vicious and evil thing in the world.

"Didn't you tell me, sir, in my house that you had no idea how things would go after our introduction? Don't you think your story has been completed? Now you'll really go to the Bar of Sweet Dreams."

"Blast you, Abu Qaed," the officer said. "That's a beautiful name."

The car took me away as my character, eyeless, continued to look at me. I no longer heard the tired flow of water at the mill, and the bright lights around the bar dissolved. Near-complete darkness descended, like in a movie theater after a show.

The icons were still asleep at the dark Catholic church, and so was Baby Jesus in his mother's lap. The church bells couldn't wait for the morning.

Sufi Blessings

The bright sun was scorching Kirkuk, but the man continued to run. He was gasping for air as he bumped into passersby and vendors' carts.

Although he was crossing streets and alleyways, he seemed blind, to-tally, for he had just one eye, and it did not seem to be functioning. He managed to cross the bridge toward the Biryadi neighborhood, but his breast now heaved like a bellows. He must have realized his throat was dry, and he slowed down and then rushed as he saw the *takya* from afar.

Jamal, whose bad eye had become part of his name, entered the *takya*. Still panting, his eye didn't seem to see the disciples, beggars, and der-vishes crowding the courtyard. He just saw the sayyid, and as soon as he approached, the sayyid raised his eyes to him. Jamal fell on his hand and kissed it in total submission to the sayyid.

"What is it?" the sayyid said.

"Master, a disaster. A catastrophe. A major one."

"Settle down, Son," the sayyid said quietly, his hand gently stroking his beard. "What has happened?"

Jamal, still panting, was soaked with sweat. "Oh, Sayyid, a disaster I just heard of and decided to let you know." He tried to collect himself. "I dropped everything and ran to tell you."

"Settle down, Son," the sayyid said and patted his shoulder. "Now, tell me what happened." He asked for water to be brought for Jamal.

Jamal gulped the water and turned to the sayyid, who was still pat-ting his shoulder.

"This is a God-forsaken city, Sayyid," he said quietly with pleading looks. "It does not deserve your guardianship. A God-forsaken city."

His eyes filled with tears. The sayyid was still patiently waiting to hear what the man had to say.

"It's not reasonable to denounce a whole city," the sayyid said. "There are those who fear Allah, and others who do not. Allah alone judges, and all we humans can do is pray for everyone to find the path of righteousness."

"Oh, Sayyid. The municipality wants to demolish the cemetery of Our Sayyid Allawi." He said the last sentence quickly. His breathing be-came more regular, and his face regained its natural color. His sole eye regained its white spot as well, but his hands were still shaking.

The sayyid's face became pale for a moment. He lowered his head and whispered to himself.

"Is it as you say?" the sayyid said after a long silence.

"I swear by Allah, Sayyid. I work at the municipality, and I heard that workers will be heading to the cemetery tomorrow morning to level it. Our city is about to commit a grave sin."

"Do not worry, Son." The sayyid was shaken, but he tried not to show it. "Allah willing, everything will be alright."

Jamal then became aware of the disciples and beggars and dervishes who were in the courtyard forming a ring around him. They had heard everything, and now they gave each other blank looks. Then all eyes resolutely turned to the sayyid.

In the early morning hours the disciples and beggars and dervishes took off with the birds and the sun toward the cemetery of Our Sayyid Allawi. Their green and black banners were everywhere.

The grass smelled of spring, and as far as the eye could see greenery blended with the season's other colors. The windows of scattered houses on the scene were open, and women with head scarves looked at the wildflowers in the cemetery. They mourned their dead there prior to the Eid and made a ritual of mourning them again the first day of the Eid. In this city cemeteries have a language of their own, unique and indigenous in its blend of mourning and jubilance.

Hasan the drunkard stood in front of the crowd heading toward the cemetery.

"People, friends," he shouted vehemently, "where are you going?"

"Damn you!" Mirza the grocer said. "It's not yet morning and you have already gulped in this poisonous liquor."

Hasan the drunkard moved toward Mirza and stared at him. "You're heading to protect the cemetery?" he said. "When are you going to wake up? Let them build the new road." His words were punctuated with uncontrollable hiccups. "The souls of the dead are with Allah, and only their bones are here. Let them build the new street so that we can see downtown. Cemeteries are a burden. Who among you passes by the cemetery at night without fear? You're making a mistake. The cemetery is full of scorpions and snakes. Give us a chance to see the city."

"Get out of here, you drunkard," Mirza said and pushed him aside. Then he shouted to the crowd, "You're not going to listen to this drunkard, are you? Let's go!"

They all moved except Hasan. "Shame on you," he shouted in the vacant marketplace. "Let's see the heart of the city."

The car stopped, and the governor stepped out. He looked at the crowd at the cemetery. The sayyid was at its center, surrounded by dervishes and beggars.

"Brothers," the governor said, "what you're doing is against the law."

"Don't the authorities also overstep the lines?" Jamal shouted, forgetting he worked for the municipality.

"The authorities know better what's good for you. And we go by the law."

"Do you follow the laws or the dictates of the party?" somebody shouted from the back. Several voices showed enthusiastic approval.

The governor's face lost all its color.

"Brothers, what's this nonsense?" he ventured. "Our purpose is to open up a paved street to the downtown area. It's for your own convenience. Please think and be reasonable. This will modernize our city. We all revere Our Sayyid Allawi. We'll remove only a few graves."

"No way," several voices shouted together. "Those who lie in this cemetery are the children of this city. They might be our sons or uncles or relatives. That's not going to happen."

A bulldozer was making its way to the cemetery at that point. A commotion erupted with shouts of "Infidels! Infidels!" Some tried to seize the bulldozer, but the sayyid raised his hand and said, "We want a reasonable solution to this problem," and when some protested, he was firm. "Quiet. We don't want violence. We'll stay here till what's right overcomes what's not. No power will prevent us from protecting Sayyid Allawi."

"You said it, Sayyid!" Jamal said as he kissed the sayyid's hand. "We're not leaving the cemetery."

The governor's face became pale again. "What you're doing is dangerous," he said. "All we are doing is for the benefit of the city and ourselves. I'm only doing my duty."

"Tell your superiors what you have seen," the sayyid said. "We'll stay here till the truth overcomes."

The governor got into his car, and a few hands waved sarcastic good-byes.

The city was divided. Some supported those who took refuge in the cemetery, others saw the futility of opposing the city's decision. Loads of food and supplies came to the cemetery. Zakiyya the baker approved of the protesters' action and reminded others of the miracles of Our Sayyid Allawi. "Our businesses will stagnate," she told some, "and women will become barren. I haven't sold a single bread loaf all morning. The protest should go on so that the blasphemers know what they have done." The imam of the big mosque also approved. "I invoke Allah's forgiveness," he said. "Right will vanquish wrong because faith is still alive and well in this city." But Abdul Qadir Jamil said, "Will people ever wake up? Everything is progressing while cobwebs continue to grow in their heads. They raise hell against a new street?" And Husniyya, a fallen woman in the community's view, bewailed her bad luck and foresaw days of hunger because people's minds were elsewhere. Hasan the drunkard kept singing the praises of having a view of downtown unimpeded by graves.

The crowd stayed for two days in the cemetery, and the city had nothing to talk about but the protesters and the cemetery. People filled the spaces between graves with all colors and the sky with black and green banners. Women had more things to look at now.

The sayyid remained a central figure in all this. He told of his meeting with the governor the previous day and the promises he had heard.

"The governor wants us to leave and promised to respect our will. The cemetery will remain under the protection of Our Sayyid Allawi. The minister himself has asked the governor to stop the whole thing. You can all go back to your homes."

"Should we trust them?" Jamal asked.

"We are the tribe of faith, Son. Promises mean a lot to us."

When the sayyid got up, the rest followed. *Riq* tunes accompanied dervishes' recitations of the ninety-nine names of Allah, and the banners preceded the march back to the city. It was noon.

In the dead hours of the night a car and a bulldozer made their way toward the shrine of Sayyid Allawi. The governor and the head of the city municipality got out of the car, and only the crescent in the night sky marked their secret presence. The head of the municipality motioned to the bulldozer, and it made its way between the graves like a monster. The governor was amused by the sayyid's naïveté. He looked at the leveled graves and started to compose in his mind the report he would submit to the leadership of the party.

Ibtisam Abdullah

Although more readily recognized in Iraq as a journalist and television figure, Ibtisam Abdullah is also one of Iraq's most productive fiction writers. Between 1985 and 2001, she published four novels and one collection of short stories. Like many Iraqi women writers, her feminist themes are intricately related to the wider social and political issues in the country. For instance, two of her novels, published in 1994 and 2001, give female characters and concerns the bulk of their attention, but also look at the first Gulf War and its aftermath. Abdullah was born in Kirkuk and has been living mostly in Baghdad. She has written for a number of newspapers and magazines and since 2001 has been editor in chief of the country's only publication dedicated to world literature, the Journal of Foreign Cultures.

The stories selected here show Abdullah's blending of feminist concerns and current events, especially the traumas of the war with Iran from 1980 to 1988 and the international economic sanctions against Iraq from 1990 to 2003. "The Other in the Mirror" makes its point through the accessible but effective metaphor of a mirror in which sameness and difference become problematic. The Iraqi soldier on leave at home is the same individual he was before he became a soldier and went to the front, but he is so changed that he loses his ability to deal with that change. His wife, who has already been victimized by a senseless war, is his most immediate victim. "The Nursery" presents a comparable situation in which analogy draws attention to the debilitating effects of economic starvation. The mother, struggling to care for her son in the absence of the father, passively watches her hungry son's slow degeneration into an animal.

"The Nursery" is a translation of "Al-bustan" from Bakhur *(Incense; Baghdad: Dar ishtar, 1999). "The Other in the Mirror" is a translation of "Al-aakhar fi al-miraat" from the same collection.*

The Nursery

Depression. It's like drops of concentrated acid falling on a metal surface and slowly corroding it. It hits the self and burrows its way slowly, mushrooming in all directions. This notion haunts me all morning like a tune I hear early in the day and keep humming ad nauseam. Like drops of concentrated acid, I tell myself on the way to the school where I work, on my way home, and as I rinse the bunches of parsley piled in front of me at the moment. My son is playing outside with the dog his father bought for us before he left. A guard of sorts and a playmate for Ahmed, he said.

It's one o'clock now, and the boy must be hungry. For breakfast he ate a piece of bread with tea, sweetened a little. We say "a little" nowadays whenever we speak of food. I think about the meal I need to prepare for both of us and of our last handful of rice from the monthly quota, but I delay doing anything so that the meal serves (both) as lunch and dinner.

The little money I get from preparing vegetables I add to my meager salary, and still we barely make ends meet. Yesterday's necessities are today's nonessentials, if not luxuries. I don't want to think about a tomorrow in which food becomes a luxury. The parsley I'm chopping now is for the restaurant whose bright lights at night ridicule the surrounding darkness.

I moved in with my father, into this nursery, after my husband sold most of our furniture to pay for his journey out of the country. The little house at the back of the nursery has two rooms. My father takes care of the nursery during the day and works as a boss boy in the restaurant at night, serving an assortment of barbecues to well-to-do commuters.

Like drops of concentrated acid falling on a metal surface and slowly corroding it, depression permeates the self through black holes, and nothing will stop it. Let's see! In the past few years I tried to find my reservoir of willpower and hummed the clichés, "Say no to despair!" and "Smile in the face of adversity!" and "Just work harder!" My optimism, smiles, and hard work got me nowhere. The little black dots became disfiguring black holes.

The little kid is pale, and his face is becoming bonier. His running is slowing down now. Does he ever think about this life we're leading? Or is life to him a colored ball to chase after in a big garden? I look at the place.

Autumn has already cast its gloomy shadows everywhere. Trees have lost their greenery, their branches covered in dust. The irrigation channels are blocked with dry leaves and fallen twigs. Last year's drought has taken its toll on the nursery. Droughts of all kinds. Debris keeps collecting despite our efforts to get rid of it. Let's hope it won't bury us beneath it.

We went to a nursery like this one for our first rendezvous. We had met at a dentist's clinic, and I talked a little with him to return his interest in me. On a later occasion he told me about a recent visit to a nursery to buy some flowering plants. He said he didn't know exactly why, but when he was there, he thought of me.

"You should see the place. It's amazing; it gives you a sense of spring. Perhaps you too want to buy some plants."

I didn't say a thing. He smiled. Behind his boldness I could see the shyness that men try awkwardly to hide.

"Let the flowers bloom. Don't nip this relationship in the bud!"

Our eyes met for a few seconds. I pretended I hadn't caught what he meant. "I'm not sure I understand your point. Anyway, I have little interest in flower shows."

His reply showed unwavering persistence. "We'll go there. How about tomorrow? The first time there I just kept thinking of you," he added. "I thought of nothing but you. This is the first time anything like this has happened to me, and I have no explanation for it. If you don't believe me, forget what I just said. I'll wait for you at the nursery tomorrow morning anyway. Ten o'clock."

The nursery was a paradise of sorts, and I said so as we walked around numerous shrubs and plants. Leaves all shades of green, creeks brimming with water, birds chirping in the trees, flowers in dazzling colors and shapes. Backs straight, healthy faces, and sparkling eyes, laughs and smiles and elegant outfits. "We'll have a good life ahead of us. We'll get married. We're in love, aren't we? You can't deny that. We'll have a small family, and we'll never separate," he said to me.

But he went away two summers ago when the specter of hunger started to threaten the whole family. I'll send for both of you as soon as I get settled there, he said. But he never settled. Ever since then he's been on the move. We are not only apart, but also falling apart—here and over there. I try to reconstruct his diminishing features, but all I can in-voke is a photo with fading colors. Only a distant picture comes through, and none of the overpowering passions that brought us together in the nursery.

The silence around me scatters with my son's approaching steps. He lifts his pale face to me and says he's hungry. I know that and I'm hungry, too. Should I try what the Bedouin woman did hundreds of years ago when she put stones and water in the pot and told her children to hold on till the food was ready? That was only once in her single year of deprivation, but ours seems to drag on forever.

"I'm starved. When are we going to eat?"

I turn to the pile of parsley bunches and say without looking at him, "In a minute, as soon as I'm done with these. It won't be long."

It's almost three o'clock now. I put the chopped parsley in a big bowl and head home to fetch the remaining rice. The kid is energetically fol-lowing my steps. I rinse the rice and put it in a small pot with water and drops of oil.

"It's not going to be long. The rice is on the stove. I've even added a piece of crushed tomato to redden it. Just the way you like it."

"But when are we going to eat?"

"In a minute. I just said so."

I pour the rice into a metal bowl and see the beaming smile on the boy's face. He's clapping his hands as he follows me, the dog after him. I put the bowl on a low table out there in the nursery. The two of them rush towards it, and the bowl tips over. In a split second rice is all over the place. Stunned, my eyes take in the still images. Dust-covered rice on the ground, the boy's pinched and pale features. For a few moments we freeze in our places, me, the boy, and the dog, like single frames of a movie. But the black reel finally spins in the projector, and the scenes come to life. The dog approaches the rice slowly, his eyes on us. I wave it away as I think of scooping up the scat-tered rice grains, but the dog comes back and starts licking the rice. The boy shouts at it and says, "Go and eat your bones!" The dog's tongue is still pick-ing up small lumps. I feel the pangs of hunger and think of the boy's hunger as my eyes move between the two. As if by pure instinct, he reads my thoughts and falls to the ground, puts out his tongue, and starts licking the dust-covered rice.

I feel heavy, and the nursery starts spinning, my eyes still going between the boy and the dog, as I hit the ground. Suffocating with hunger and a leadlike fist in my chest, I feel the drops of concentrated acid falling, falling.

The Other in the Mirror

I'm alone, and it doesn't look like that's going to change anytime soon. I can put up with that. All I have learned these years is how to pass or kill time with silence. It's a profession I began to master after he went to war. Or after he was drafted. Anyway, loneliness soon followed. Mornings go on reasonably well, but evenings and nights are heavy. They wear down my shoulders and eyelids, and by night's end dim lines spread across my face. My nose alone sticks out, presiding over a landscape of features vanquished by the barriers of mute darkness. Then I slowly fall into sleep. I lull myself with sighs of relief as I repeat for the hundredth time, "There goes another long day, and tomorrow might bring something else."

Hours of sleep bring some energy to my body, and I rise as soon as I wake up. Then comes the daily routine of eating breakfast, cleaning our two-bedroom house, cooking, bathing. As I work, I feel his presence as if he has never departed, and as if he'd walk in any moment and hold me in his arms. I often talk to him during meals. I place his teacup on the small table in the kitchen and talk to him. Joke with him or reproach him. Sometimes I even create scenes and quarrel with him. His vacant seat has always seemed filled with his presence.

We've been in love with each other, and the past two years of our married life have only intensified our initial passions. We were practically inseparable during evening hours whether we stayed at home or went out. The time that flies unnoticeable during the day we would seize and fill with pleasure at its end. These little pleasures died out bit by bit after he was drafted.

We, or he, started to change over a period of several months. A few little things would happen when he was on leave. I would think about them for a while and then dismiss them. I didn't want to spoil the joy of our brief reunions. The little things multiplied and came into focus with his sharper changes a few months later. He withdrew and almost seemed a different person.

Emotions have spent themselves, and silence envelops me again. Like a dormant volcano, I can go over what happened and think about it. I think it all started with his reluctance to speak. His spells of absent-mindedness increased, and he seemed to lose touch with his surroundings. Whenever I tried to break the shell of silence around him, he'd jump, terrified; his face muscles would contract, and he'd look at me with scared suspicions.

He used to stare for long frightened moments at his face in the mirror. He'd stand close to it or retreat, all the time staring at his eyes and his paling features. Sometimes he smiled, at others he looked distressed, but whenever he realized I was watching him, he left the mirror alone and distracted himself with something else.

One night he gazed at his face in the mirror, but after some scrutiny turned to me and surprised me with a question, "What has changed in me?"

Depressed, I looked at him, wondering what to say. He repeated the question, "What has changed in me?"

"What do you think?"

"I don't know. I don't seem to know myself anymore. A strong feeling tells me I've changed. That much I'm sure of."

"What has changed? The way you do things, for instance?"

He shook his head in disagreement and said, "No, not that. I mean my face. My features. Don't you see that?"

I looked at his face for some time, the way he had been doing, and shook my head. "I don't know," I said. "Perhaps some paleness in the face."

He picked up a hand mirror and stared at it, then whispered to himself, "Yes, I'm sure I've changed. No, it's not the paleness. What I mean is that I have a different face."

I laughed, sensing how close to me he seemed at that moment. I took his head in my hands and laid it on my breasts. "It's a better face," I said, and I lifted his face to me and kissed his eyes and forehead. "I'd still love you even if the change were for the worse. Do you hear me? I'd still love you."

I don't know if he really believed me, for he said nothing, not even when I pressed him a little afterwards. He turned his back to me and left the house without saying where he was going.

The quiet and silence that fell then drowned me with past memories. Yes, he's changed, I thought. At the beginning he used to avoid talking about the war and ignored all my questions for months or gave only cryptic answers. "What do you do there at the front?" I'd ask. "The usual," he'd say. His stony silence shielded me from a world that for him had become the usual.

"How do you spend your days there?"

"Oh, the usual."

"What's the usual?" I try to break that wall of silence.

"Oh, all these questions! But you know what war is about, right? You read about it, right? It's on television every evening."

But during his last leave it was the war that he talked about when he talked at all. It was he who broke the silence, and with that he made a hole in the heavy bag of withdrawal he carried on his back for months. He'd talk even without my prompting, with loving embraces, his head often on my breasts. Long talks about incoming fire and engulfing flames. Smoke and explosions and dead soldiers and POWs. And the state of mental collapse that seized them in moments of weakness so devastating to both body and soul. I'd listen, not daring to interrupt.

I'd hold his head close to me, overprotectively, and let my fingers go over his cropped hair. His voice would rise occasionally or falter during these prolonged talks, like a wave peaking to its height only to withdraw soon after. Scattered words sometimes died on his lips before they reached me. During those moments of retreat I used to shower him with love, draw him close to me, and feel his face when he thrust it through my dress opening. The feel of his rugged complexion on my neck and of my welling desire to make love to him.

As he looked into the mirror one evening, a happy smile parted his lips. "This is me. I haven't changed. The eyes are mine, and so are the thin face, the mouth, the moustache. Everything as it used to be."

"I told you a million times," I said.

"But—"

"What, not those doubts again!"

"Well, they don't quite go away. They might contract a little like a stream of molten iron when cold water is poured on it, but they start flowing again as soon as the temperature rises again."

Indeed, I was sensing the change he underwent, as if nothing but molten iron flowed in and pulverized his insides. His eyes would squint sometimes, and their light would fade as if a curtain of dense fog separated him from the world around him. But they were also the eyes I loved so much, and they would sparkle again with dazzling radiance, like dashes of lightning emerging from dark clouds.

Oh, when those dark clouds dissipated and he was himself again! Gentle and cheerful, telling me silly stories about his fellow soldiers and what they all did when he was away. But when he was not himself, I simply waited for him. I became very much the wall he needed to lean against during those times of ebb and flow that left the psyche drained. The wall occasionally sagged and whined under his pressing pains, but didn't buckle under them. If it did, that would have broken him into pieces.

Alone, in the midst of this engulfing silence, I keep remembering his previous leave. His volatility and long hours outside the house by himself alarmed me. "You hardly spend any time with me now," I said one day.

"Oh, there's nothing there. The Baghdad I've almost become a stranger to is calling me back. The lights, the frenzy, the attractions, the streets, the hotels resounding with laughter, the extravagance displayed on faces and bodies. You have things we've forgotten. Over there, everything is calculated, light, words, singing, even silence, and the meager space for movement. Over there I'm a different being."

I was struck by his last sentence. It brought me vague fears, but I had to suppress them then. "What's the difference between the one I know here and the other over there?" I said with a calculated laugh.

"I'm in better touch with myself over there. When you see this, you'll see the difference. Two things control me there, defending what I need to defend and preserving myself, and the two cross over all the time. They make me do things I'd have shuddered to think of before." Then he said, "Would you believe it, I have no fears when the battle surges. What scares me is the lull when we stay in the trenches, the silent wait when we run out of words. The silence we sometimes try to kill with meaningless words. When the wait wears us down, we fall asleep without losing the feeling that our exhausted bodies have tiny sharp needles shot through every single cell."

On another evening he told me, "During those quiet times one of us would explode in a fit of hysterical laughing or crying or lurch out of the underground trench; that's when the silence comes to an end. We make a move, and one of us might even try to choke the contagious frenzy that's about to spread to the rest." He also told me, "Over there I know who I am and what's at stake, to kill or be killed. But here all certainties disappear. Your quiet fills me with questions and draws me toward you and our home and the pleasures of the past. This scares me."

I wanted to say something, but his words came out instead, "Being divided like that frightens me, as if I'm literally being torn apart."

A roaring laugh contracted his face for a while. The flashing light in his eyes unsettled me.

During his most recent leave it was only the paleness that I saw. At least this is how he looked to me when I met him at the door. A face with almost no color, like the white masks some Japanese actors wear. Lifeless or nearly so. His masks were paleness and silence. On the first day he barely moved. He was nailed to a chair in the living room, chain smoking, and completely ignoring me and my anxiety. The second day was no different. He moved only when he had to and ate only a light lunch. The next four days were like that.

It was on the seventh day that he picked up the mirror and stared at his face. His features contracted, and the paleness intensified.

"What is it?" I said.

"I've changed a lot," he said almost to himself.

"You paint an exaggerated picture of your condition."

"What do you know about my condition?"

I came close to him and tried to hug him the way I did during his fits of talking. He let me hold him for a few seconds, but he stiffened when I tried to take away the mirror from him. His hands clung to it in despair. He raised his eyes to me, and there I saw the frenzied look. I pulled at the mirror, but his grip tightened.

"Are you crazy? It's just a mirror," I said.

"No, it's the truth."

His hand was still clinging to the mirror when I withdrew. His eyes widened and flashed. He raised his hand and threw the mirror at me. Its broken pieces flew all over the room. A long wound opened on my chest, and blood flowed between the two of us.

Ibrahim Ahmed

Born in Heet, the Anbar governorate, in 1946, Ibrahim Ahmed had to sneak out of Iraq in 1979 because he was under travel restriction owing to political oppression. His life in exile led him to Syria, Algeria, Romania, and finally Sweden. Some of his works had been published in Iraq, but they were censored, so Ahmed republished them outside Iraq. He is among a very small number of Arab writers who have been trying since the late 1960s to popularize the genre of the very short story. He writes literary and political essays, and some of his stories have been translated into English, Russian, German, Danish, and Swedish.

"The Arctic Refugee" brings humor to a theme that is common in contemporary Arab literature but not always presented in natural, humorous terms. The gaiety is representative of Ahmed's work, where writing and play converge, and indeed is representative of the Iraqi disposition to resort to jokes to subvert political adversity. The piece certainly draws on autobiographical material, but it goes beyond the personal to present a notion of home in bonding and friendship with those considered strangers. Like Abdul Sattar Nasir's "Good-bye, Hippopotamus," the story dramatizes a departure, but the divide between its refugee and the homeland seems sharper than in Nasir's.

"The Arctic Refugee" is a translation of "Laji' inda al-eskimo" from Lara . . . Zahrat al-barari (Lara . . . Flower of the Wilderness; Dar al-manfa, 2001).

The Arctic Refugee

From the hole in an igloo at the top of the world I looked at the universal abyss widening in front of me. The moon and the stars danced by my side, and I thought Allah would be so close that I could see him. But my mind was elsewhere as I waited in fear for the Eskimo chief's decision. Would they grant me asylum, or would they push me over this icy edge into the world to come?

Countries kicked me around the way we played with a rag ball in our muddy ally back home, but, fortunately, they did not hand me over to the Iraqi authorities. At the airport in Stockholm the police questioned me for hours and denied me asylum. I told them I came from Libya after the Libyans terminated my work contract. They told me that Libya was a signatory to the 1951 Geneva Refugee Convention and that I should have applied for asylum there. I was too embarrassed to tell them that I had tried in vain with the Arab brothers there to let me stay in their wide, warm country. I even reminded them of our blood ties, which they used to say were thicker than the ink of conventions. My naïveté and the urge to tell the truth had plagued my life.

The Germans turned me down at the borders because I came from Sweden, also a signatory to the 1951 Geneva Refugee Convention, and the Danes because I was coming from Germany, also a signatory to the 1951 Geneva Refugee Convention. And Norway. I wondered if that Geneva Convention was written in ink or in mercury, on paper in elegant closets or on my grandma's gravestone.

My attention was divided between an endless highway buzzing with semis loaded with mobile homes and a massive frozen ocean. If we could survive underwater, I thought, then the hazards of living next to killer whales and sharks would not be too bad in comparison to human insults.

"Am I heading in the right direction?" an old man asked me. He was on a dog sledge, and snow was falling from his beard.

"What do you mean?"

"Don't you know the Eskimo country? Don't you know me?"

I felt flattered and elated. If the man thought I knew his way, then perhaps I knew my own way. My intuition, dead for years, came to life.

"You are," I said with confidence.

I felt embarrassed when I realized I was pointing to the sea, but it seemed my intuition was flawless.

"You saved me from myself," the old man said gleefully. "I have been telling myself for the past hour that I came from this direction."

He moved, then pulled at his eight dogs and stopped.

"Do you want to come with me?" he said as soon as he turned his head. His warmth reminded me of the village I had left thirty years earlier. I decided to stop being naïve and accepted his invitation. The land of the Eskimos was just one more frontier before the Bermuda Triangle.

The old man had me sit on the part of the seat he had been sitting on, and I felt the warmth. He pulled out three bottles of alcohol and told me he exchanged them in Oslo for fox and polar bear and seal hides. A whole year's worth of hunting. That was an excellent deal, I told him. If I were to return to Iraq I'd exchange all the hides I could think of for a bottle of arak. That, too, would be an excellent deal, he said.

He opened a bottle and said, "Let's introduce our names to alcohol." I pronounced my name, but it froze as soon as it came out of my mouth. His came out fine, but I wondered if my frozen head got it. He started calling me "Ki," probably the part he heard from "Iraqi."

"*Ki* in our tongue means 'lock,' and I think it means 'key' in English," he said smiling. "What does it mean in your language?"

"Lock and key and belly dancing," I said.

"That's what I thought," he said and opened another bottle. We took turns drinking from the bottle. For some reason the odor from the sweat of the running dogs reminded me of our own odor in an ancient political demonstration. I started singing to the dogs hoping to prompt them to hurry, but the old man thought my voice was too sad and, if anything, would induce the dogs to pee. We had slices of raw sea-lion liver with the alcohol, and I started to better appreciate the effort and the skill of the running dogs over the frozen ocean. They stayed away from all those warm undercurrents going south.

"Ki, will you mind if I keep half this bottle for my wife?" the old man asked. "I want to wipe away half her years tonight."

Then he closed his eyes and went to sleep. I was scared because I didn't even know how to steer the sleigh. And which way to go in this Arctic region? Moonlight was gliding over the snow, and the sleigh seemed to be airborne. I decided to leave matters to the dogs and the moon. Perhaps the dogs had their clue from the old man's breathing. I went back to thinking of the Geneva Convention and must have fallen asleep. I awoke as the old man shook my shoulders.

"Ki, Ki. Wake up. You have arrived in the land of the Eskimo."

I saw men and women with round, red faces teasing my chin and nose with fishtails. That was their warmest greeting, the old man explained.

Their chief summoned me as soon as I arrived. He wanted to introduce himself, I was told. I was overwhelmed by that humility, but some old grudges against rulers brought me enough depressing trepidation.

The chief placed a small fish in my hand and had me sit on a seal hide. His consoling smiles dissipated my confusion. His entourage was there, and I thought that if he intended to interrogate me, then the Eskimos must be some of the most considerate people. He took me by surprise when he asked me how my people treated dogs. I was thinking of the Geneva Convention all the time, and I had prepared some really impressive answers in response to several of its articles. I was inspired in that long snow ride, and I told myself just to lie and lie. The chief's question made me feel I wanted to sleep.

"We treat them with the utmost respect," I said without thinking. "We give them the highest positions. They tear our flesh apart, but we worship them."

"Who pulls the sleighs?" he asked.

I yawned, and when I saw that my head was not cut off for yawning in the presence of royalty, I said with some ease, "We have automobiles and oil. A lot of oil, and we'll give you some of it."

"No, thanks, we're fine," the chief said with the mortification of a virgin shying away from the first kiss. He gulped a handful of snow and added, "How about the fish? How do you treat them?"

Another question I was not prepared for. What would my prepared lies do with that? I decided to tell the truth.

"Very generously, sir. We feed them the flesh of our enemy soldiers and that of our own."

The chief seemed disgusted and spit out the raw fish he was chewing. His entourage became restless. The chief was evidently disappointed and even upset. He sat back in his chair, and everybody appeared stressed. Fear came back, and I started blaming myself again for my naïveté and sheer stupidity. That part of me was incorrigible.

They then brought me to this igloo, but in a manner much nicer than what I had seen at airports. The sound of running feet on snow reached me, and I saw three men carrying lanterns. The lanterns burned with the smell of fish oil, and their light fell on a beautiful woman's face.

They were carrying a word from the chief, and they unrolled a piece of dried wolf skin and read respectfully. "Do not ask him to return to his country before you know that his people have stopped eating the flesh of their own in the fish they eat." Then they introduced the woman. They said she fell in love with me when she saw me disembark from the sleigh, still under the spell of sleep. The chief had blessed her love, they said.

That night I missed only Iraq's golden palm dates.

Shmuel Moreh

Shmuel Moreh grew up in Baghdad and began publishing his own poetry as well as translations of English poems in Iraqi newspapers. He left Iraq for Israel in 1951, but pursued his interest in Arabic literature in the following years, earning a doctorate in modern Arabic poetry in 1965. Valuable scholarship informs much of his published work on Arabic literature and criticism as well as on Jewish writers of Arab descent. He is the founder and chairman of the Association of Jewish Academics from Iraq and the chairman of the Academic Committee of the Babylonian Jewry Heritage Center, Or-Yehuda, Israel.

"A Belly Dancer from Baghdad" presents intriguing aspects of the Iraqi Jewish experience. The detached narrator is a Jewish man, and the principal character is a Muslim woman, but because they meet in London, they feel free to talk about Iraqi society, including ethnic tensions. Their perspectives converge and diverge owing to their different perspectives on Muslims and Jews, but there is an unmistakable bond between the two. Fawziyya, the belly dancer, tells the Jewish narrator, "You're like a brother to me," and there is every indication that she means what she says. Ironically, she reveals how conventional social dictates regarding boys and girls in Iraq alienated her from her own biological brother when she started to grow up. Like Samir Naqqash's "Tantal," Moreh's story is a valuable document in presenting Jewish writers' view of ethnic relations in Iraq, but, unlike that story, it presents a detached assessment because in many senses the story is Fawziyya's, a Muslim woman's, and Jewish issues are peripheral to her experiences.

"A Belly Dancer from Baghdad" is a translation of "Raqisa min Baghdad" from the collection Al-qissah al-qasirah ind yahood al-Iraq (Short Stories by Jewish Writers from Iraq), edited by Shmuel Moreh (Jerusalem: Magnes Press, 1981).

A Belly Dancer from Baghdad

Those mesmerizing Middle Eastern features were a rare sight in a London night club. Her exotic belly-dancing outfit made her look even more shapely despite the extra flesh she carried. Makeup had revived her receding beauty and charm, especially her full-lipped, inscrutable smile, which, because of her profession, she had to use cautiously in dealing with clients. When our eyes met, her smile beamed with more charm.

"Are you from Iraq?" she asked when she approached me. Her broken English had a strong accent.

"Yes. How did you know?" I was indeed surprised.

"From the mark on your left cheek. Isn't this *habbet Baghdad?* I'm from Baghdad, too. A stranger sees all natives as his own family. I can't tell you how happy I am to find someone I can talk to in my own language."

I smiled and blushed a little. This was the first time I had talked to a dancer.

"This mark helps Baghdadis recognize each other abroad and helps to draw them closer," I said. "Some Iraqis brag to foreign women that it's a war scar. When did you leave Iraq?"

"I have been here for a bunch of years," she suddenly said in Iraqi Arabic. "I have been trying to forget Iraq, but I simply can't. Iraq is the only place I long for, but as much as I love it, I can't even look at its men. They're the reason behind my estrangement in the West. Nothing compares to Baghdad's river or sun. Here, the river flows with stagnant water, and it rains all year long. The sun comes out for a few seconds and then goes behind the clouds. No wonder you see people nearly naked crowding the parks on sunny days."

She had probably picked up the weather talk from the British, I thought.

"It baffles me," she added with an apologetic smile, "how I feel at home with an Iraqi woman, but other than that I'm like the stranger of our Iraqi proverb who sees only closed doors as soon as night falls."

Tango music was playing, inviting people to dance, and couples soon started dancing. I remained seated, looking at dancers in front of me.

"When did you leave Baghdad?" she said suddenly. "Not a long time ago, I hope."

"Just two weeks ago," I said.

"So, you still smell of Baghdad. Are you Muslim or Jewish?"

She asked her last question as if to apologize for not asking sooner. The question was customary among Baghdadis, Muslims, and Jews alike.

"Jewish," I said, expecting an end to the conversation, as often happened in Baghdad with Muslims.

"So what? We all are alike since we all drink the waters of the Tigris," she said smiling. "Our neighbors were the Hisqail family, the china trader, and I used to play with his daughters. I still love them to this day. What a pity those days are gone now. We have come a long way from the days when Jews were seen like animals. Tell me, do you still make *tibeet* every Saturday? Allah knows how much I loved it. The only thing I couldn't stomach about Jewish food was sesame oil. It made me barf."

She laughed, and I laughed with her. I remembered then how Muslims used to refer to Jews as those "who stink of sesame oil" and how we used to speak derogatorily of the oils that Muslims use and of their ways of slaughtering chicken and animals.

She didn't wait for my answer.

"You don't know where we used to live," she went on in English with a good deal of Iraqi Arabic. "It was in Bab al-Sheikh, and my family was very conservative. I was their only child, and it pained me when my father would say whenever I approached him, 'Get away from me, may you perish! Why didn't Allah give me a son?' I wondered then about the difference between a girl and a boy, and the only one I saw between me and the neighborhood boys was my long hair and dress.

"When my mother gave birth to a boy, my father was elated. He gave lavish parties, and I wondered if he gave such parties when I was born. I asked my mother, and she said, 'No one is overjoyed when they have a girl. A girl is a curse from Allah.' I felt jealous, but I thought that boys must be better than girls. When my brother came home after his first day in school, there was such a commotion—ululations and 'Allahu Akbars' and sweets sprinkled over his head as if he had just achieved an undisputable victory. As for me, needless to say, I stayed home and learned what good homemakers needed to learn—sewing and cooking and preparing myself to serve my husband. I wanted to go to school, but no one would listen to me. Not even my mother. 'You were a girl, too,' I told her once, 'so how can you accept this preferential treatment of boys?' The long-honored tradition always wins of course.

"Years later when my brother became a young man, I was told to abide by the rules of modesty in his presence. 'But he's my brother,' I protested, and again convention, not reason, ruled. I had to wear the *abaya* whenever I was outside and could never go alone—always with either mother or the maid. I was closely observed as if I were a scandal about to happen, but my brother could go anywhere and do whatever he could. Nightclubs, brothels, and he would share his adventures with my father. My father even bragged about the true son who wore down the town prostitutes. I'm sorry if my language offends, but I'm really upset. And you're like a brother to me.

"Anyway, I waited for the good man to come along, and that finally happened. The day of good—or bad—omen came when a middle-aged man expressed interest in me. An idiot nibbling on a big inheritance and knowing nothing but sinful living. My father turned down educated young men because they were 'penniless' he said. I don't want to bore you with stories of my husband's behavior, but he was just like other men—consumed by bad company, alcohol, and women of all sorts. When I became pregnant, I had hopes he would settle down and become a family man. He tortured me day and night with his threats that if the child was a girl he would send me back to my father. I was scared, and I prayed for a boy, but can one change one's own fate?

"I gave birth to a girl and nearly collapsed from anxiety. My husband completely lost his mind. He didn't spit on the floor and curse me the way my father did the day I was born, but he left for a life of orgies, and before a week had passed I got the news of his death. Killed by the lover of a dancer, Badia, for whom he had bought a furnished house.

"I remained a luckless widow, and his mother took me with her to Turkey. After she died, I lost my source of sustenance, and I had to work at nightclubs in Istanbul. I made sure my daughter got the best education and sent her to a boarding school to keep her from knowing what I did. I wanted her to become a doctor, and I started to work for the owner of this club after meeting him in Istanbul. My daughter will soon finish medical school."

She felt proud enough to repeat, "Yes, my daughter will soon become a doctor. She knows my suffering, and she's sworn to liberate me from this humiliating job. No dancer is immune to drunkards' bawdy comments or roaming hands, and they have to put up with this and more to keep the patrons happy. After she becomes a doctor, I'll repent and go to Mecca for the hajj. I'm proud to save my daughter from the fate that all Iraqi women face when they have no provider. To work, that is, as a maid, which means sleeping with the men of the house, or as a dancer or singer. What else can they do? Either a whore or a maid."

"Fawziyya, you're next," the owner of the club told her.

She smiled to me. "Here, they respect dancing," she whispered. "It's art. In Baghdad, if you play the violin, you're a pimp, and if you sing, you're a whore. Good-bye, sweetheart. Come visit us when you have the time."

When she got up, her smile showed pride and perhaps something else I couldn't tell for sure. Was it wounded dignity?

Glossary

abaya: a black cloak worn by conservative Iraqi women

Allahu Akbar: an Arabic phrase meaning "Allah is greater." In Iraq and several other Muslim countries, the phrase expresses a range of meanings, not all of them religious. Here it merely denotes jubilation.

athan: the call for prayer

bember: a fruit whose stone is covered with a sweet and sticky pulp

Bibi: "Grandma" in Iraqi Arabic

delillol: the opening word of a common lullaby in Iraq; little is known of its origin or meaning

dellak: a public bath masseur

dinar: the Iraqi currency

dishdasha: a long, loose garment worn mostly by men

egal: usually a two-tier round headwear used to hold the kaffiyeh in place

Eid: religious celebration; Muslims have two major Eids

fils: the smallest Iraqi coin

futa: cloth usually worn by women in Iraq to cover the head and torso

habbet Baghdad: a skin infection afflicting Iraqi children as recently as the 1950s that left a round scar the size of a U.S. quarter

halal: foods prepared in accordance with the Islamic code of law known as Sharia

hussainiyya: a small Shia mosque

ibdalak: a word in Iraq Jewish dialect meaning "I offer myself in sacrifice for you"

Imam Ali bin Abi Talib: the central figure of Shiism, recognized by Muslims as a pious caliph

kushki: soup made with *kushk,* or bulgur wheat dough kneaded with dried yogurt

lawash: very thin bread

madrasa: a Muslim school or college often attached to a mosque

misbaha: a string of prayer beads, among Muslims the equivalent of a rosary

muqri: the person who recites the Qur'an, usually as a profession

riq: a big, plain tambourine

sayyid: the spiritual leader of a Sufi order

Shafi'i: one of the four major Sunni doctrines

Sharia: code of Islamic law

Shubayk, Lubayk: in Arab folkloric tales, phrase blurted out by the genie as it emerges from the magic lamp, implying its readiness to fulfill the desires of the master of the lamp

takya: the lodging of a Sufi order

tannur: a small clay oven

Tantal: in Iraqi folklore, a creature of massive height and playful temperament

tasht: a big bathing basin

tbaGat: in Iraqi Arabic, derogatory term for a person with faltering judgment

tibeet: a Jewish Sabbath dish of rice and stuffed chicken, slow cooked on the Sabbath eve

Ya satir!: an Arabic phrase that implies the seeking of refuge in Allah's protection